Tarl Cabot was of Earth. Or at least so he had believed for all of his twenty-odd years. He had no inkling of the fantastic event that was to occur one winter's night in the frosty woods of America's New England.

Nothing had prepared him for the great wild tarns that screamed across an alien sky, for the dreaded, omniscient Priest Kings of the Sardar Mountains, for the Scribes and Warriors and Slaves and Assassins of Gor.

Yet Tarl was the chosen one—the one picked out of millions, to be trained and schooled and disciplined by the best teachers, swordsmen, bowmen on Gor. Toward what end, what mission, what purpose?

Only Gor—Counter-Earth—held the answer.

By John Norman

THE
GOREAN
CYCLE

TARNSMAN OF GOR

OUTLAW OF GOR

PRIEST-KINGS OF GOR

NOMADS OF GOR

ASSASSIN OF GOR

RAIDERS OF GOR

Available from Ballantine Books

This is an original publication—not a reprint.

TARNSMAN OF GOR

John Norman

BALLANTINE BOOKS • NEW YORK

SBN 345-02485-0-095

First Printing: December, 1966
Second Printing: January, 1970
Third Printing: December, 1971

First Canadian Printing: January, 1968

Printed in the United States of America

Cover Painting: Robert Foster

BALLANTINE BOOKS, INC.
101 Fifth Avenue, New York, New York 10003
An Intext Publisher

CONTENTS

TARNSMAN
OF
GOR

1

A Handful of Earth

MY NAME IS TARL CABOT. The name is supposed to have been shortened in the fifteenth century from the Italian surname Caboto. As far as I know, however, I have no connection with the Venetian explorer who carried the banner of Henry VII to the New World. Such a connection seems unlikely for a number of reasons, among them the fact that my people were simple tradesmen of Bristol, and uniformly fair-complexioned and topped with a blaze of the most outrageous red hair. Nonetheless, such coincidences, even if they are only geographical, linger in family memory—our small challenge to the ledgers and arithmetic of an existence measured in bolts of cloth sold. I like to think there may have been a Cabot in Bristol, one of us, who watched our Italian namesake weigh anchor in the early morning of that second of May, 1497.

You may remark my first name, and I assure you that it gave me quite as much trouble as it might you, particularly during my early school years, when it occasioned almost as many contests of physical skill as my red hair. Let us say simply that it is not a common name, not common on this world of ours. It was given to me by my father, who disappeared when I was quite young. I thought him dead until I received his strange message, more than twenty years after he had vanished. My mother, whom he inquired after, had died when I was about six, somewhere about the time I entered school. Biographical details are tedious, so suffice it to say that I was a bright child, fairly large for my age, and was given a creditable upbringing by an aunt who furnished everything that a child might need, with the possible exception of love.

Surprisingly enough, I managed to gain entrance to the University of Oxford, but I shall not choose to embarrass my college by entering its somewhat too revered name in this narrative. I graduated decently, having failed to astound either myself or my tutors. Like a large number of young men, I found myself passably educated, able to parse a sentence or so in Greek, and familiar enough with the abstractions of philosophy and economics to know that I would not be likely to fit into that world to which they claimed to bear some obscure relation. I was not, however, reconciled to ending up on the shelves of my aunt's shop, along with the cloth and ribbon, and so I embarked upon a wild, but not too wild, adventure, all things considered.

Being literate and not too dull, and having read enough history to tell the Renaissance from the Industrial Revolution, I applied to several small American colleges for an instructorship in history—English history, of course. I told them I was somewhat more advanced academically than I was, and they believed me, and my tutors, in their letters of recommendation, being good fellows, were kind enough not to disabuse them of this illusion. I believe my tutors thoroughly enjoyed the situation, which they, naturally, did not officially allow me to know they understood. It was the Revolutionary War all over again. One of the colleges to which I applied, one perhaps somewhat less perceptive than the rest, a small liberal arts college for men in New Hampshire, entered into negotiations, and I had soon received what was to be my first and, I suppose, my last appointment in the academic world.

In time I assumed I would be found out, but meanwhile I had my passage to America paid and a position for at least one year. This outcome struck me as being a pleasant if perplexing state of affairs. I admit I was annoyed by the suspicion that I had been given the appointment largely on the grounds that I would be faculty *exotica.* Surely I had no publications, and I am confident there must have been several candidates from American universities whose credentials and capacities would have far outshone my own, except for the desiderated British accent. Yes, there would be the round of teas and the cocktail and supper invitations.

I liked America very much, though I was quite busy the first semester, smashing through numerous texts in an undignified manner, attempting to commit enough English history to memory to keep at least a reign or so ahead of my students. I discovered, to my dismay, that being English does not automatically qualify one as an authority on English history. Fortunately, my departmental chairman, a gentle, bespectacled man, whose speciality was American economic history, knew even less than I did, or, at least, was considerate enough to allow me to believe so.

The Christmas vacation helped greatly. I was especially counting on the time between the semesters to catch up, or, better, to lengthen my lead on the students. But after the term papers, the tests, and the grading of the first semester, I was afflicted with a rather irresistible desire to chuck the British Empire and go for a long, long walk

—indeed, even a camping trip in the nearby White Mountains.

I borrowed some camp gear, mostly a knapsack and a sleeping bag, from one of the few friends I had made on the faculty—an instructor also, but in the deplorable subject of physical education. He and I had fenced occasionally and had gone for infrequent walks. I sometimes wonder if he is curious about what happened to his camp gear or to Tarl Cabot. Surely the administration of the college was curious, and angry at the inconvenience of having to replace an instructor in the middle of the year, for Tarl Cabot was never heard of again on the campus of that college.

My friend in the physical education department drove me a few miles into the mountains and dropped me off. We agreed to meet again in three days at the same place. The first thing I did was check my compass, as if I knew what I was up to, and then proceeded to leave the highway well behind me. More quickly than I realized, I was alone and in the woods, climbing. Bristol, as you know, is a heavily urbanized area, and I was not well prepared for my first encounter with nature. Surely the college, though somewhat rural, was at least one of the outworks of, say, material civilization. I was not frightened, being confident that walking steadily in any given direction would be sure to bring me to one highway or another, or some stream or another, and that it would be impossible to become lost, or at least for long. Primarily, I was exhilarated, being alone, with myself and the green pines and patches of snow.

I trudged along for the better part of two hours before I finally yielded to the weight of the pack. I ate a cold lunch and was on my way again, getting deeper into the mountains. I was pleased that I had regularly taken a turn or two around the college track.

That evening I dropped my pack near a rock platform and set about gathering some wood for a fire. I had gone a bit from my makeshift camp when I stopped, startled for a moment. Something in the darkness, to the left, lying on the ground, seemed to be glowing. It held a calm, hazy blue radiance. I put down the wood I had gathered and approached the object, more curious than anything else. It appeared to be a rectangular metal envelope, rather thin, not much larger than the normal envelope one customarily uses for correspondence. I touched it; it seemed to be hot. My hair rose on the back of my head; my eyes widened. I read, in a rather archaic English script inscribed on the envelope, two words—my name, Tarl Cabot.

It was a joke. Somehow my friend had followed me, must be hiding somewhere in the darkness. I called his name, laughing. There was no answer. I raced about in the woods a moment, shaking bushes, batting the snow from the low-hanging branches of pines. I then walked more slowly, more carefully, being quiet. I would find him!

Some fifteen minutes passed, and I was growing cold, angry. I shouted to him. I widened my search, keeping that strange metal envelope with its blue ambience the center of my movements. At last I realized he must have planted the odd object, left it for me to discover, and was probably on his way home by now or was perhaps camping somewhere nearby. I was confident he was not within earshot or he would have eventually responded. It was no longer funny, not if he was near.

I returned to the object and picked it up. It seemed to be cooler now, though I still had the distinct impression of warmth. It was a strange object. I brought it back to my camp and built my fire, against the darkness and cold. I was shivering in spite of my heavy clothing. I was sweating. My heart was beating. My breath was short. I was frightened.

Accordingly, slowly and calmly, I set about tending the fire, opened a can of chili, and set up sticks to hold the tiny cooking pot over the fire. These domestic activities slowed my pulse and succeeded in convincing me that I could be patient and was even not too much interested in the contents of the metal envelope. When the chili was heating, and not before, I turned my attention to the puzzling object.

I turned it over and over in my hands and studied it by the light of the campfire. It was about twelve inches long and four inches high. It weighed, I guessed, about four ounces. The color of the metal was blue, and something of its ambience continued to characterize it, but the glow was fading. Also, the envelope no longer seemed warm to the touch. How long had it lain waiting for me in the woods? How long ago had it been placed there?

While I considered this, the glow faded abruptly. If it had faded earlier, I never would have discovered it in the woods. It was almost as if the glow had been connected with the intent of the sender, as if the glow, no longer needed, had been allowed to fade. "The message has been delivered," I said to myself, feeling a bit silly as I said it. I did not find my private joke very funny.

I looked closely at the lettering. It resembled some now outdated English script, but I knew too little about such things to hazard much of a guess at the date. Something about the lettering reminded me of that on a colonial charter, a page of which had been photocopied for an illustration in one of my books. Seventeenth century perhaps? The lettering itself seemed to be inset in the envelope, bonded in its metallic structure. I could find no seam or flap in the envelope. I tried to crease the envelope with my thumbnail, but failed.

Feeling rather foolish, I took out the can opener I had used on the chili can and attempted to force the metal point through the envelope. Light as the envelope seemed to be, it resisted the point as if I were trying to open an anvil. I leaned on the can opener with both arms, pressing down with all my weight. The point of the can opener bent into a right angle, but the envelope had not been scratched.

I handled the envelope carefully, puzzled, trying to determine if it might be opened. There was a small circle on the back of the envelope, and in the circle seemed to be the print of a thumb. I wiped it on my sleeve, but it did not disappear. The other prints on the envelope, from my fingers, wiped away immediately. As well as I could, I scrutinized the print in the circle. It, too, like the lettering, seemed a part of the metal, yet its ridges and lineaments were exceedingly delicate.

At last I was confident that it was a part of the envelope. I pressed it with my finger; nothing happened. Tired of this strange business, I set the envelope aside and turned my attention to the chili, which was now bubbling over the small campfire. After I had eaten, I removed my boots and coat and crawled into the sleeping bag.

I lay there beside the dying fire, looking up at the branch-lined sky and the mineral glory of the unconscious universe. I lay awake for a long time, feeling alone, yet not alone, as one sometimes does in the wilderness, feeling as if one were the only living object on the planet and as if the closest things to one—one's fate and destiny perhaps—lay outside our small world, somewhere in the remote, alien pastures of the stars.

A thought struck me with sudden swiftness, and I was afraid, but I knew what I must do. The matter of the envelope was not a hoax, not a trick. Somewhere, deep in whatever I am, I knew that and had known it from the beginning. Almost as if dreaming, yet with vivid clarity, I inched partly out of my sleeping bag. I rolled over and threw some wood on the fire and reached for the envelope. Sitting in the sleeping bag, I waited for the fire to rise a bit. Then I carefully placed my right thumb on the impression in the envelope, pressing down firmly. It answered to my touch, as I had expected it to, as I had feared it would. Perhaps only one man could open that envelope—he whose print fitted the strange lock, he whose name was Tarl Cabot. The apparently seamless envelope crackled open, almost with the sound of cellophane.

An object fell from the envelope, a ring of red metal bearing the simple crest "C." I barely noticed it in my excitement. There was lettering on the inside of the envelope, which had opened in a manner surprisingly like a foreign air-mail letter, where the envelope serves also as stationery. The lettering was in the same script as my name on the outside of the envelope. I noticed the date and froze, my hands clenched on the metallic paper. It was dated the third of February, 1640. It was dated more than three hundred years ago, and I was reading it in the sixth decade of the twentieth century. Oddly enough, also, the day on which I was reading it was the third of February. The signature at the bottom was not in the old script, but might have been done in modern cursive English.

I had seen the signature once or twice before, on some letters my aunt had saved. I knew the signature, though I could not remember the man. It was the signature of my father, Matthew Cabot, who had disappeared when I was an infant.

I was dizzy, unsettled. It seemed my vision reeled; I couldn't move. Things grew black for a moment, but I shook myself and clenched my teeth, breathed in the sharp, cold mountain air, once, twice, three times, slowly, gathering the piercing contact of reality into my lungs, reassuring myself that I was alive, not dreaming, that I held in my hands a letter with an incredible date, delivered more than three hundred years later in the mountains of New Hampshire, written by a man who presumably, if still alive, was, as we reckon time, no more than fifty years of age—my father.

Even now I can remember the letter to the last word. I think I will carry its simple, abrupt message burned into the cells of my brain until, as it is elsewhere said, I have returned to the Cities of Dust.

The third day of February, in the
Year of Our Lord 1640.

Tarl Cabot, Son:

Forgive me, but I have little choice in these matters. It has been decided. Do whatever you think is in your own best interest, but the fate is upon you, and you will not escape. I wish health to you and to your mother. Carry on your person the ring of red metal, and bring me, if you would, a handful of our green earth.

Discard this letter. It will be destroyed.

With affection,
Matthew Cabot

I read and reread the letter and had become unnaturally calm. It seemed clear to me that I was not insane, or if I was, that insanity was a state of mental clarity and comprehension quite apart from the torment that I had conceived it to be. I placed the letter in my knapsack.

What I must do was fairly obvious—make my way out of the mountains as soon as it was light. No, that might be too late. It would be mad, scrambling about in the darkness, but there seemed to be nothing else that would serve. I did not know how much time I had, but even if it was only a few hours, I might be able to reach some highway or stream or perhaps a cabin.

I checked my compass to get the bearing back to the highway. I looked uneasily about in the darkness. An owl hooted once, perhaps a hundred yards to the right. Something out there might be watching me. It was an unpleasant feeling. I pulled on my boots and coat, rolled my sleeping bag, and fixed the pack. I kicked the fire to pieces, stamping out the embers, scuffing dirt over the sparks.

Just as the fire was sputtering out, I noticed a glint in the ashes. Bending down, I retrieved the ring. It was warm from the ashes, hard, substantial—a piece of reality. It was there. I dropped it into the pocket of my coat and started off on my compass-bearing, trying to make my way back to the highway.

I felt stupid trying to hike in the dark. I was asking for a broken leg or ankle, if not a neck. Still, if I could put a mile or so between myself and the old camp, that should be sufficient to give myself the margin of safety I needed—from what I didn't know. I might then wait until morning and start off in the light, secure, confident. Moreover, it would be a simple matter to cover one's tracks in the light. The important thing was not to be at the old camp.

I had made my way perilously through the darkness for perhaps twenty minutes when, to my horror, my knapsack and bedroll seemed to burst into blue flame on my back. It was an instant's action to hurl them from me, and I gazed, bewildered, awe-stricken, at what seemed to be a furious blue combustion that lit the pines on all sides as if with acetylene flames. It was like staring into a furnace. I knew that it was the envelope that had burst into flame, taking with it my knapsack and bedroll. I shuddered, thinking of what might have happened if I had been carrying it in the pocket of my coat.

Strangely enough, now that I think of it, I didn't run headlong from the spot, though I can't see why, and the thought did cross my mind that the bright, flarelike luminescence would reveal my position, if it was of interest to anyone or anything. With a small flashlight I knelt beside the flakes of my knapsack and bedroll. The stones on which they had fallen were blackened. There was no trace of the envelope. It seemed to have been totally consumed. There was an unpleasant, acrid odor in the air, some fumes of a sort that I was not familiar with.

The thought came to me that the ring, which I had dropped in my pocket, might similarly burst into flame, but, unaccountably perhaps, I doubted it. There might be a point in someone's destroying the letter, but presumably there would be little point or no point in destroying the ring. Why should it have been sent if not to have been kept?

Besides, I had been warned about the letter—a warning I had foolishly neglected—but had been asked to carry the ring. Whatever it was, father or no, that was the source of these frightening events, it did not seem to wish me harm, but then, I thought, somewhat bitterly, floods and earthquakes presumably wish no one harm either. Who knew the nature of the things or forces that were afoot that night in the mountains, things and forces that might perhaps smash me, casually, as one innocently steps on an insect without being aware of it or caring?

I still had the compass, and that constituted a firm link to reality. The silent but intense explosion of the envelope into flames had caused me momentarily to become confused—that and the sudden return to the darkness from the hideous glaring light of the disintegrating envelope. My compass would get me out. With my flashlight I examined it. As the thin, sharp beam struck the face of the compass, my heart stopped. The needle was spinning crazily, and oscillating backward and forward, as if the laws of nature had suddenly been abridged in its vicinity.

For the first time since I had opened the envelope, I began to lose my control. The compass had been my anchor and trust. I had counted on it. Now it had gone crazy. There was a loud noise, but I now think it must have been the sound of my own voice, a sudden frightened shriek for which I shall always bear the shame.

The next thing I was running like a demented animal, in any direction, every direction. How long I ran I don't know. It may have been hours, perhaps only a few minutes. I slipped and fell dozens of times and ran into the prickly branches of the pines, the needles stabbing at my face. I may have been sobbing; I remember the taste of salt in my mouth. But mostly I remember a blind, headlong flight, a panic-stricken, unworthy, sickening flight. Once I saw two eyes in the darkness and screamed and ran from them, hearing the flap of wings behind me and the startled cry of an owl. Once I startled a small band of deer and found myself in the midst of their bounding shapes buffeting me in the darkness.

The moon came out, and the mountainside was suddenly lit with its cold beauty, white on the snow in the trees and on the side of the slope, sparkling on the rocks. I could run no further. I fell to the ground, gasping for breath, suddenly asking myself why I had run. For the first time in my life I had felt full, unreasoning fear, and it had gripped me like the paws of some grotesque predatory animal. I had surrendered to it for just a moment, and it had become a force that had carried me, hurling me about as if I were a swimmer captured in surging waves—a force that could not be resisted. It had departed now. I must never surrender to it again. I looked around and recognized the platform of rock near which I had set my bedroll. I saw the ashes of my fire. I had returned to my camp. Somehow I'd known that I would.

As I lay there in the moonlight, I felt the earth beneath me, against my aching muscles and the body that was covered with the foul-smelling sheen of fear and sweat. I felt then that it was good even to feel pain. Feeling was the important thing. I was alive.

I saw the ship descend. For a moment it looked like a falling star, but then it suddenly became clear and substantial, like a broad, thick disk of silver. It was silent and settled on the rock platform, scarcely disturbing the light snow that was scattered on it. There was a slight wind in the pine needles, and I rose to my feet. As I did so, a door in the side of the ship slid quietly upward. I must go in. My father's words recurred in my memory: "The fate is upon you." Before entering the ship, I stopped at the side of the large, flat rock on which it rested. I bent down and scooped up, as my father had asked, a handful of our green earth. I, too, felt that it was important to take something with me, something which, in a way, was my native soil. The soil of my planet, my world.

2

The Counter-Earth

I REMEMBERED NOTHING, FROM THE time I'd boarded the silver disk in the mountains of New Hampshire until now. I awoke, feeling rested, and opened my eyes, half expecting to see my room in the alumni house at the college. I turned my head, without pain or discomfort. I seemed to be lying on some hard, flat object, perhaps a table, in a circular room with a low ceiling some seven feet high. There were five narrow windows, not large enough to let a man through; they rather reminded me of ports for bowmen in a castle tower, yet they admitted sufficient light to allow me to recognize my surroundings.

There was a tapestry to the right, a well-woven depiction of some hunting scene, I took it, but fancifully done, the spear-carrying hunters mounted on birds of a sort and attacking an ugly animal that reminded me of a boar, except that it appeared to be too large, out of proportion to the hunters. Its jaws carried four tusks, curved like scimitars. It reminded me, with the vegetation and background and the classic serenity of the faces, of a Renaissance tapestry I had once seen on a vacation tour I had taken to Florence in my second year at the University.

Opposite the tapestry—for decoration, I assumed—hung a round shield with crossed spears behind it. The shield was rather like the old Greek shields on some of the red-figured vases in the London Museum. The design on the shield was unintelligible to me. I could not be sure that it was supposed to mean anything. It might have been an alphabetic monogram or perhaps a mere delight to the artist. Above the shield was suspended a helmet, again reminiscent of a Greek helmet, perhaps of the Homeric period. It had a somewhat "Y"-shaped slot for the eyes, nose, and mouth in the nearly solid metal. There was a savage dignity about it, with the shield and spears, all of them stable on the wall, as if ready, like the famous colonial rifle over the fireplace, for instant use; they were all polished and gleamed dully in the half light.

Aside from these things and two stone blocks, perhaps chairs, and a mat on one side, the room was bare; the walls and ceiling and floor were smooth as marble, and a classic white. I could see no door in the room. I rose from the stone table, which was indeed what it was, and went to the window. I looked out and saw the sun—our sun it had to be. It seemed perhaps a fraction larger, but it was difficult to be sure. I was confident that it was our own brilliant yellow star. The sky, like that of the earth, was blue. My first thought was that this must be the earth and the sun's apparent size an illusion.

Obviously, I was breathing, and that meant necessarily an atmosphere containing a large percentage of oxygen. It must be the earth. But as I stood at the window, I knew that this could not be my mother planet. The building in which I found myself was apparently one of an indefinite number of towers, like endless flat cylinders of varying sizes and colors, joined by narrow, colorful bridges that arched lightly between them.

I could not lean far enough outside the window to see the ground. In the distance I could see hills covered with some type of green vegetation, but I could not determine whether or not it was grass. Wondering at my predicament, I turned back to the table. I strode over to it and nearly bruised my thigh on the stone structure. I felt for a moment as though I must have stumbled, have been dizzy. I walked around the room. I leaped to the top of the table almost as I would have climbed a stair in the alumni house. It was different, a different movement. Less gravity. It had to be. The planet, then, was smaller than our earth, and, given the apparent size of the sun, perhaps somewhat closer to it.

My clothes had been changed. My hunting boots were gone, my fur cap and the heavy coat and the rest of it. I was clad in some sort of tunic of a reddish color, which was tied at the waist with a yellow cord. It occurred to me that I was clean, in spite of my adventures, my panic-stricken rout in the mountains. I had been washed. I saw that the ring of red metal, with the crest of a "C," had been placed on the second finger of my right hand. I was hungry. I tried to put my thoughts together, sitting on the table, but there was too much. I felt like a child, knowing nothing, taken to some complex factory or store, unable to sort out his impressions, unable to comprehend the new and strange things that flash incessantly upon him.

A panel in the wall slid sideways, and a tall red-haired man, somewhere in his late forties, dressed much as I was, stepped through. I hadn't known what to expect, what these people would be like. This man was an earthman, apparently. He smiled at me and came forward, placing his hands on my shoulders and looking into my eyes. He said, I thought rather proudly, "You are my son, Tarl Cabot."

"I am Tarl Cabot," I said.

"I am your father," he said, and shook me powerfully by the shoulders. We shook hands, on my part rather stiffly, yet this gesture of our common homeland somehow reassured me. I was surprised to find myself accepting this stranger not only as a being of my world, but as the father I couldn't remember.

"Your mother?" he asked, his eyes concerned.

"Dead, years ago," I said.

He looked at me. "She, of all of them, I loved most," he said, turning away, crossing the room. He appeared to be affected keenly, shaken. I wanted to feel no sympathy with him, yet I found that I could not help it. I was angry with myself. He had deserted my mother and me, had he not? And what was it now that he felt some regret? And how was it that he had spoken so innocently of "all of them," whoever they might be? I did not want to find out.

Yet, somehow, in spite of these things, I found that I wanted to cross the room, to put my hand on his arm, to touch him. I felt somehow a kinship with him, with this stranger and his sorrow. My eyes were moist. Something stirred in me, obscure, painful memories that had been silent, quiet for many years—the memory of a woman I had barely known, of a gentle face, of arms that had protected a child who had awakened frightened in the night. And I remembered suddenly another face, behind hers.

"Father," I said.

He straightened and turned to face me across that simple, strange room. It was impossible to tell if he had wept. He looked at me with sadness in his eyes, and his rather stern features seemed for a moment to be tender. Looking into his eyes, I realized, with an incomprehensible suddenness and a joy that still bewilders me, that someone existed who loved me.

"My son," he said.

We met in the center of the room and embraced. I wept, and he did, too, without shame. I learned later that on this alien world a strong man may feel and express emotions, and that the hypocrisy of constraint is not honored on this planet as it is on mine.

At last we moved apart.

My father regarded me evenly. "She will be the last," he said. "I had no right to let her love me."

I was silent.

He sensed my feeling and spoke brusquely. "Thank you for your gift, Tarl Cabot," he said.

I looked puzzled.

"The handful of earth," he said. "A handful of my native ground."

I nodded, not wanting to speak, wanting him to tell me the thousand things I had to know, to dispel the mysteries that had torn me from my native world and brought me to this strange room, this planet, to him, my father.

"You must be hungry," he said.

"I want to know where I am and what I am doing here," I said.

"Of course," he said, "but you must eat." He smiled. "While you satisfy your hunger, I shall speak to you."

He clapped his hands twice, and the panel slid back again. I was startled. Through the opening came a young girl, somewhat younger than myself, with blond hair bound back. She wore a sleeveless garment of diagonal stripes, the brief skirt of which terminated some inches above her knees. She was barefoot, and as her eyes shyly met mine, I saw they were blue and deferential. My eyes suddenly noted her one piece of jewelry—a light, steel-like band she wore as a collar. As quickly as she had come, she departed.

"You may have her this evening if you wish," said my father, who had scarcely seemed to notice the girl.

I wasn't sure what he meant, but I said no.

At my father's insistence, I began to eat, reluctantly, never taking my eyes from him, hardly tasting the food, which was simple but excellent. The meat reminded me of venison; it was not the meat of an animal raised on domestic grains. It had been roasted over an open flame. The bread was still hot from the oven. The fruit—grapes and peaches of some sort—was fresh and as cold as mountain snow. After the meal I tasted the drink, which might not inappropriately be described as an almost incandescent wine, bright, dry, and powerful. I learned later it was called Ka-la-na. While I ate, and afterward, my father spoke.

"Gor," he said, "is the name of this world. In all the languages of this planet, the word means Home Stone." He paused, noting my lack of comprehension. "Home Stone," he repeated. "Simply that.

"In peasant villages on this world," he continued, "each hut was originally built around a flat stone which was placed in the center of the circular dwelling. It was carved with the family sign and was called the Home Stone. It was, so to speak, a symbol of sovereignty, or territory, and each peasant, in his own hut, was a sovereign."

"Later," said my father, "Home Stones were used for villages, and later still for cities. The Home Stone of a village was always placed in the market; in a city, on the top of the highest tower. The Home Stone came naturally, in time, to acquire a mystique, and something of the same hot, sweet emotions as our native peoples of Earth feel toward their flags became invested in it."

My father had risen to his feet and had begun to pace the room, and his eyes seemed strangely alive. In time I would come to understand more of what he felt. Indeed, there is a saying on Gor, a saying whose origin is lost in the past of this strange planet, that one who speaks of Home Stones should stand, for matters of honor are here involved, and honor is respected in the barbaric codes of Gor.

"These stones," said my father, "are various, of different colors, shapes, and sizes, and many of them are intricately carved. Some of the largest cities have small, rather insignificant Home Stones, but of incredible antiquity, dating back to the time when the city was a village or only a mounted pride of warriors with no settled abode."

My father paused at the narrow window in the circular room and looked out onto the hills beyond and fell silent.

At last he spoke again.

"Where a man sets his Home Stone, he claims, by law, that land for himself. Good land is protected only by the swords of the strongest owners in the vicinity."

"Swords?" I asked.

"Yes," said my father, as if there were nothing incredible in this admission. He smiled. "You have much to learn of Gor," he said. "Yet there is a hierarchy of Home Stones, one might say, and two soldiers who would cut one another down with their steel blades for an acre of fertile ground will fight side by side to the death for the Home Stone of their village or of the city within whose ambit their village lies.

"I shall show you someday," he said, "my own small Home Stone, which I keep in my chambers. It encloses a handful of soil from the Earth, a handful of soil that I first brought with me when I came to this world—a long time ago." He looked at me evenly. "I shall keep the handful of earth you brought," he said, his voice very quiet, "and someday it may be yours." His eyes seemed moist. He added, "If you should live to earn a Home Stone."

I rose to my feet and looked at him.

He had turned away, as if lost in thought. "It is the occasional dream of a conqueror or statesman," he said, "to have but a single Supreme Home Stone for the planet." Then, after a long moment, not looking at me, he said, "It is rumored there is such a stone, but it lies in the Sacred Place and is the source of the Priest-Kings' power."

"Who are the Priest-Kings?" I asked.

My father faced me, and he seemed troubled, as if he might have said more than he intended. Neither of us spoke for perhaps a minute.

"Yes," said my father at last, "I must speak to you of Priest-Kings." He smiled. "But let me begin in my own way, that you may better understand the nature of that whereof I speak." We both sat down again, the stone table between us, and my father calmly and methodically explained many things to me.

As he spoke, my father often referred to the planet Gor as the Counter-Earth, taking the name from the writings of the Pythagoreans who had first speculated on the existence of such a body. Oddly enough, one of the expressions in the tongue of Gor for our sun was Lar-Torvis, which means The Central Fire, another Pythagorean expression, except that it had not been, as I understand it, originally used by the Pythagoreans to refer to the sun but to another body. The more common expression for the sun was Tor-tu-Gor, which means Light Upon the Home Stone. There was a sect among the people that worshiped the sun, I later learned, but it was insignificant both in numbers and power when compared with the worship of the Priest-Kings who, whatever they were, were accorded the honors of divinity. Theirs, it seems, was the honor of being enshrined as the most ancient gods of Gor, and in time of danger a prayer to the Priest-Kings might escape the lips of even the bravest men.

"The Priest-Kings," said my father, "are immortal, or so most here believe."

"Do you believe it?" I asked.

"I don't know," said my father. "I think perhaps I do."

"What sort of men are they?" I asked.

"It is not known that they are men," said my father.

"Then what are they?"

"Perhaps gods."

"You're not serious?"

"I am," he said. "Is not a creature beyond death, of immense power and wisdom, worthy to be so spoken of?"

I was quiet.

"My speculation, however," said my father, "is that the Priest-Kings are indeed men—men much as we, or humanoid organisms of some type—who possess a science and technology as far beyond our normal ken as that of our own twentieth century would be to the alchemists and astrologers of the medieval universities."

His supposition seemed plausible to me, for from the very beginning I had understood that in something or someone existed a force and clarity of understanding beside which the customary habits of rationality as I knew them were little more than the tropisms of the unicellular animal. Even the technology of the envelope with its patterned thumb-lock, the disorientation of my compass, and the ship that had brought me, unconscious, to this strange world, argued for an incredible grasp of unusual, precise, and manipulable forces.

"The Priest-Kings," said my father, "maintain the Sacred Place in the Sardar Mountains, a wild vastness into which no man penetrates. The Sacred Place, to the minds of most men here, is taboo, perilous. Surely none have returned from those mountains." My father's eyes seemed faraway, as if focused on sights he might have preferred to forget. "Idealists and rebels have been dashed to pieces on the frozen escarpments of those mountains. If one approaches the mountains, one must go on foot. Our beasts will not approach them. Parts of outlaws and fugitives who have sought refuge in them have been found on the plains below, like scraps of meat cast from an incredible distance to the beaks and teeth of wandering scavengers."

My hand clenched on the metal goblet. The wine moved in the vessel. I saw my image in the wine, shattered by the tiny forces in the vessel. Then the wine was still.

"Sometimes," said my father, his eyes still faraway, "when men are old or have had enough of life, they assault the mountains, looking for the secret of immortality in the barren crags. If they have found their immortality, none have confirmed it, for none have returned to the Tower Cities." He looked at me. "Some think that such men in time become Priest-Kings themselves. My own speculation, which I judge as likely or unlikely to be true as the more popular superstitious stories, is that it is death to learn the secret of the Priest-Kings."

"You do not know that," I said.

"No," admitted my father. "I do not know it."

My father then explained to me something of the legends of the Priest-Kings, and I gathered that they seemed to be true to this degree at least—that the Priest-Kings could destroy or control whatever they wished, that they were, in effect, the divinities of this world. It was supposed that they were aware of all that transpired on their planet, but, if so, I was informed that they seemed, on the whole, to take little note of it. It was rumored, according to my father, that they cultivated holiness in their mountains, and in their contemplation could not be concerned with the realities and evils of the outside and unimportant world. They were, so to speak, absentee divinities, existent but remote, not to be bothered with the fears and turmoil of the mortals beyond their mountains. This conjecture, the seeking of holiness, however, seemed to me to fit not well with the sickening fate apparently awaiting those who attempted the mountains. I found it difficult to conceive of one of those theoretical saints rousing himself from contemplation to hurl the scraps of interlopers to the plains below.

"There is at least one area, however," said my father, "in which the Priest-Kings do take a most active interest in this world, and that is the area of technology. They limit, selectively, the technology available to us, the Men Below the Mountains. For example, incredibly enough, weapon technology is controlled to the point where the most powerful devices of war are the crossbow and lance. Further, there is no mechanized transportation or communication equipment or detection devices such as the radar and sonar equipment so much in evidence in the military establishments of your world.

"On the other hand," he said, "you will learn that in lighting, shelter, agricultural techniques, and medicine, for example, the Mortals, or the Men Below the Mountains, are relatively advanced." He looked at me—amused, I think. "You wonder," he said, "why the numerous, rather obvious deficits in our technology have not been repaired—in spite of the Priest-Kings. It crosses your mind that there must exist minds on this world capable of designing such things as, say, rifles and armored vehicles."

"Surely these things must be produced," I urged.

"And you are right," he said grimly. "From time to time they are, but their owners are then destroyed, bursting into flame."

"Like the envelope of blue metal?"

"Yes," he said. "It is Flame Death merely to possess a weapon of the interdicted sort. Sometimes bold individuals create or acquire such war materials and sometimes for as long as a year escape the Flame Death, but sooner or later they are struck down." His eyes were hard. "I once saw it happen," he said.

Clearly, he did not wish to discuss the topic further.

"What of the ship that brought me here?" I asked. "Surely that is a marvelous example of your technology?"

"Not of our technology, but of that of the Priest-Kings," he said. "I do not believe the ship was manned by any of the Men Below the Mountains."

"By Priest-Kings?" I asked.

"Frankly," said my father, "I believe the ship was remotely controlled from the Sardar Mountains, as are said to be all the Voyages of Acquisition."

"Of Acquisition?"

"Yes," said my father. "And long ago I made the same strange journey. As have others."

"But for what end, to what purpose?" I demanded.

"Each perhaps for a different end, for each perhaps a different purpose," he said.

My father then spoke to me of the world on which I found myself. He said, from what he could learn from the Initiates, who claimed to serve as the intermediaries of Priest-Kings to men, that the planet Gor had originally been a satellite of a distant sun, in one of the fantastically remote Blue Galaxies. It was moved by the science of the Priest-Kings several times in its history, seeking again and again a new star. I regarded this story as improbable, at least in part, for several reasons, primarily having to do with the sheer spatial improbabilities of such a migration, which, even at a speed approximating light, would have taken billions of years. Moreover, in moving through space, without a sun for photosynthesis and warmth, all life would surely have been destroyed.

If the planet had been moved at all, and I knew enough to understand that this was empirically possible, it must have been brought into our system from a closer star. Perhaps it had once been a satellite of Alpha Centauri, but, even so, the distances still seemed almost unimaginable. Theoretically, I did admit that the planet might have been moved without destroying its life, but the engineering magnitude of such a feat staggered the imagination. Perhaps life might have been suspended temporarily or hidden beneath the planet's surface with sufficient sustenance and oxygen for the incredible journey. In effect, the planet would have functioned as a gigantic sealed spacecraft.

There was another possibility I mentioned to my father—perhaps the planet had been in our system all the time, but had been undiscovered, unlikely though that might be, given the thousands of years of study of the skies by men, from the shambling creatures of the Neander Valley to the brilliant intellects of Mount Wilson and Palomar. To my surprise, this absurd hypothesis was welcomed by my father.

"That," he said with animation, "is the Theory of the Sun Shield." He added, "That is why I like to think of the planet as the Counter-Earth, not only because of its resemblance to our native world, but because, as a matter of fact, it is placed as a counterpoise to the Earth. It has the same plane of orbit and maintains its orbit in such a way as always to keep The Central Fire between it and its planetary sister, our Earth, even though this necessitates occasional adjustments in its speed of revolution."

"But surely," I protested, "its existence could be discovered. One can't hide a planet the size of the Earth in our own solar system! It's impossible!"

"You underestimate the Priest-Kings and their science," said my father, smiling. "Any power that is capable of moving a planet—and I believe the Priest-Kings possess this power—is capable of effecting adjustments in the motion of the planet, such adjustments as might allow it to use the sun indefinitely as a concealing shield."

"The orbits of the other planets would be affected," I pointed out.

"Gravitational perturbations," said my father, "can be neutralized." His eyes shone. "It is my belief," he said, "that the Priest-Kings can control the forces of gravity, at least in localized areas, and, indeed, that they do so. In all probability their control over the motion of the planet is somehow connected with this capacity. Consider certain consequences of this power. Physical evidence, such as light or radio waves, which might reveal the presence of the planet, can be prevented from doing so. The Priest-Kings might gravitationally warp the space in their vicinity, causing light or radio waves to be diffused, curved, or deflected in such a way as not to expose their world."

I must have appeared unconvinced.

"Exploratory satellites can be similarly dealt with," added my father. He paused. "Of course, I only propose hypotheses, for what the Priest-Kings do and how it is done is known only to them."

I drained the last sip of the heady wine in the metal goblet.

"Actually," said my father, "there is evidence of the existence of the Counter-Earth."

I looked at him.

"Certain natural signals in the radio band of the spectrum," said my father.

My astonishment must have been obvious.

"Yes," he said, "but since the hypothesis of another world is regarded as so incredible, this evidence has been interpreted to accord with other theories; sometimes even imperfections in instrumentation have been supposed rather than admit the presence of another world in our solar system."

"But why would this evidence not be understood?" I asked.

"Surely you know," he laughed, "one must distinguish between the data to be interpreted and the interpretation of the data, and one chooses, normally, the interpretation that preserves as much as possible of the old world view, and, in the thinking of the Earth, there is no place for Gor, its true sister planet, the Counter-Earth."

My father had finished speaking. He rose and gripped me by the shoulders, held me for a moment and smiled. Then silently the door in the wall slid aside, and he strode from the room. He had not spoken to me of my role or destiny, whatever it was to be. He did not wish to discuss the reason for which I had been brought to the Counter-Earth, nor did he explain to me the comparatively minor mysteries of the envelope and its strange letter. Most keenly perhaps, I missed that he had not spoken to me of himself, for I wanted to know him, that kindly, remote stranger whose bones were in my body, whose blood flowed in mine—my father.

I now inform you that what I write of my own experience I know to be true, and that what I have accepted on authority I believe to be true, but I shall not be offended if you disbelieve, for I, too, in your place, would refuse to believe. Indeed, on the small evidence I can present in this narrative, you are obliged, in all honesty, to reject my testimony or at the very least to suspend judgment. In fact, there is so little probability that this tale will be believed that the Priest-Kings of Sardar, the Keepers of the Sacred Place, have apparently granted that it may be recorded. I am glad of this, because I must tell this story. I have seen things of which I must speak, even if, as it is said here, only to the Towers.

Why have the Priest-Kings been so lenient in this case —those who control this second earth? I think the answer is simple. Enough humanity remains in them, if they are human, for we have never seen them, to be vain; enough vanity remains in them to wish to inform you of their existence, if only in a way that you will not accept or be able to consider seriously. Perhaps there is humor in the Sacred Place, or irony. After all, suppose you should accept this tale, should learn of the Counter-Earth and of the Voyages of Acquisition, what could you do? You could do nothing, you with your rudimentary technology of which you are so proud—you could do nothing at least for a thousand years, and by that time, if the Priest-Kings choose, this planet will have found a new sun, and new peoples to populate its verdant surface.

3

The Tarn

"Ho!" CRIED TORM, THAT MOST improbable member of the Caste of Scribes, throwing his blue robes over his head as though he could not bear to see the light of day. Out of the robes then popped the sandy-haired head of the scribe, his pale blue eyes twinkling on each side of that sharp needle of a nose. He looked me over. "Yes," he cried, "I deserve it!" Back went the head into the robes. Muffled, his voice reached me. "Why must I, an idiot, be always afflicted with idiots?" Out came the head.

"Have I nothing better to do? Have I not a thousand scrolls gathering dust on my shelves, unread, unstudied?"

"I don't know," I said.

"Look," he cried in actual despair, waving his blue-robed arms hopelessly at the messiest chamber I had seen on Gor. His desk, a vast wooden table, was piled with papers and pots of ink, and pens and scissors and leather fasteners and binders. There was no square foot of the chamber that did not contain racks of scrolls, and others, hundreds perhaps, were piled like cord wood here and there. His sleeping mat was unrolled, and his blankets must not have been aired for weeks. His personal belongings, which seemed to be negligible, were stuffed into the meanest of the scroll racks.

One of the windows into Torm's chamber was quite irregular, and I noted that it had been forcibly enlarged. I imagined him with a carpenter's hammer, angrily cracking and banging away at the wall, chipping away the stone that more light might enter his room. And always under his table a brazier filled with hot coals burned near the feet of the scribe, perilously close to the scholarly litter with which the floor was strewn. It seemed that Torm was always cold or, at best, never quite warm enough. The hottest days would be likely to find him wiping his nose on the sleeve of his blue robes, shivering miserably and lamenting the price of fuel.

Torm was of slight build and reminded me of an angry bird which enjoys nothing so much as scolding squirrels. His blue robes were worn through in a dozen spots, only two or three of which had been ineptly attacked by thread. One of his sandals had a broken strap that had been carelessly knotted back together. The Goreans I had seen in the past few weeks had tended to be meticulous in their dress, taking great pride in their appearance, but Torm apparently had better things on which to spend his time. Among these things, unfortunately, was berating those like myself who were hapless enough to fall within the ambit of his wrath.

Yet, in spite of his incomparable eccentricities, his petulance and exasperation, I felt drawn to the man and sensed in him something I admired—a shrewd and kind spirit, a sense of humor, and a love of learning, which can be one of the deepest and most honest of loves. It was this love for his scrolls and for the men who had written them, perhaps centuries before, that most impressed me about Torm. In his way, he linked me, this moment, and himself with generations of men who had pondered on the world and its meaning. Incredible as it may seem, I did not doubt that he was the finest scholar in the City of Cylinders, as my father had said.

With annoyance, Torm poked through one of the enormous piles of scrolls and at last, on his hands and knees, fished out one skimpy scroll, set it in the reading device —a metal frame with rollers at the top and bottom— and, pushing a button, spun the scroll to its opening mark, a single sign.

"Al-Ka!" said Torm, pointing one long, authoritative finger at the sign. "Al-Ka," he said.

"Al-Ka," I repeated.

We looked at one another, and both of us laughed. A tear of amusement formed along the side of his sharp nose, and his pale blue eyes twinkled.

I had begun to learn the Gorean alphabet.

In the next few weeks I found myself immersed in intensive activity, interspersed with carefully calculated rest and feeding periods. At first only Torm and my father were my teachers, but as I began to master the language of my new home, numerous others, apparently of Earth stock, assumed responsibility for my lessons in special areas. Torm's English, incidentally, was spoken with a Gorean accent. He had learned our tongue from my father. Most Goreans would have regarded it as a worthless tongue, since it is nowhere spoken on the planet, but Torm had mastered it, apparently only for the delight of seeing how living thought could express itself in yet another garb.

The schedule that was forced upon me was meticulous and grueling, and except for rest and feeding, alternated between times of study and times of training, largely in arms, but partly in the use of various devices as common to the Goreans as adding machines and scales are to us.

One of the most interesting was the Translator, which could be set for various languages. Whereas there was a main common tongue on Gor, with apparently several related dialects or sublanguages, some of the Gorean languages bore in sound little resemblance to anything I had heard before, at least as languages; they resembled rather the cries of birds and the growls of animals; they were sounds I knew could not have been produced by a human throat. Although the machines could be set for various languages, one term of the translation symmetry, at least in the machines I saw, was always Gorean. If I set the machine to, say, Language A and spoke Gorean into it, it would, after a fraction of a second, emit a succession of noises, which was the translation of my Gorean sentences into A. On the other hand, a new succession of noises in A would be received by the machine and emitted as a message in Gorean.

My father, to my delight, had taped one of these translation devices with English, and accordingly it was a most useful tool in working out equivalent phrases. Also, of course, he and Torm worked intensively with me. The machine, however, particularly to Torm's relief, allowed me to practice on my own. These translation machines are a marvel of miniaturization, each of them, about the size of a portable typewriter, being programmed for four non-Gorean languages. The translations, of course, are rather literal, and the vocabulary is limited to recognitions of only about 25,000 equivalencies for each language.

Accordingly, for subtle communication or the fullest expression of thought, the machine was inferior to a skilled linguist. The machine, however, according to my father, retained the advantage that its mistakes would not be intentional, and that its translations, even if inadequate, would be honest.

"You must learn," Torm had said matter-of-factly, "the history and legends of Gor, its geography and economics, its social structures and customs, such as the caste system and clan groups, the right of placing the Home Stone, the Places of Sanctuary, when quarter is and is not permitted in war, and so on."

And I learned these things, or as much as I could in the time I was given. Occasionally Torm would cry out in horror as I made a mistake, incomprehension and disbelief written large on his features, and he would then sadly take up a large scroll, containing the work of an author of whom he disapproved, and strike me smartly on the head with it. One way or another, he was determined that I should profit by his instruction.

Oddly enough, there was little religious instruction, other than to encourage awe of the Priest-Kings, and what there was, Torm refused to administer, insisting it was the province of the Initiates. Religious matters on this world tend to be rather carefully guarded by the Caste of Initiates, who allow members of other castes little participation in their sacrifices and ceremonies. I was given some prayers to the Priest-Kings to memorize, but they were in Old Gorean, a language cultivated by the Initiates but not spoken generally on the planet, and I never bothered to learn them. To my delight, I learned that Torm, whose memory was phenomenal, had forgotten them years ago. I sensed that a certain distrust existed between the Caste of Scribes and the Caste of Initiates.

The ethical teachings of Gor, which are independent of the claims and propositions of the Initiates, amount to little more than the Caste Codes—collections of sayings whose origins are lost in antiquity. I was specially drilled in the Code of the Warrior Caste.

"It's just as well," said Torm. "You would never make a Scribe."

The Code of the Warrior was, in general, characterized by a rudimentary chivalry, emphasizing loyalty to the Pride Chiefs and the Home Stone. It was harsh, but with a certain gallantry, a sense of honor that I could respect. A man could do worse than live by such a code.

I was also instructed in the Double Knowledge—that is, I was instructed in what the people, on the whole, believed, and then I was instructed in what the intellectuals were expected to know. Sometimes there was a surprising discrepancy between the two. For example, the population as a whole, the castes below the High Castes, were encouraged to believe that their world was a broad, flat disk. Perhaps this was to discourage them from exploration or to develop in them a habit of relying on commonsense prejudices—something of a social control device.

On the other hand, the High Castes, specifically the Warriors, Builders, Scribes, Initiates, and Physicians, were told the truth in such matters, perhaps because it was thought they would eventually determine it for themselves, from observations such as the shadow of their planet on one or another of Gor's three small moons during eclipses, the phenomenon of sighting the tops of distant objects first, and the fact that certain stars could not be seen from certain geographical positions; if the planet had been flat, precisely the same set of stars would have been observable from every position on its surface.

I wondered, however, if the Second Knowledge, that of the intellectuals, might not be as carefully tailored to preclude inquiry on their level as the First Knowledge apparently was to preclude inquiry on the level of the Lower Castes. I would guess that there is a Third Knowledge, that reserved to the Priest-Kings.

"The city-state," said my father, speaking to me late one afternoon, "is the basic political division on Gor—hostile cities controlling what territory they can in their environs, surrounded by a no-man's land of open ground on every side."

"How is leadership determined in these cities?" I asked.

"Rulers," he said, "are chosen from any High Caste."

"High Caste?" I asked.

"Yes, of course," was his answer. "In fact, in the First Knowledge, there is a story told to the young in their public nurseries, that if a man from Lower Caste should come to rule in a city, the city would come to ruin."

I must have appeared annoyed.

"The caste structure," said my father patiently, with perhaps the trace of a smile on his face, "is relatively immobile, but not frozen, and depends on more than birth. For example, if a child in his schooling shows that he can raise caste, as the expression is, he is permitted to do so. But, similarly, if a child does not show the aptitude expected of his caste, whether it be, say, that of physician or warrior, he is lowered in caste."

"I see," I said, not much reassured.

"The High Castes in a given city," said my father, "elect an administrator and council for stated terms. In times of crisis, a war chief, or Ubar, is named, who rules without check and by decree until, in his judgment, the crisis is passed."

"In his judgment?" I asked skeptically.

"Normally the office is surrendered after the passing of the crisis," said my father. "It is part of the Warrior's Code."

"But what if he does not give up the office?" I asked. I had learned enough of Gor by now to know that one could not always count on the Caste Codes being observed.

"Those who do not desire to surrender their power," said my father, "are usually deserted by their men. The offending war chief is simply abandoned, left alone in his palace to be impaled by the citizens of the city he has tried to usurp."

I nodded, imagining a palace, empty save for one man sitting alone on his throne, clad in his robes of state, waiting for the angry people outside the gates to break through and work their wrath.

"But," said my father, "sometimes such a war chief, or Ubar, wins the hearts of his men, and they refuse to withdraw their allegiance."

"What happens then?" I asked.

"He becomes a tyrant," said my father, "and rules until eventually, in one way or another, he is ruthlessly deposed." My father's eyes were hard and seemed fixed in thought. It was not mere political theory he spoke to me. I gathered that he knew of such a man. "Until," he repeated slowly, "he is ruthlessly deposed."

The next morning it was back to Torm and his interminable lessons.

In large outline Gor, as would be expected, was not a sphere, but a spheroid. It was somewhat heavier in its southern hemisphere and was shaped somewhat like the Earth—like a rounded, inverted top. The angle of its axis was somewhat sharper than the Earth's, but not enough to prevent its having a glorious periodicity of seasons. Moreover, like the Earth, it had two polar regions and an equatorial belt, interspersed with northern and southern temperate zones. Much of the area of Gor, surprisingly enough, was blank on the map, but I was overwhelmed trying to commit as many of the rivers, seas, plains, and peninsulas to memory as I could.

Economically, the base of the Gorean life was the free peasant, which was perhaps the lowest but undoubtedly the most fundamental caste, and the staple crop was a yellow grain called Sa-Tarna, or Life-Daughter. Interestingly enough, the word for meat is Sa-Tassna, which means Life-Mother. Incidentally, when one speaks of food in general, one always speaks of Sa-Tassna. The expression for the yellow grain seems to be a secondary expression, derivative. This would seem to indicate that a hunting economy underlay or was prior to the agricultural economy. This would be the normal supposition in any case, but what intrigued me here, perhaps for no sufficient reason, was the complex nature of the expressions involved. This suggested to me that perhaps a well-developed language or mode of conceptual thought existed prior to the primitive hunting groups that must have flourished long ago on the planet. People had come, or had been brought to Gor possibly, with a fully developed language. I wondered at the possible antiquity of the Voyages of Acquisition I had heard my father speak of. I had been the object of one such voyage, he, apparently, of another.

I had little time for speculation, however, as I was trying to bear up under an arduous schedule which seemed designed to force me to become a Gorean in a matter of weeks or perhaps see me die in the attempt. But I enjoyed those weeks, as one is likely to when learning and developing oneself, though to what end I was still ignorant. I met many Goreans, other than Torm, in these weeks—free Goreans, mostly of the Caste of Scribes and the Caste of Warriors. The Scribes, of course, are the scholars and clerks of Gor, and there are divisions and rankings within the group, from simple copiers to the savants of the city.

I had seen few women, but knew that they, when free, were promoted or demoted within the caste system according to the same standards and criteria as the men, although this varied, I was told, considerably from city to city. On the whole, I liked the people I met, and I was confident that they were largely of Earth stock, that their ancestors had been brought to the planet in Voyages of Acquisition. Apparently, after having been brought to the planet, they had simply been released, much as animals might be released in a forest preserve, or fish stocked free in a river.

The ancestors of some of them might have been Chaldeans or Celts or Syrians or Englishmen brought to this world over a period of centuries from different civilizations. But the children, of course, and their children eventually became simply Gorean. In the long ages on Gor almost all traces of Earth origin had vanished. Occasionally, however, an English word in Gorean, like "ax" or "ship," would delight me. Certain other expressions seemed clearly to be of Greek or German origin. If I had been a skilled linguist, I undoubtedly would have discovered hundreds of parallels and affinities, grammatical and otherwise, between Gorean and various of the Earth Languages. Earth origin, incidentally, was not a part of the First Knowledge, though it was of the Second.

"Torm," I once asked, "why is Earth origin not part of the First Knowledge?"

"Is it not self-evident?" he asked.

"No," I said.

"Ah!" he said, and closed his eyes very slowly and kept them shut for about a minute, during which time he was apparently subjecting the matter to the most intense scrutiny.

"You're right," he said at last, opening his eyes. "It is not self-evident."

"Then what do we do?" I asked.

"We continue with our lessons," said Torm.

The caste system was socially efficient, given its openness with respect to merit, but I regarded it as somehow ethically objectionable. It was still too rigid, in my opinion, particularly with respect to the selection of rulers from the High Castes and with respect to the Double Knowledge. But far more deplorable than the caste system was the institution of slavery. There were only three statuses conceivable to the Gorean mind outside of the caste system: slave, outlaw, and Priest-King. A man who refused to practice his livelihood or strove to alter status without the consent of the Council of High Castes was, by definition, an outlaw and subject to impalement.

The girl I had originally seen had been a slave, and what I had taken to be the jewlery at her throat had been a badge of servitude. Another such badge was a brand concealed by her clothing. The latter marked her as a slave, and the former identified her master. One might change one's collar, but not one's brand. I had not seen the girl since the first day. I wondered what had become of her, but I did not inquire. One of the first lessons I was taught on Gor was that concern for a slave was out of place. I decided to wait. I did learn, casually from a Scribe, not Torm, that slaves were not permitted to impart instruction to a free man, since it would place him in their debt, and nothing was owed to a slave. If it was in my power, I resolved to do what I could to abolish what seemed to me a degrading condition. I once talked to my father about the matter, and he merely said that there were many things on Gor worse than the lot of slavery, particularly that of a Tower Slave.

Without warning, with blinding speed, the bronze-headed spear flew toward my breast, the heavy shaft blurred like a comet's tail behind it. I twisted, and the blade cut my tunic cleanly, creasing the skin with a line of blood as sharp as a razor. It sunk eight inches into the heavy wooden beams behind me. Had it struck me with that force, it would have passed through my body.

"He's fast enough," said the man who had cast the spear. "I shall accept him."

This was my introduction to my instructor in arms, whose name was also Tarl. I shall call him the Older Tarl. He was a blond Viking giant of a man, a bearded fellow with a cheerful, craggy face and fierce blue eyes, who strode about as though he owned the earth on which he stood. His whole body, his carriage, the holding of his head bespoke the warrior, a man who knew his weapons and, on the simple world of Gor, knew that he could kill almost any man who might stand against him. If there was one outstanding impression I gathered of the Older Tarl in that first terrifying meeting, it was that he was a proud man, not arrogant, but proud, and rightfully so. I would come to know this skilled, powerful, proud man well.

Indeed, the largest part of my education was to be in arms, mostly training in the spear and sword. The spear seemed light to me because of the gravity, and I soon developed a dexterity in casting it with considerable force and accuracy. I could penetrate a shield at close distance, and I managed to develop a skill sufficient to hurl it through a thrown hoop about the size of a dinner plate at twenty yards. I was also forced to learn to throw the spear with my left hand.

Once I objected.

"What if you are wounded in the right arm?" demanded the Older Tarl. "What will you do then?"

"Run?" suggested Torm, who occasionally observed these practice sessions.

"No!" cried the Older Tarl. "You must stand and be slain like a warrior!"

Torm tucked a scroll, which he had been pretending to read, under his arm. He wiped his nose sagely on the sleeve of his blue robe. "Is that rational?" he asked.

The Older Tarl seized a spear, and Torm, lifting his robes, hastily departed the training area.

In despair, with my left arm I lifted another spear from the spear-rack, to try once more. Eventually, perhaps more to my surprise than that of the Older Tarl, my performance became almost creditable. I had increased my margin of survival by some obscure percentage.

My training in the short, stabbing sword of the Goreans

was as thorough as they could make it. I had belonged to a fencing club at Oxford and had fenced for sport and pleasure at the college in New Hampsire, but this current business was serious. Once again, I was supposed to learn to wield the weapon equally well with either hand, but, again, I could never manage to develop the skill to my genuine satisfaction. I acknowledged to myself that I was inveterately, stubbornly right-handed, for better or worse.

During my training with the sword, the Older Tarl cut me unpleasantly a number of times, shouting out, annoyingly enough, I thought, "You are dead!" At last, near the end of my training, I managed to break through his guard and, pulling my stroke, to drive my blade against his chest. I withdrew it bright with his blood. He flung down his sword with a crash on the stone tiles and clasped me to his bleeding chest, laughing.

"I am dead!" he shouted in triumph. He slapped me on the shoulders, proud as a father who has taught his son chess and has been defeated for the first time.

I also learned the use of the shield, primarily to meet the cast spear obliquely so that it would deflect harmlessly. Toward the end of my training I always fought with shield and helmet. I would have supposed that armor, or chain mail perhaps, would have been a desirable addition to the accouterments of the Gorean warrior, but it had been forbidden by the Priest-Kings. A possible hypothesis to explain this is that the Priest-Kings may have wished war to be a biologically selective process in which the weaker and slower perish and fail to reproduce themselves. This might account for the relatively primitive weapons allowed to the Men Below the Mountains. On Gor it was not the case that a cavern-chested toothpick could close a switch and devastate an army. Also, the primitive weapons guaranteed that what selection went on would proceed with sufficient slowness to establish its direction, and alter it, if necessary.

Besides the spear and sword, the crossbow and longbow were permitted, and these latter weapons perhaps tended to redistribute the probabilities of survival somewhat more broadly than the former. It may be, of course, that the Priest-Kings controlled weapons as they did simply because they feared for their own safety. I doubted that they stood against one another, man to man, sword to sword, in their holy mountains, putting their principles of selection to the test in their own cases. Incidentally, speaking of the crossbow and longbow, I did receive some instruction in them, but not much. The Older Tarl, my redoubtable instructor in arms, did not care for them, regarding them as secondary weapons almost unworthy for the hand of a warrior. I did not share his contempt, and occasionally during my rest periods had sought to improve my proficiency with them.

I gathered that my education was coming to an end. Perhaps it was in the lengthening of the rest periods; perhaps it was in the repetition of materials I had already encountered; perhaps it was something in the attitude of my instructors. I felt that I was nearly ready—but for what I had no idea. One pleasure of these final days was that I had begun to speak Gorean with the facility that comes from constant contact with and intensive study of a language. I had begun to dream in Gorean and to understand easily the small talk of my teachers among themselves when they were speaking for one another and not for the ears of an outlander. I had begun to think in Gorean as well, and after a time I was conscious of a deliberate mental shift involved in thinking in English. After a few English sentences or a page or so in one of my father's books, I would be at home again in my native tongue, but the shift was there, and necessary. I was fluent in Gorean. Once, when struck by the Older Tarl, I had cursed in Gorean, and he had laughed.

This afternoon, when it was time for our lesson, he

was not laughing. He entered my apartment, carrying a metal rod about two feet long, with a leather loop attached. It had a switch in the handle, which could be set in two positions, on and off, like a simple torch. He wore another such instrument slung from his belt. "This is not a weapon," he said. "It is not to be used as a weapon."

"What is it?" I asked.

"A tarn-goad," he replied. He snapped the switch in the barrel to the "on" position and struck the table. It showered sparks in a sudden cascade of yellow light, but left the table unmarked. He turned off the goad and extended it to me. As I reached for it, he snapped it on and slapped it in my palm. A billion tiny yellow stars, like pieces of fiery needles, seemed to explode in my hand. I cried out in shock. I thrust my hand to my mouth. It had been like a sudden, severe electric charge, like the striking of a snake in my hand. I examined my hand; it was unhurt. "Be careful of a tarn-goad," said the Older Tarl. "It is not for children." I took it from him, this time being careful to take it near the leather loop, which I fastened around my wrist.

The Older Tarl was leaving, and I understood that I was to follow him. We ascended a spiral staircase inside the cylinder and climbed for what must have been dozens of apartment levels. At last we emerged on the flat roof of the cylinder. The wind swept across the flat, circular roof, tugging one toward the edge. There was no protective rail. I braced myself, wondering what was to occur. Some dust blew against my face. I shut my eyes. The Older Tarl took a tarn whistle, or tarn call, from his tunic and blew a piercing blast.

I had never seen one of the tarns before, except on the tapestry in my apartment and in illustrations in certain books I had studied devoted to the care, breeding, and equipment of tarns. That I had not been trained for this moment was intentional, as I later discovered.

The Goreans believe, incredibly enough, that the capacity to master a tarn is innate and that some men possess this characteristic and that some do not. One does not learn to master a tarn. It is a matter of blood and spirit, of beast and man, of a relation between two beings which must be immediate, intuitive, spontaneous. It is said that a tarn knows who is a tarnsman and who is not, and that those who are not die in this first meeting.

My first impression was that of a rush of wind and a great snapping sound, as if a giant might be snapping an enormous towel or scarf; then I was cowering, awe-stricken, in a great winged shadow, and an immense tarn, his talons extended like gigantic steel hooks, his wings sputtering fiercely in the air, hung above me, motionless except for the beating of his wings.

"Stand clear of the wings," shouted the Older Tarl.

I needed no urging. I darted from under the bird. One stroke of those wings would hurl me yards from the top of the cylinder.

The tarn dropped to the roof of the cylinder and regarded us with his bright black eyes.

Though the tarn, like most birds, is surprisingly light for its size, this primarily having to do with the comparative hollowness of the bones, it is an extremely powerful bird, powerful even beyond what one would expect from such a monster. Whereas large Earth birds, such as the eagle, must, when taking flight from the ground, begin with a running start, the tarn, with its incredible musculature, aided undoubtedly by the somewhat lighter gravity of Gor, can with a spring and a sudden flurry of its giant wings lift both himself and his rider into the air. In Gorean, these birds are sometimes spoken of as Brothers of the Wind.

The plumage of tarns is various, and they are bred for their colors as well as their strength and intelligence. Black tarns are used for night raids, white tarns in winter campaigns, and multicolored, resplendent tarns are bred for warriors who wish to ride proudly, regardless of the lack of camouflage. The most common tarn, however, is greenish brown. Disregarding the disproportion in size, the Earth bird which the tarn most closely resembles is the hawk, with the exception that it has a crest somewhat of the nature of a jay's.

Tarns, who are vicious things, are seldom more than half tamed and, like their diminutive earthly counterparts, the hawks, are carnivorous. It is not unknown for a tarn to attack and devour his own rider. They fear nothing but the tarn-goad. They are trained by men of the Caste of Tarn Keepers to respond to it while still young, when they can be fastened by wires to the training perches. Whenever a young bird soars away or refuses obedience in some fashion, he is dragged back to the perch and beaten with the tarn-goad. Rings, comparable to those which are fastened on the legs of the young birds, are worn by the adult birds to reinforce the memory of the hobbling wire and the tarn-goad. Later, of course, the adult birds are not fastened, but the conditioning given them in their youth usually holds, except when they become abnormally disturbed or have not been able to obtain food. The tarn is one of the two most common mounts of a Gorean warrior; the other is the high tharlarion, a species of saddle-lizard, used mostly by clans who have never mastered tarns. No one in the City of Cylinders, as far as I knew, maintained tharlarions, though they were supposedly quite common on Gor, particularly in the lower areas—in swampland and on the deserts.

The Older Tarl had mounted his tarn, climbing up the five-rung leather mounting ladder which hangs on the left side of the saddle and is pulled up in flight. He fastened himself in the saddle with a broad purple strap. He tossed me a small object which nearly fell from my fumbling hands. It was a tarn whistle, with its own note, which would summon one tarn, and one tarn only, the mount which was intended for me. Never since the panic of the disoriented compass back in the mountains of New Hampshire had I been so frightened, but this time I refused to allow my fear the fatal inch it required. If I was to die, it would be; if I was not to die, I would not.

I smiled to myself in spite of my fear, amused at the remark I had addressed to myself. It sounded like something out of the Code of the Warrior, something which, if taken literally, would seem to encourage its believer to take not the slightest or most sane precautions for his safety. I blew a note on the whistle, and it was shrill and different, of a new pitch from that of the Old Tarl.

Almost immediately from somewhere, perhaps from a ledge out of sight, rose a fantastic object, another giant tarn, even larger than the first, a glossy sable tarn which circled the cylinder once and then wheeled toward me, landing a few feet away, his talons striking on the roof with a sound like hurled gauntlets. His talons were shod with steel—a war tarn. He raised his curved beak to the sky and screamed, lifting and shaking his wings. His enormous head turned toward me, and his round, wicked eyes blazed in my direction. The next thing I knew his beak was open; I caught a brief sight of his thin, sharp tongue, as long as a man's arm, darting out and back, and then, snapping at me, he lunged forward, striking at me with that monstrous beak, and I heard the Older Tarl cry out in horror, "The goad! The goad!"

4

The Mission

I THREW MY RIGHT ARM up to protect myself, the goad, attached by its strap to my wrist, flying wildly. I seized it, using it like a puny stick, striking at the great snapping beak that was trying to seize me, as if I were a scrap of food on the high, flat plate of the cylinder's roof. He lunged twice, and I struck it twice. He drew back his head again, spreading his beak, preparing to slash downward again. In that instant I switched the tarn-goad to the "on" position, and when the great beak flashed downward again, I struck it viciously, trying to force it away from me. The effect was startling: there was the sudden bright flash of yellow glittering light, the splash of sparks, and a scream of pain and rage from the tarn as he immediately beat his wings, lifting himself out of my reach in a rush of air that nearly forced me over the edge of the roof. I was on my hands and knees, trying to get back on my feet, too near the edge. The tarn was circling the cylinder, uttering piercing cries; then he began to fly away from the city.

Without knowing why, and thinking I was better off to have the thing in retreat, I seized my tarn whistle and blew its shrill note. The giant bird seemed almost to shudder in the air, and then he reeled, losing altitude, gaining it again. If he had not been simply a winged beast, I would have believed him to be struggling with himself, a creature locked inwardly in mental torture. It was the wild nature of the tarn, the call of the distant hills, the open sky, against the puny conditioning he had been subjected to, against the will of tiny men with their private objectives, their elementary psychology of stimulus and response, their training wires and tarn-goads.

At last, with a wild cry of rage, the tarn returned to the cylinder. I seized the short mounting ladder swinging wildly from the saddle and climbed it, seating myself in the saddle, fastening the broad purple belt that would keep me from tumbling to my death.

The tarn is guided by virtue of a throat strap, to which are attached, normally, six leather streamers, or reins, which are fixed in a metal ring on the forward portion of the saddle. The reins are of different colors, but one learns them by ring position and not color. Each of the reins attaches to a small ring on the throat strap, and the rings are spaced evenly. Accordingly, the mechanics are simple. One draws on the streamer, or rein, which is attached to the ring most nearly approximating the direction in which one wishes to go. For example, to land or lose altitude, one uses the four-strap which exerts pressure on the four-ring, which is located beneath the throat of the tarn. To rise into flight, or gain altitude, one draws on the one-strap, which exerts pressure on the one-ring, which is located on the back of the tarn's neck. The throat-strap rings, corresponding to the position of the reins on the main saddle ring, are numbered in a clockwise fashion.

The tarn-goad also is occasionally used in guiding the bird. One strikes the bird in the direction opposite to which one wishes to go, and the bird, withdrawing from the goad, moves in that direction. There is very little precision in this method, however, because the reactions of the bird are merely instinctive, and he may not withdraw in the exact tangent desired. Moreover, there is danger in using the goad excessively. It tends to become less effective if often used, and the rider is then at the mercy of the tarn.

I drew back on the one-strap and, filled with terror and exhilaration, felt the power of the gigantic wings beating on the invisible air. My body lurched wildly, but the saddle belt held. I couldn't breathe for a minute, but clung, frightened and thrilled, to the saddle-ring, my hand wrapped in the one-strap. The tarn continued to climb, and I saw the City of Cylinders dropping far below me, like a set of rounded children's blocks set in the gleaming green hills. I had never experienced anything like this, and if man ever felt godlike I suppose I did in those first savage, exhilarating moments. I looked below and saw the Older Tarl, mounted on his own tarn, climbing to overtake me. When he was near, he shouted to me, the words merry but indistinct in the rush of air.

"Ho, child," he called. "Do you seek to climb to the Moons of Gor?"

I suddenly realized I felt dizzy, or slightly so, but the magnificent black tarn was still climbing, though now struggling, his wings beating fiercely with frustrated persistence against the thinning, less resistant air. The hills and plains of Gor were a blaze of colors far below me, and it may have been my imagination, but it seemed almost as if I could see the curve of the world. I realize now it must have been the thin air and my excitement.

Fortunately, before losing consciousness, I drew on the four-strap, and the tarn leveled out and then lifted his wings over his back and dropped like a striking hawk, with a speed that left me without breath in my body. I released the reins, letting them hang on the saddle-ring, which is the signal for a constant and straight flight, no pressure on the throat strap. The great tarn snapped his wings out, catching the air under them, and smoothly began to fly a straight course, his wings beating slowly but steadily in a cruising speed that would soon take us far beyond the towers of the city. The Older Tarl, who seemed pleased, drew near. He pointed back toward the city, which was now several miles in the distance.

"I'll race you," I cried.

"Agreed!" he shouted, wheeling his tarn in the instant he spoke, and turning him to the city. I was dismayed. His skill was such that he had taken a lead that it would be impossible to overcome. At last I managed to turn the bird, and we were streaking along in the wake of the Older Tarl. Certain of his cries drifted back to us. He was urging his tarn to greater speed by a series of shouts intended to communicate his own excitement to his winged mount. The thought flashed through my mind that tarns should be trained to respond to voice commands as well as to the numbered straps and the tarn-goad. That they had not been seemed astounding to me.

I shouted to my tarn, in Gorean and in English. "Har-ta! Har-ta! Faster! Faster!"

The great bird seemed to sense what I intended, or perhaps it was merely his sudden realization that the other tarn was in the lead, but a remarkable transformation swept over my sable, plumed steed. His neck straightened and his wings suddenly cracked like whips in the sky; his eyes became fiery and his every bone and muscle seemed to leap with power. In a dizzying minute or two we had passed the Older Tarl, to his amazement, and had settled again in a flurry of wings on the top of the cylinder from which we had departed a few minutes before.

"By the beards of the Priest-Kings," roared the Older Tarl as he brought his bird to the roof, "that is a tarn of tarns!"

The tarns, released, winged their way back to the tarn cots, and the Older Tarl and I descended to my apartment. He was bursting with pride. "What a tarn!" he marveled. "I had a full pasang start, and yet you passed me!" The pasang is a measure of distance on Gor, equivalent approximately to .7 of a mile. "That tarn," he said, "was bred for you, specially selected from the best broods of the finest of our war tarns. It was with you in mind that the keepers of the tarns worked, breeding and crossbreeding, training and retraining."

"I thought," I said, "on the roof it would kill me. It seems the tarn keepers do not train their prodigies as well as they might."

"No!" cried the Older Tarl. "The training is perfect. The spirit of the tarn must not be broken, not that of a war tarn. He is trained to the point where it is necessary for a strong master to decide whether he shall serve him or slay him. You will come to know your tarn, and he will come to know you. You will be as one in the sky, the tarn the body, you the mind and will. You will live in an armed truce with the tarn. If you become weak or helpless, he will kill you. As long as you remain strong, his master, he will serve you, respect you, obey you." He paused. "We were not sure of you, your father and myself, but today I am sure. You have mastered a tarn, a war tarn. In your veins must flow the blood of your father, once Ubar, War Chieftain, now Administrator of Ko-ro-ba, this City of Cylinders."

I was surprised, for this was the first time I had known that my father had been War Chieftain of the city, or that he was even now its supreme civil official, or, for that matter, that the city was named Ko-ro-ba, a now archaic expression for a village market. The Goreans have a habit of not revealing names easily. For themselves, particularly among the Lower Castes, they often have a real name and what is called a use name. Often only the closest relatives know the real name.

On the level of the First Knowledge, it is maintained that knowing the real name gives one a power over a person, a capacity to use that name in spells and insidious magical practices. Perhaps something of the same sort lingers even on our native Earth, where the first name of a person is reserved for use by those who know him intimately and presumably wish him no harm. The second name, which would correspond to the use-name on Gor, is common property, a public sound not sacred or to be protected. At the level of the Second Knowledge, of course, the High Castes, at least in general, recognize the baseless superstition of the Lower Castes and use their own names comparatively freely, usually followed by the name of their city. For example, I would have given my name as Tarl Cabot of Ko-ro-ba, or, more simply, as Tarl of Ko-ro-ba. The Lower Castes, incidentally, commonly believe that the names of the High Castes are actually use-names and that the High Castes conceal their real names.

Our discussion terminated abruptly. There was a rush of wings outside the window of my apartment, and the Older Tarl flung himself across the room and dragged me to the floor. At the same moment the iron bolt of a crossbow, fired through one of the narrow windows, struck the wall behind my chair-stone and ricocheted viciously about the room. I caught a glimpse of a black helmet through the port as a warrior, still clutching a crossbow and mounted on his tarn, hauled up on the one-strap and flew from the window. There were shouts, and, rushing to the window, I saw several answering bolts leave the cylinder and fly in the direction of the retreating assailant, who was now almost half a pasang away and making good his escape.

"A member of the Caste of Assassins," said the Older Tarl, gazing at the retreating speck in the distance. "Marlenus, who would be Ubar of all Gor, knows of your existence."

"Who is Marlenus?" I asked, shaken.

"You will learn in the morning," said the Older Tarl.

"And in the morning you will learn why you have been brought to Gor."

"Why can't I know now?" I demanded.

"Because the morning will come soon enough," said the Older Tarl.

I looked at him.

"Yes," he said, "tomorrow will be soon enough."

"And tonight?" I asked.

"Tonight," he said, "we will get drunk."

In the morning I awoke on the sleeping mat in the corner of my apartment, cold and shivering. It was shortly before dawn. I turned off the power switch on the mat and folded back its blanket sides. It was chilly to the touch now, because I had set the chronometric temperature device to turn to cold an hour before the first light. One has little inclination to remain in a freezing bed. I decided I disapproved of the Gorean devices for separating mortals from their beds as much as I loathed the alarm clocks and clock radios of my own world. Besides, I had a headache like the beating of spears on a bronze shield, a headache that drove all lesser considerations, such as the attempt on my life yesterday, from my mind. The planet might be exploding and a man would stop to remove a burr from his sandal. I sat up, cross-legged, on the mat, which was now returning to room temperature. I struggled to my feet and staggered to the laving bowl on the table and splashed some water in my face.

I could remember something of the night before, but not much. The Older Tarl and I had made a round of taverns in the various cylinders, and I recall toddling precariously, singing obscene camp lyrics, along different narrow bridges, about a yard wide without rails, and the earth somewhere below—how far I had no idea at the time. If we were on the high bridges, it would have been more than a thousand feet away. The Older Tarl and I may have drunk too much of that fermented brew concocted with fiendish skill from the yellow grain, Sa-Tarna, and called Pagar-Sa-Tarna, Pleasure of the Life-Daughter, but almost always "Paga" for short. I doubted that I would ever touch the stuff again.

I remembered, too, the girls in the last tavern, if it was a tavern, lascivious in their dancing silks, pleasure slaves bred like animals for passion. If there were natural slaves and natural free men, as the Older Tarl had insisted, those girls were natural slaves. It was impossible to conceive of them as other than they had been, but somewhere they, too, must be awakening painfully, struggling to their feet, needing to clean themselves. One in particular I remembered, young, her body like a cheetah, her black hair wild on her brown shoulders, the bangles on her ankles, their sound in the curtained alcove. I found the thought crossing my mind that I would like to have owned that one for more than the hour I had paid for. I shook the thought from my aching head, made an unsuccessful effort to muster a decent sense of shame, failed, and was belting my tunic when the Older Tarl entered the room.

"We are going to the Chamber of the Council," he said.

I followed him.

The Chamber of the Council is the room in which the elected representatives of the High Castes of Ko-ro-ba hold their meetings. Each city has such a chamber. It was in the widest of cylinders, and the ceiling was at least six times the height of the normal living level. The ceiling was lit as if by stars, and the walls were of five colors, applied laterally, beginning from the bottom—white, blue, yellow, green, and red, caste colors. Benches of stone, on which the members of the Council sat, rose in five monumental tiers about the walls, one tier for each of the High Castes. These tiers shared the color of that portion of the wall behind them, the caste colors.

The tier nearest the floor, which denoted some preferential status, the white tier, was occupied by Initiates, Interpreters of the Will of the Priest-Kings. In order, the ascending tiers, blue, yellow, green, and red, were occupied by representatives of the Scribes, Builders, Physicians, and Warriors.

Torm, I observed, was not seated in the tier of Scribes. I smiled to myself. "I am," Torm had said, "too practical to involve myself in the frivolities of government." I supposed the city might be under siege and Torm would fail to notice.

I was pleased to note that my own caste, that of the Warriors, was accorded the least status; if I had had my will, the warriors would not have been a High Caste. On the other hand, I objected to the Initiates being in the place of honor, as it seemed to me that they, even more than the Warriors, were nonproductive members of society. For the Warriors, at least, one could say that they afforded protection to the city, but for the Initiates one could say very little, perhaps only that they provided some comfort for ills and plagues largely of their own manufacture.

In the center of the amphitheater was a throne of office, and on this throne, in his robe of state—a plain brown garment, the humblest cloth in the hall—sat my father, Administrator of Ko-ro-ba, once Ubar, War Chieftain of the city. At his feet lay a helmet, shield, spear, and sword.

"Come forward, Tarl Cabot," said my father, and I stood before his throne of office, feeling the eyes of everyone in the chamber on me. Behind me stood the Older Tarl. I had noted that those blue Viking eyes showed almost no evidence of the previous night. I hated him, briefly.

The Older Tarl was speaking. "I, Tarl, Swordsman of Ko-ro-ba, give my word that this man is fit to become a member of the High Caste of Warriors."

My father answered him, speaking in ritual phrases. "No tower in Ko-ro-ba is stronger than the word of Tarl, this Swordsman of our city. I, Matthew Cabot of Ko-ro-ba, accept his word."

Then, beginning with the lowest tier, each member of the Council spoke in succession, giving his name and pronouncing that he, too, accepted the word of the blond swordsman. When they had finished, my father invested me with the arms which had lain before the throne. About my shoulder he slung the steel sword, fastened on my left arm the round shield, placed in my right hand the spear, and slowly lowered the helmet on my head.

"Will you keep the Code of the Warrior?" asked my father.

"Yes," I said, "I will keep the Code."

"What is your Home Stone?" asked my father.

Sensing what was wanted, I replied, "My Home Stone is the Home Stone of Ko-ro-ba."

"Is it to that city that you pledge your life, your honor, and your sword?" asked my father.

"Yes," I said.

"Then," said my father, placing his hands solemnly on my shoulders, "in virtue of my authority as Administrator of this city and in the presence of the Council of High Castes, I declare you to be a Warrior of Ko-ro-ba."

My father was smiling. I removed my helmet, feeling proud as I heard the approval of the Council, both in voice and by Gorean applause, the quick, repeated striking of the left shoulder with the palm of the right hand. Aside from candidates for the status of Warrior, none of my caste was permitted to enter the Council armed. Had they been armed, my caste brothers in the last tier would have struck their spear blades on their shields. As it was, they smote their shoulders in the civilian manner, more exuberantly perhaps than was compatible with the decorum of that weighty chamber. Somehow I had the feeling they were genuinely proud of me, though I had no idea why. I had surely done nothing to warrant their commendation.

With the Older Tarl I left the Chamber of the Council and entered a room off the chamber to wait for my father. In the room was a table, and on the table was a set of maps. The Older Tarl immediately went to the maps, and, calling me to his side, began to pore over them, pointing out this mark and that. "And there," he said, poking downward with his finger, "is the City of Ar, hereditary enemy of Ko-ro-ba, the central city of Marlenus, who intends to be Ubar of all Gor."

"This has something to do with me?" I asked.

"Yes," said the Older Tarl. "You are going to Ar. You are going to steal the Home Stone of Ar and bring it to Ko-ro-ba."

5

Lights of the Planting Feast

I MOUNTED MY TARN, THAT fierce, black magnificent bird. My shield and spear were secured by saddle straps; my sword was slung over my shoulder. On each side of the saddle hung a missile weapon, a crossbow with a quiver of a dozen quarrels, or bolts, on the left, a longbow with a quiver of thirty arrows on the right. The saddle pack contained the light gear carried by raiding tarnsmen —in particular, rations, a compass, maps, binding fiber, and extra bowstrings. Bound in the saddle in front of me, drugged, her head completely covered with a slave hood buckled under her chin, was a girl. It was Sana, the Tower Slave whom I had seen on my first day in Gor.

I waved a farewell to the Older Tarl and to my father, drew back on the one-strap, and was off, leaving the tower and their tiny figures behind me. I leveled the tarn and drew on the six-strap, setting my course for Ar. As I passed the cylinder in which Torm kept his scrolls, I was happy to catch a glimpse of the little scribe standing at his rough-hewn window. I now realize he might have been waiting there for hours. He lifted his blue-clad arm in a gesture of farewell—rather sadly, I thought. I waved back at him and then turned my eyes away from Ko-ro-ba and toward the hills beyond. I felt little of the exhilaration I had felt in my first soaring venture on the back of the tarn. I was troubled and angry, dismayed at the ugly details of the project before me. I thought of the innocent girl bound senseless before me.

How surprised I had been when she had appeared in the small room outside the Chamber of the Council, after my father! She had knelt at his feet in the position of the Tower Slave as he had explained to me the plan of the Council.

The power of Marlenus, or much of it, lay in the mystique of victory that had never ceased to attend him, acting like a magic spell on his soldiers and the people of his city. Never defeated in combat, Ubar of Ubars, he had boldly refused to relinquish his title after a Valley War some twelve years ago, and his men had refused to withdraw from him, refused to abandon him to the traditional fate of the overambitious Ubar. The soldiers, and the Council of his city, had succumbed to his blandishments, his promises of wealth and power for Ar.

Indeed, it seemed their confidence had been well placed, for now Ar, instead of being a single beleaguered city like so many others on Gor, was a central city in which were kept the Home Stones of a dozen hitherto free cities. There was now an empire of Ar, a robust, arrogant, warlike polity only too obviously involved in the work of dividing its enemies and extending its political hegemony city by city across the plains, hills, and deserts of Gor.

In a matter of time Ko-ro-ba would be forced to match its comparative handful of tarnsmen against those of the Empire of Ar. My father, in his office as Administrator of Ko-ro-ba, had attempted to develop an alliance against Ar, but the free cities of Gor had, in their pride and suspicion, their almost fanatical commitment to protecting their own independent destinies, refused the alliance. Indeed, they had, in the fashion of Gor, driven my father's envoys from their Council Chambers with the whips normally used on slaves, an insult which, at another time, would have been answered by the War Call of Ko-ro-ba. But, as my father knew, strife among the free cities would be the very madness which Marlenus of Ar would welcome most; better even that Ko-ro-ba should suffer the indignity of being thought a city of cowards. Yet if the Home Stone of Ar, the very symbol and significance of the empire, could be removed from Ar, the spell of Marlenus might be broken. He would become a laughingstock, suspect to his own men, a leader who had lost the Home Stone. He would be fortunate if he was not publicly impaled.

The girl on the saddle before me stirred, the effect of the drug wearing off. She moaned softly and leaned back against me. As soon as we had taken flight, I had unfastened the restraining straps on her legs and wrists, leaving only the broad belt which lashed her securely to the back of the tarn. I would not permit the plan of the Council to be followed completely, not in her case, even though she had agreed to play her part in the plan, knowing it meant her life. I knew little more about her than her name, Sana, and the fact that she was a slave from the City of Thentis.

The Older Tarl had told me that Thentis is a city famed for its tarn flocks and remote in the mountains from which the city takes its name. Raiders from Ar had struck at the tarn flocks and the outlying cylinders of Thentis, and the girl had been captured. She had been sold in Ar on the Day of the Love Feast and had been purchased by an agent of my father. He, in accordance with the plan of the Council, had need of a girl who would be willing to give her life to be avenged on the men of Ar.

I could not help feeling sorry for her, even in the stern world of Gor. She had been through too much and was clearly not of the stock of the tavern girls; slavery would not have been a good life for her, as it might have been for them. I felt that, somehow, in spite of her collar, she was free. I had felt this even when my father had commanded her to rise and submit to me, accepting me as her new master. She had risen and walked across the room, her feet bare on the stone floor, and dropped to her knees before me, lowering her head and lifting and extending her hands to me, the wrists crossed. The ritual significance of the gesture of submission was not lost on me; her wrists were offered to me, as if for binding. Her part in the plan was simple, though ultimately fatal.

The Home Stone of Ar, like most Home Stones in the cylinder cities, was kept free on the tallest tower, as if in open defiance of the tarnsmen of rival cities. It was, of course, kept well-guarded and at the first sign of serious danger would undoubtedly be carried to safety. Any attempt on the Home Stone was regarded by the citizens of a city as sacrilege of the most heinous variety and punishable by the most painful of deaths, but, paradoxically, it was regarded as the greatest of glories to purloin the Home Stone of another city, and the warrior who managed this was acclaimed, accorded the highest honors of the city, and was believed to be favored by the Priest-Kings themselves.

The Home Stone of a city is the center of various rituals. The next would be the Planting Feast of Sa-Tarna, the Life-Daughter, celebrated early in the growing season to insure a good harvest. This is a complex feast, celebrated by most Gorean cities, and the observances are numerous and intricate. The details of the rituals are arranged and mostly executed by the Initiates of a given city. Certain portions of the ceremonies, however, are often allotted to members of the High Castes.

In Ar, for example, early in the day, a member of the Builders will go to the roof on which the Home Stone is kept and place the primitive symbol of his trade, a metal angle square, before the Stone, praying to the Priest-Kings for the prosperity of his caste in the coming year; later in the day a Warrior will, similarly, place his arms before the Stone, to be followed by other representatives of each caste. Most significantly, while these members of the High Castes perform their portions of the ritual, the Guards of the Home Stone temporarily withdraw to the interior of the cylinder, leaving the celebrant, it is said, alone with the Priest-Kings.

Lastly, as the culmination of Ar's Planting Feast, and of the greatest importance to the plan of the Council of Ko-ro-ba, a member of the Ubar's family goes to the roof at night, under the three full moons with which the feast is correlated, and casts grain upon the stone and drops of a red, winelike drink made from the fruit of the Ka-la-na tree. The member of the Ubar's family then prays to the Priest-Kings for an abundant harvest and returns to the interior of the cylinder, at which point the Guards of the Home Stone resume their vigil.

This year the honor of the grain sacrifice was to be accorded to the daughter of the Ubar. I knew nothing about her, except that her name was Talena, that she was rumored to be one of the beauties of Ar, and that I was supposed to kill her.

According to the plan of the Council of Ko-ro-ba, exactly at the time of the sacrifice, at the twentieth Gorean hour, or midnight, I was to drop to the roof of the highest cylinder in Ar, slay the daughter of the Ubar, and carry away her body and the Home Stone, discarding the former in the swamp country north of Ar and carrying the latter home to Ko-ro-ba. The girl, Sana, whom I carried on the saddle before me, would dress in the heavy robes and veils of the Ubar's daughter and return in her place to the interior of the cylinder. Presumably, it would be at least a matter of minutes before her identity was discovered, and, before that, she would take the poison provided by the Council.

Two girls were supposed to die that I might have time to escape with the Home Stone before the alarm could be given. In my heart I knew I would not carry out this plan. Abruptly I changed course, drawing on the four-strap, guiding my tarn toward the blue, shimmering wave of a mountain range in the distance. The girl before me groaned and shook herself, her hands, unsteady, going to the slave hood, which was buckled over her head.

I helped her unbuckle the hood and felt delighted at the sudden flash of her long blond hair streaking out beside my cheek. I placed the hood in the saddle pack, admiring her, not only her beauty but even more that she did not seem frightened. Surely there was enough to frighten any girl—the height at which she found herself, the savage mount on which she rode, the prospect of the terrible fate that she believed to await her at our journey's end. But she was, of course, a girl of mountainous Thentis, famed for its fierce tarn flocks. Such a girl would not frighten easily.

She didn't turn to look at me, but she examined her

wrists, rubbing them gently. The marks of the original restraining straps, which I had removed, were just visible.

"You unbound me," she said. "And you removed my hood—why?"

"I thought you would be more comfortable," I replied.

"You treat a slave with unexpected consideration," she said. "Thank you."

"You're not—frightened?" I asked, stumbling on the words, feeling stupid. "I mean—about the tarn. You must have ridden tarns before. I was frightened my first time."

The girl looked back at me, puzzled. "Women are seldom permitted to ride on the backs of tarns," she said. "In the carrying baskets, but not as a warrior rides." She paused, and the wind whistled past, a steady sound mingling with the rhythmical stroke of the tarn's beating wings. "You said you were frightened—when you first rode a tarn," she said.

"I was," I laughed, recalling the excitement and the sense of danger.

"Why do you tell a slave that you were frightened?" she asked.

"I don't know," I replied. "But I was."

She turned her head away again and looked, unseeing, at the head of the great tarn as he plowed the wind.

"I did ride once before on the back of a tarn," she said bitterly, "to Ar, bound across the saddle, before I was sold in the Street of Brands."

It was not easy to talk on the back of the great tarn, with the wind, and, besides, though I wanted to communicate with the girl, I felt I could not.

She was looking at the horizon, and suddenly her body tensed. "This is not the way to Ar," she cried.

"I know," I said.

"What are you doing?" She turned bodily in the straps, looking at me, her eyes wide. "Where are you going, Master?"

The word "Master," though it had come appropriately enough from the girl, who was, legally at least, my property, startled me.

"Don't call me Master," I said.

"But you are my Master," she said.

I took from my tunic the key my father had given me, the key to Sana's collar. I reached to the lock behind her neck, inserted the key and turned it, springing open the mechanism. I jerked the collar away from her throat and threw it and the key from the tarn's back and watched them fly downward in a long, graceful parabola.

"You are free," I said. "And we are going to Thentis."

She sat before me, stunned, her hands unbelievingly at her throat. "Why?" she asked. "Why?"

What could I tell her? That I had come from another world, that I was determined that all the ways of Gor should not be mine, or that I had cared for her, somehow, so helpless in her condition—that she had moved me to regard her not as an instrumentality of mine or of the Council, but as a girl, young, rich with life, not to be sacrificed in the games of statecraft?

"I have my reasons for freeing you," I said, "but I am not sure that you would understand them," and I added, under my breath, to myself, that I was not altogether sure I understood them myself.

"My father," she said, "and my brothers will reward you."

"No," I said.

"If you wish, they are bound in honor to grant me to you, without bride price."

"The ride to Thentis will be long," I said.

She replied proudly, "My bride price would be a hundred tarns."

I whistled softly to myself—my ex-slave would have come high. On a Warrior's allowance I would not have been able to afford her.

"If you wish to land," said Sana, apparently determined to see me compensated in some fashion, "I will serve your pleasure."

It occurred to me that there was at least one reply which she, bred in the honor codes of Gor, should understand, one reply that should silence her. "Would you diminish the worth of my gift to you?" I asked, feigning anger.

She thought for a moment and then gently kissed me on the lips. "No, Tarl Cabot of Ko-ro-ba," she said, "but you well know that I could do nothing that would diminish the worth of your gift to me. Tarl Cabot, I care for you."

I realized that she had spoken to me as a free woman, using my name. I put my arms around her, sheltering her as well as I could from the swift, chilling blast of the wind. Then I thought to myself, a hundred tarns indeed! Forty perhaps, because she was a beauty. For a hundred tarns one might have the daughter of an Administrator, for a thousand perhaps even the daughter of the Ubar of Ar! A thousand tarns would make a formidable addition to the cavalry force of a Gorean warlord. Sana, collar or no, had the infuriating, endearing vanity of the young and beautiful of her sex.

On a tower of Thentis I left her, kissing her, removing from my neck her clinging hands. She was crying, with all the incomprehensible absurdity of the female kind. I hauled the tarn aloft, waving back at the small figure still wearing the diagonally striped livery of the slave. Her white arm was lifted, and her blond hair was swept behind her on the windy roof of the cylinder. I turned the tarn toward Ar.

As I crossed the Vosk, that mighty river, some forty pasangs in width, which hurtles past the frontiers of Ar to pour into the Tamber Gulf, I realized that I was at last within the borders of the Empire of Ar. Sana had insisted that I keep the pellet of poison which the Council had given her to spare her from the otherwise inevitable tortures that would follow the disclosure of her identity in the cylinders of Ar. However, I took the pellet from my tunic and dropped it into the wide waters of the Vosk. It constituted a temptation to which I had no inclination to succumb. If death was easy, I might seek life less strenuously. There would come times when, in my weakness, I would regret my decision.

It took three days to reach the environs of the city of Ar. Shortly after crossing the Vosk, I had descended and made camp, thereafter traveling only at night. During the day I freed my tarn, to allow him to feed as he would. They are diurnal hunters and eat only what they catch themselves, usually one of the fleet Gorean antelopes or a wild bull, taken on the run and lifted in the monstrous talons to a high place, where it is torn to pieces and devoured. Needless to say, tarns are a threat to any living matter that is luckless enough to fall within the shadow of their wings, even human beings.

During the first day, sheltered in the occasional knots of trees that dot the border plains of Ar, I slept, fed on my rations, and practiced with my weapons, trying to keep my muscles vital in spite of the stiffness that attends prolonged periods on tarnback. But I was bored. At first even the countryside was depressing, for the men of Ar, as a military policy, had devastated an area of some two or three hundred pasangs on their borders, cutting down fruit trees, filling wells, and salting the fertile areas. Ar had, for most practical purposes, surrounded itself with an invisible wall, a bleached region, forbidding and almost impassable to those on foot.

I was more pleased on the second day and made camp in a grassy veldt, dotted with the Ka-la-na trees. The night before, I had ridden over fields of grain, silvery yellow beneath me in the light of the three moons. I kept my course by the luminescent dial of my Gor compass, the needle of which pointed always to the Sardar Mountain Range, home of the Priest-Kings. Sometimes I guided my tarn by the stars, the same fixed stars I had seen from another angle above my head in the mountains of New Hampshire.

The third day's camp was made in the swamp forest that borders the city of Ar on the north. I had chosen this area because it is the most uninhabitable area within tarn strike of Ar. I had seen too many village cooking fires on the last night, and twice I had heard the tarn whistles of nearby patrols—groups of three warriors flying their rounds. The thought crossed my mind of giving up the project, turning outlaw, if you will, deserter, if you like, but of saving my own skin, trying to get out of this mad scheme if only with my life, and that only for a time.

But an hour before midnight, on the day I knew was the Planting Feast of Sa-Tarna, I climbed again to the saddle of my tarn, drew back on the one-strap, and rose above the lush trees of the swamp forest. Almost simultaneously I heard the raucous cry of a patrol leader of Ar, "We have him!"

They had followed my tarn, trailing it back from its feeding in the swamp forest, and now, like the points of a rapidly converging triangle, three warriors of Ar were closing in on me. They apparently had no intention of taking me prisoner, for an instant after the shout the sharp hiss of a bolt from a crossbow passed over my head. Before I had time to gather my senses, a dark winged shape had materialized in front of me, and, in the light of the three moons, I saw a warrior on a tarn passing, thrusting out with his spear.

He surely would have struck home had not my tarn veered wildly to the left, almost colliding with another tarn and its rider, who fired a bolt that sank deep in the saddle pack with a sound like slapping leather. The third of the warriors of Ar was sweeping in from behind. I turned, raising the tarn-goad, which was looped to my wrist, to ward off the stroke of his blade. Sword and tarn-goad met in a ringing clash and a shower of glittering yellow sparks. Somehow I must have turned the goad on. Both my tarn and that of the attacker withdrew as if by instinct from the flash of the goad, and I had inadvertently purchased a moment of time.

I unslung my longbow and fitted an arrow, yanking my tarn in an abrupt wing-shuddering arc. I think the first of my pursuers had not realized I would turn the bird. He had been expecting a chase. As I passed him, I saw his eyes wide in the "Y" of his helmet, as, in that split second, he knew I could not miss. I saw him stiffen suddenly in the saddle and was dimly aware of his tarn streaking away, screaming.

Now the other two men of the patrol were circling for their attack. They swept toward me, about five yards apart, to close on either side of me, to force the wings of my tarn up and hold it for the moment they would need, trapped motionless between their own mounts.

I had no time to think, but somehow I was aware that my sword was now in my hand and the tarn-goad thrust in my belt. As we crashed in the air, I sharply jerked back the one-strap, bringing the steel-shod talons of my war tarn into play. And to this day I bless the tarn keepers of Ko-ro-ba for the painstaking training they had given the great bird. Or perhaps I should bless the fighting spirit of that plumed giant, my war tarn, that terrible thing the Older Tarl had called a tarn of tarns. Beak and talons rending, uttering ear-shattering screams, my tarn slashed at the other two birds.

I crossed swords with the nearer of the two warriors in a brief passage that could have lasted only an instant. I was suddenly aware, dizzily conscious, that one of the enemy tarns was sinking downward, flopping wildly, falling into the recesses of the swamp forest below. The other warrior pulled his tarn about as if for another passage at arms, but then, as if suddenly realizing that his duty was to give the alarm, he shouted at me in rage and wheeled his tarn again, streaking for the lights of Ar.

With his start, he would be confident, but I knew that my tarn could overtake him easily. I brought my tarn into line with the retreating speck and gave him his rein. As we neared the fleeing warrior, I fitted a second arrow to my bow. Rather than kill the warrior, I loosed the arrow into the wing of his tarn. The tarn spun about and began to favor the injured wing. The warrior could no longer control the mount, and I saw the tarn dropping awkwardly, descending in drunken circles to the darkness below.

I drew back on the one-strap, and when we had climbed to a height where my breath came in gasps, I leveled our course for Ar. I wished to fly above the normal patrol runs. When I neared Ar, I crouched low in the saddle and hoped that the speck against a moon which might be seen by the watchmen of the outlying towers would be taken for a wild tarn, flying high over the city.

The city of Ar must have contained more than a hundred thousand cylinders, each ablaze with the lights of the Planting Feast. I did not question that Ar was the greatest city of all known Gor. It was a magnificent and beautiful city, a worthy setting for the jewel of empire, that awesome jewel that had proved so tempting to its Ubar, the all-conquering Marlenus. And now, down there, somewhere in that monstrous blaze of light, was a humble piece of stone, the Home Stone of that great city, and I must seize it.

6

Nar the Spider

I HAD LITTLE DIFFICULTY MAKING out the tallest tower in Ar, the cylinder of the Ubar Marlenus. As I dropped closer, I saw that the bridges were lined with the celebrants of the Planting Feast, many perhaps reeling home drunk on Paga. Flying among the cylinders were tarnsmen, cavalry warriors reveling in the undisciplined liberty of the feast, racing one another, essaying mock passages at arms, sometimes dropping their tarns like thunderbolts toward the bridges, only to jerk them upward just inches above the terrified heads of the celebrants.

Boldly I dipped my tarn downward, into the midst of the cylinders, just another of the wild tarnsmen of Ar. I brought him to rest on one of the steel projections that occasionally jut forth from the cylinders and serve as tarn perches. The great bird opened and closed his wings, his steel-shod talons ringing on the metal perch as he changed his position, moving back and forth upon it. At last, satisfied, he brought his wings against his body and remained still, except for the alert movements of his great head and the flash of those wicked eyes scrutinizing the streams of men and women on the nearby bridges.

My heart began to beat wildly, and I considered the

facility with which I might yet wing my way from Ar. Once a warrior without a helmet flew near, drunk, and challenged me for the perch, a wild tarnsman of low rank, spoiling for a fight. If I had yielded the perch, it would have aroused suspicion immediately, for on Gor the only honorable reply to a challenge is to accept it promptly.

"May the Priest-Kings blast your bones," I shouted, as cheerfully as I could, adding, for good measure, "and may you thrive upon the excrement of tharlarions!" The latter recommendation, with its allusion to the loathed riding lizards used by many of the primitive clans of Gor, seemed to please him.

"May your tarn lose its feathers," he roared, slapping his thigh, bringing his tarn to rest on the perch. He leaned over and tossed me a skin bag of Paga, from which I took a long swig, then hurled it contemptuously back into his arms. In a moment he had taken flight again, bawling out some semblance of a song about the woes of a camp girl, the bag of Paga flying behind him, dangling from its long straps.

Like most Gor compasses, mine contained a chronometer, and I took the compass, turned it over, and pressed the tab that would snap open the back and reveal the dial. It was two minutes past the twentieth hour! Vanished were my thoughts of escape and desertion. I abruptly forced my tarn into flight, streaking for the tower of the Ubar.

In a moment it was below me. I dropped immediately, for no one without good reason rides a tarn in the vicinity of the tower of a Ubar. As I descended, I saw the wide, round roof of the cylinder. It seemed to be translucently lit from beneath—a bluish color. In the center of the circle was a low, round platform, some ten paces in diameter, reached by four circular steps that extended about the perimeter of the platform. On the platform, alone, was a dark robed figure. As my tarn struck down on the platform and I leaped from its back, I heard a girl's scream.

I lunged for the center of the platform, breaking under my foot a small ceremonial basket filled with grain, kicking from my path a Ka-la-na container, splashing the fermented red liquid across the stone surface. I raced to the pile of stones at the center of the platform, the girl's screaming in my ears. From a short distance away I heard the shouts of men and the clank of arms as warriors raced up the stairs to the roof. Which was the Home Stone? I kicked apart the rocks. One of them must be the Home Stone of Ar, but which? How could I tell it from the others, the Home Stones of those cities which had fallen to Ar?

Yes! It would be the one that would be red with Ka-la-na, that would be sprinkled with the seeds of grain! I felt the stones in frenzy, but several were damp and dotted with the grains of Sa-Tarna. I felt the heavily robed figure dragging me back, tearing at my shoulders and throat with her nails, pitting against me all the fury of her enraged body. I swung back, forcing her from me. She fell to her knees and suddenly crawled to one of the stones, seized it up, and turned to flee. A spear shattered on the platform near me. The Guards were on the roof!

I leaped after the heavily robed figure, seized her, spun her around and tore from her hands the stone she carried. She struck at me and pursued me to the tarn, which was excitedly shaking his wings, preparing to forsake the tumultuous roof of the cylinder. I leaped upward and seized the saddle ring, inadvertently dislodging the mounting ladder. In an instant I had attained the saddle of the tarn and drew back savagely on the one-strap. The heavily robed figure was trying to climb the mounting ladder, but was impeded by the weight and ornate inflexibility of her garments. I cursed as an arrow creased my shoulder, as the tarn's great wings smote the air and the monster took to flight. He was in the air, and the passage of arrows sang in my ears, the cries of enraged men, and the long, piercing, terrified scream of a girl.

I looked down, dismayed. The heavily robed figure was still clinging desperately to the mounting ladder. She was now clear of the roof, swinging free below the tarn, with the lights of Ar dropping rapidly into the distance below her. I drew my sword from its sheath, to cut the mounting ladder from the saddle, but stopped, and angrily drove the blade back into its sheath. I couldn't afford to carry the extra weight, but neither could I bring myself to cut the ladder free and send the girl hurtling to her death.

I cursed as the frenzied notes of tarn whistles drifted up from below. All the tarnsmen of Ar would be flying tonight. I passed the outermost cylinders of Ar and found myself free in the Gorean night, streaking for Ko-ro-ba. I placed the Home Stone in the saddle pack, snapping the lock shut, and then reached down to haul in the mounting ladder.

The girl was whimpering in terror, and her muscles and fingers seemed frozen. Even after I had drawn her to the saddle before me and belted her securely to the saddle ring, I had to force her fingers from the rung of the mounting ladder. I folded the ladder and fastened it in its place at the side of the saddle. I felt sorry for the girl, a helpless pawn in this sorry man's game of empire, and the tiny animal noises she uttered moved me to pity.

"Try not to be afraid," I said.

She trembled, whimpering.

"I won't hurt you," I said. "Once we're beyond the swamp forest, I'll set you down on some highway to Ar. You'll be safe." I wanted so to reassure her. "By morning you'll be back in Ar," I promised.

Helplessly, she seemed to stammer some incoherent word of gratitude and turned trustfully to me, putting her arms around my waist as though for additional security; I felt her trembling, innocent body against mine, her dependence on me, and then she suddenly locked her arms around my waist and with a cry of rage hurled me from the saddle. In the sickening instant of falling I realized I had not fastened my own saddle belt in the wild flight from the roof of the Ubar's cylinder. My hands flung out, grasping nothing, and I fell headlong downward into the night.

I remember hearing for a moment, fading like the wind, her triumphant laughter. I felt my body stiffening in the fall, setting itself for the impact. I remember wondering if I would feel the crushing jolt, and supposing that I would. Absurdly, I tried to loosen my body, relaxing the muscles, as if it would make any difference. I waited for the shock, was conscious of the flashing pain of breaking through branches and the plunge into some soft, articulated yielding substance. I lost consciousness.

When I opened my eyes, I found myself partially adhering to a vast network of broad, elastic strands that formed a structure, perhaps a pasang in width, and through which at numerous points projected the monstrous trees of the swamp forest. I felt the network, or web, tremble, and I struggled to rise, but found myself unable to gain my feet. My flesh adhered to the adhesive substance of the broad strands. Approaching me, stepping daintily for all its bulk, prancing over the strands, came one of the Swamp Spiders of Gor. I fastened my eyes on the blue sky, wanting it to be the last thing I looked upon. I shuddered as the beast paused near me, and I felt the light stroke of its forelegs, felt the tactile investigation of the sensory hairs on its appendages. I looked at it, and it peered down, with its four pairs of pearly eyes—quizzically, I thought. Then, to my astonishment, I heard a mechanically reproduced sound say, "Who are you?"

I shuddered, believing that my mind had broken at

last. In a moment the voice repeated the question, the volume of the sound being slightly increased, and then added, "Are you from the City of Ar?"

"No," I said, taking part in what I believed must be some fantastic hallucination in which I madly conversed with myself. "No, I am not," I said. "I am from the Free City of Ko-ro-ba."

When I said this, the monstrous insect bent near me, and I caught sight of the mandibles, like curved knives. I tensed myself for the sudden lateral chopping of those pincerlike jaws. Instead, saliva or some related type of secretion or exudate was being applied to the web in my vicinity, which loosened its adhesive grip. When freed, I was lifted lightly in the mandibles and carried to the edge of the web, where the spider seized a hanging strand and scurried downward, placing me on the ground. He then backed away from me on his eight legs, but never taking the pearly gaze of his several eyes from me.

I heard the mechanically reproduced sound again. It said, "My name is Nar, and I am of the Spider People." I then saw for the first time that strapped to his abdomen was a translation device, not unlike those I had seen in Ko-ro-ba. It apparently translated sound impulses, below my auditory threshold, into the sounds of human speech. My own replies were undoubtedly similarly transformed into some medium the insect could understand. One of the insect's legs twiddled with a knob on the translation device. "Can you hear this?" he asked. He had reduced the volume of the sound to its original level, the level at which he had asked his original question.

"Yes," I said.

The insect seemed relieved. "I am pleased," he said. "I do not think it is appropriate for rational creatures to speak loudly."

"You have saved my life," I said. "Thank you."

"My web saved your life," corrected the insect. He was

still for a moment, and then, as if sensing my apprehension, said, "I will not hurt you. The Spider People do not hurt rational creatures."

"I am grateful for that," I said.

The next remark took my breath away.

"Was it you who stole the Home Stone of Ar?"

I paused, then, being confident the creature had no love for the men of Ar, answered affirmatively.

"That is pleasing to me," said the insect, "for the men of Ar do not behave well toward the Spider People. They hunt us and leave only enough of us alive to spin the Cur-lon Fiber used in the mills of Ar. If they were not rational creatures, we would fight them."

"How did you know the Home Stone of Ar was stolen?" I asked.

"The word has spread from the city, carried by all the rational creatures, whether they crawl or fly or swim." The insect lifted one foreleg, the sensory hairs trembling on my shoulder. "There is great rejoicing on Gor, but not in the city of Ar."

"I lost the Home Stone," I said. "I was tricked by her I suppose to be the daughter of the Ubar, thrown from my own tarn, and saved from death only by your web. I think tonight there will again be gladness in Ar, when the daughter of the Ubar returns the Home Stone."

The mechanical voice spoke again. "How is it that the daughter of the Ubar will return the Home Stone of Ar when you carry in your belt the tarn-goad?"

Suddenly I realized the truth of what he had said and was amazed that it had not occurred to me before. I imagined the girl alone on the back of the fierce tarn, unskilled in the mastery of such a mount, without even a tarn-goad to protect herself if the bird should turn on her. Her chances of survival seemed now more slim than if I had cut the ladder over the cylinders of Ar when she hung helplessly in my power, the treacherous daughter of the Ubar Marlenus. Soon the tarn would be feeding. It must have been light for several hours.

"I must return to Ko-ro-ba," I said. "I have failed."

"I will take you to the edge of the swamp if you like," said the insect. I assented, thanking him, this rational creature who lifted me gently to his back and moved with such dainty rapidity, picking his way exquisitely through the swamp forest.

We had proceeded for perhaps an hour when Nar, the spider, abruptly stopped and lifted his two forelegs into the air, testing the odors, straining to sift out something in the dense, humid air.

"There is a carnivorous tharlarion, a wild tharlarion, in the vicnity," he said. "Hold tightly."

Luckily I did immediately as he had advised, fixing my grip deep in the long black hairs that covered his thorax, for Nar suddenly raced to a nearby swamp tree and scuttled high into its branches. About two or three minutes later I heard the hunger grunt of a wild tharlarion and a moment afterward the piercing scream of a terrified girl.

From the back of Nar I could see the marsh, with its reeds and clouds of tiny flying insects below. From a wall of reeds about fifty paces to the right and thirty feet below, stumbling and screaming, came the bundled figure of a human being, running in horror, its hands flung out before it. In that instant I recognized the heavy brocaded robes, now mud-splattered and torn, of the daughter of the Ubar.

Scarcely had she broken into the clearing, splashing through the shallow greenish waters near us, than the fearsome head of a wild tharlarion poked through the reeds, its round, shining eyes gleaming with excitement, its vast arc of a mouth swung open. Almost too rapid to be visible, a long brown lash of a tongue darted from its mouth and curled around the slender, helpless figure of the girl. She screamed hysterically, trying to force the adhesive band from her waist. It began to withdraw toward the mouth of the beast.

Without thinking, I leaped from the back of Nar, seizing one of the long, tendril-like vines that parasitically interlace the gnarled forms of the swamp trees. In an instant I had splashed into the marsh at the foot of the tree and raced toward the tharlarion, my sword raised. I rushed between its mouth and the girl, and with a swift downward slash of my blade severed that foul brown tongue.

A shattering squeal of pain rent the heavy air of the swamp forest, and the tharlarion actually reared on its hind legs and spun about in pain, sucking the brown stump of its tongue back into its mouth with an ugly popping noise. Then it splashed on its back in the water, rolled quickly onto its legs, and began to move its head in rapid scanning motions. Almost immediately its eyes fixed on me; its mouth, now filled with a colorless scum, opened, revealing its teeth ridges.

It charged, its great webbed feet striking the marsh water like explosions. In an instant the mouth had snapped for me, and I had left the mark of my blade deep in the teeth ridges of its lower jaw. It snapped again, and I knelt, the jaws passing over me as I thrust upward with the sword, piercing the neck. It backed away to about four or five paces, slowly, unsteadily. The tongue, or rather its stump, flitted in and out of its mouth two or three times, as if the creature could not understand that it was no longer at its disposal.

The tharlarion sunk a bit lower in the marsh, half closing its eyes. I knew the fight was over. More of the colorless exudate was seeping from its throat. About its flanks, as it settled into the mud, there was a stirring in the water, and I realized the small water lizards of the swamp forest were engaged in their grisly work. I bent down and washed the blade of my sword as well as I could in the green water, but my tunic was so splattered and soaked that I had no way to dry the blade. Accordingly, carrying the sword in my hand, I waded back to the foot of the swamp tree and climbed the small, dry knoll at its base.

I looked around. The girl had fled. This made me angry, for some reason, though I thought myself well rid of her. After all, what did I expect? That she would thank me for saving her life? She had undoubtedly left me to the tharlarion, rejoicing in the luck of a Ubar's daughter, that her enemies might destroy one another while she escaped with her life. I wondered how far she would get in the swamps before another tharlarion caught her scent. I called out "Nar!", looking for my spider comrade, but he, like the girl, had disappeared. Exhausted, I sat with my back against the tree, my hand never leaving the hilt of my sword.

Idly, with repulsion, I watched the body of the tharlarion in the swamp. As the water lizards had fed, the carcass, lightened, had shifted position, rolling in the water. Now, in a matter of minutes, the skeleton was visible, picked almost clean, the bones gleaming except where small lizards skittered about on them, seeking a last particle of flesh.

There was a sound. I leaped to my feet, sword ready. But across the marsh, with his swift prancing stride, came Nar, and in his mandibles, held gently but firmly, the daughter of the Ubar Marlenus. She was striking at Nar with her tiny fists, cursing and kicking in a manner I thought most improper for the daughter of a Ubar. Nar pranced onto the knoll and set her down before me, his pearly luminescent eyes fixed on me like blank, expressionless moons.

"This is the daughter of the Ubar Marlenus," said Nar, and added ironically, "She did not remember to thank you for saving her life, which is strange, is it not, for a rational creature?"

"Silence, Insect," said the daughter of the Ubar, her

voice loud, clear, and imperious. She seemed to have no fear of Nar, perhaps because of the familiarity of the citizens of Ar with the Spider People, but it was obvious she loathed the touch of his mandibles, and she shivered slightly as she tried to wipe the exudate from the sleeves of her gown.

"Also," said Nar, "she speaks rather loudly for a rational creature, does she not?"

"Yes," I said.

I regarded the daughter of the Ubar, now a sorry sight. Her Robes of Concealment were splattered with mud and marsh water, and in several places the heavy brocade had stiffened and cracked. The dominant colors of her Robes of Concealment were subtle reds, yellows, and purples, arrayed in intricate, overlapping folds. I guessed it would have taken her slave girls hours to array her in such garments. Many of the free women of Gor and almost always those of High Caste wear the Robes of Concealment, though, of course, their garments are seldom as complex or splendidly wrought as those of a Ubar's daughter. The Robes of Concealment, in function, resemble the garments of Muslim women on my own planet, though they are undoubtedly more intricate and cumbersome. Normally, of men, only a father and a husband may look upon the woman unveiled.

In the barbaric world of Gor, the Robes of Concealment are deemed necessary to protect the women from the binding fibers of roving tarnsmen. Few warriors will risk their lives to capture a woman who may be as ugly as a tharlarion. Better to steal slaves, where the guilt is less and the charms of the captive are more readily ascertainable in advance.

Now the eyes of the daughter of the Ubar were blazing at me furiously from the narrow aperture in her veil. I noted that they were greenish in cast, fiery and untamed, the eyes of a Ubar's daughter, a girl accustomed to command men. I also noted, though with considerably less pleasure, that the daughter of the Ubar was several inches taller than myself. Indeed, her body seemed somehow to be out of proportion.

"You will release me immediately," announced the daughter of the Ubar, "and dismiss this filthy insect."

"Spiders are, as a matter of fact, particularly clean insects," I remarked, my eyes informing her that I was inspecting her comparatively filthy garments.

She shrugged haughtily.

"Where is the tarn?" I demanded.

"You should ask," she said, "where is the Home Stone of Ar."

"Where is the tarn?" I repeated, more interested at the moment in the fate of my fierce mount than in the ridiculous piece of rock I had risked my life to obtain.

"I don't know," she said, "nor do I care."

"What happened?" I wanted to know.

"I do not care to be questioned further," she announced.

I clenched my fists in rage.

Then, gently, the mandibles of Nar closed around the girl's throat. A sudden tremor of fear shook her heavily robed body, and the girl's hands tried to force the implacable chitinous pincers from her throat. Apparently the Spider Person was not as harmless as she had arrogantly assumed. "Tell it to stop," she gasped, writhing in the insect's grip, her fingers helplessly trying to loosen the mandibles.

"Do you wish her head?" asked the mechanical voice of Nar.

I knew that the insect, who would allow his kind to be exterminated before he would injure any rational creature, must have some plan in mind, or at least I assumed he did. At any rate, I said, "Yes." The mandibles began to close on her throat like the blades of giant scissors.

"Stop!" screamed the girl, her voice a frenzied whisper.

I motioned to Nar to relax his grip.

"I was trying to bring the tarn back to Ar," said the girl. "I was never on a tarn before. I made mistakes. It knew it. There was no tarn-goad."

I gestured, and Nar removed his mandibles from the girl's throat.

"We were somewhere over the swamp forest," said the girl, "when we flew into a flock of wild tarns. My tarn attacked the leader of the flock."

She shuddered at the memory, and I pitied her for what must have been a horrifying experience, lashed helpless to the saddle of a giant tarn reeling in a death struggle for the mastery of a flock, high over the trees of the swamp forest.

"My tarn killed the other," said the girl, "and followed it to the ground, where he tore it to pieces." She shook with the memory. "I slipped free and ran under the wing and hid in the trees. After a few minutes, his beak and talons wet with blood and feathers, your tarn took flight. I last saw him at the head of the tarn flock."

That was that, I thought. The tarn had turned wild, all his instincts triumphant over the tarn whistle, the memory of men.

"And the Home Stone of Ar?" I asked.

"In the saddle pack," she said, confirming my expectation. I had locked the pack when I had placed the Home Stone inside, and the pack is an integral part of the tarn saddle. When she had spoken, her voice had burned with shame, and I sensed the humiliation she felt at having failed to save the Home Stone. So now the tarn was gone, returned to his natural wild state, the Home Stone was in the saddle pack, and I had failed, and the daughter of the Ubar had failed, and we stood facing one another on a green knoll in the swamp forest of Ar.

7

A Ubar's Daughter

THE GIRL STRAIGHTENED, SOMEHOW PROUD but ludicrous in her mud-bedaubed regalia. She stepped away from Nar, as if apprehensive that those fierce mandibles might threaten her again. Her eyes flashed from the narrow opening in her veil. "It pleased the daughter of Marlenus," she said, "to inform you and your eight-legged brother of the fate of your tarn and of the Home Stone you sought."

Nar's mandibles opened and shut once in annoyance. It was the nearest to anger I had ever seen the gentle creature come.

"You will release me immediately," announced the daughter of the Ubar.

"You are free now," I said.

She looked at me, stunned, and backed away, being careful to avoid Nar by a safe distance. She kept her eyes on my sword, as if she expected me to strike her down if she turned her back.

"It is well," she finally said, "that you obey my command. Perhaps your death will be made easier in consequence."

"Who could refuse anything to the daughter of a Ubar?" I said, and then added—maliciously, it seems now—"Good luck in the swamps."

She stopped and shuddered. Her robes still bore the wide lateral stain where the tongue of the tharlarion had wrapped itself. I glanced no more at her, but put my hand on the foreleg of Nar, gently, so that I might not injure any of the sensory hairs.

"Well, Brother," I said, remembering the insult of the daughter of the Ubar, "shall we continue our journey?" I wanted Nar to understand that not all humankind were as contemptuous of the Spider People as the daughter of the Ubar.

"Indeed, Brother," responded the mechanical voice of Nar. And surely I would rather have been a brother to that gentle, rational monster than many of the barbarians I had met on Gor. Indeed, perhaps I should be honored that he had addressed me as brother—I who failed to meet his standards, I who had so many times, intentionally or unintentionally, injured those of the rational kind.

Nar, with me on his back, moved from the knoll.

"Wait!" cried the daughter of the Ubar. "You can't leave me here!" She stumbled a bit from the knoll, tripped and fell in the water. She knelt in the green stagnant water, her hands held out to me, pleading, as if she suddenly realized the full horror of her plight, what it would mean to be abandoned in the swamp forest. "Take me with you," she begged.

"Wait," I said to Nar, and the giant spider paused.

The Ubar's daughter tried to stand up, but, ridiculously enough, it seemed as if one leg were suddenly far shorter than the other. She stumbled again and fell once more into the water. She swore like a tarnsman. I laughed and slid from Nar's back. I waded to her side and lifted her to carry her back to the knoll. She was surprisingly light, considering her apparent size.

I had hardly taken her in my arms when she struck my face viciously with one muddy hand. "How dare you touch the daughter of a Ubar!" she exclaimed. I shrugged and dropped her back in the water. Angrily she scrambled to her feet as best she could and, hopping and stumbling, regained the knoll. I joined her there and examined her leg. One monstrous platformlike shoe had broken from her small foot and flopped beside her ankle, still attached by its straps. The shoe was at least ten inches high. I laughed. This explained the incredible height of the Ubar's daughter.

"It's broken," I said. "I'm sorry."

She tried to rise, but one foot was, of course, some ten inches higher than the other. She fell again, and I unstrapped the remaining shoe. "No wonder you can hardly walk," I said. "Why do you wear these silly things?"

"The daughter of a Ubar must look down on her subjects," was the simple if extraordinary reply.

When she stood up, now barefoot, her head came only a little higher than my chin. She might have been a bit taller than the average Gorean girl, but not much. She kept her eyes sullenly down, unwilling to raise them to look into my own. The daughter of a Ubar looked up to no man.

"I order you to protect me," she said, never taking her eyes from the ground.

"I do not take orders from the daughter of the Ubar of Ar," I said.

"You must take me with you," she said, eyes still downcast.

"Why?" I asked. After all, according to the rude codes of Gor, I owed her nothing; indeed, considering her attempt on my life, which had been foiled only by the fortuitous net of Nar's web, I would have been within my rights to slay her, abandoning her body to the water lizards. Naturally, I was not looking at things from precisely the Gorean point of view, but she would have no way of knowing that. How could she know that I would not treat her as—according to the rough justice of Gor—she deserved?

"You must protect me," she said. There was something of a pleading note in her voice.

"Why?" I asked, feeling angry.

"Because I need your help," she said. Then she angrily snapped, "You need not have made me say that!" She had lifted her head in fury, and she looked up into my eyes for an instant, and then suddenly lowered her head again, trembling with rage.

"Do you ask my favor?" I asked, which, on Gor, was much like asking if the person was willing to make a request—more simply, to say, "Please." To that small particle of respect it seemed I had a right.

Suddenly she seemed strangely docile.

"Yes," she said. "Stranger, I, the daughter of the Ubar of Ar, ask your favor. I ask you to protect me."

"You tried to kill me," I said. "For all I know, you may still be an enemy."

There was a long pause in which neither of us spoke.

"I know what you are waiting for," said the daughter of the Ubar, strangely calm after her earlier fury—unnaturally calm, it seemed to me. I didn't understand her. What was it she thought I was waiting for? Then, to my astonishment, the daughter of the Ubar Marlenus, daughter of the Ubar of Ar, knelt before me, a simple warrior of Ko-ro-ba, and lowered her head, lifting and extending her arms, the wrists crossed. It was the same simple ceremony that Sana had performed before me in the chamber of my father, back at Ko-ro-ba—the submission of the captive female. Without raising her eyes from the ground, the daughter of the Ubar said in a clear, distinct voice: "I submit myself."

Later I wished that I had had binding fiber to lash her so innocently profferred wrists. I was speechless for a moment, but then, remembering that harsh Gorean custom required me either to accept the submission or slay the captive, I took her wrists in my hands and said, "I accept your submission." I then lifted her gently to her feet.

I led her by the hand toward Nar, helped her to the glossy, hairy back of the spider, and climbed up after her. Wordlessly Nar moved rapidly through the marsh, his eight delicate feet scarcely seeming to dip into the greenish water. Once he stepped into quicksand, and his back tilted suddenly. I held the daughter of the Ubar tightly as the insect righted himself, floating in the muck for a second, and then managing to free himself with his eight scrambling legs.

After a journey of an hour or so Nar stopped and pointed ahead with one of his forelegs. About three or four pasangs distant, through the thinning swamp trees, I could see the verdant meadows of Ar's Sa-Tarna land. The mechanical voice of Nar spoke. "I do not wish to approach nearer to the land. It is dangerous for the Spider People."

I slid from his back and helped the daughter of the Ubar down. We stood together in the shallow water at the side of the gigantic insect. I placed my hand on Nar's grotesque face, and the gentle monster lightly closed his mandibles on my arm and then opened them. "I wish you well," said Nar, using a common Gorean phrase of farewell.

I responded similarly and further wished health and safety to his people.

The insect placed his forelegs on my shoulders. "I do not ask your name, Warrior," he said, "nor will I repeat the name of your city before the Submitted One, but know that you and your city are honored by the Spider People."

"Thank you," I said. "My city and I are honored."

The mechanical voice spoke once more. "Beware the daughter of the Ubar."

"She has submitted herself," I replied, confident that the promise of her submission would be fulfilled.

As Nar raced backward, he lifted a foreleg in a gesture that I interpreted as an attempt to wave. I waved back at him, touched, and my grotesque ally disappeared into the marshes.

"Let's go," I said to the girl, and I made for the fields of Sa-Tarna. The daughter of the Ubar followed, some yards behind.

We had been wading for about twenty minutes when the girl suddenly screamed, and I spun around. She had sunk to her waist in the marsh water. She had slipped into a pocket of quicksand. She cried out hysterically. Cautiously I tried to approach her, but felt the ooze slipping away beneath my feet. I tried to reach her with my sword belt, but it was too short. The tarn-goad, which had been thrust in the belt, dropped into the water, and I lost it.

The girl sank deeper in the mire, the surface of the water circling her armpits. She was screaming wildly, all control lost in the face of the slow, ugly death awaiting her. "Don't struggle!" I cried. But her movements were hysterical, like those of a mad animal. "The veil!" I cried. "Unwind it, throw it to me!" Her hands tried to tear at the veil, but she was unable to unwind it, in her terror and in the moment of time left to her. Then the muck crept upward to her horrified eyes, and her head slipped under the greenish waters, her hands clutching wildly at the air.

I frantically looked about, caught sight of a half-submerged log some yards away, protruding upward out of the marsh water. Regardless of the possible danger, not feeling my way, I splashed to the log, jerking on it, hauling on it with all my might. In what seemed like hours but must have been a matter of only a few seconds, it gave, leaping upward out of the mud. I half-carried, half-floated it, shoving it toward the place where the daughter of the Ubar had slipped under the water. I clung to the log, floating in the shallow water over the quicksand, and reached down again and again into the mire.

At last my hand clutched something—the girl's wrist—and I drew her slowly upward out of the sand. My heart leaped with joy as I heard her whimpering, choking gasps, her lungs spasmodically sucking in the fetid but vivifying air. I shoved the log back and finally, carrying the filthy body soaked in its absurd garments, made my way to a ledge of green, dry land at the edge of the swamp.

I set her down on a bed of green clover. Beyond it, some hundred yards away, I could see the border of a yellow field of Sa-Tarna and a yellow thicket of Ka-la-na trees. I sat beside the girl, exhausted. I smiled to myself; the proud daughter of the Ubar in all her imperial regalia quite literally stank, stank of the swamps and the mud and of the perspiration exuded beneath that heavy covering, stank of heat and fear.

"You have saved my life again," said the daughter of the Ubar.

I nodded, not wanting to talk about anything.

"Are we out of the swamp?" she asked.

I assented.

This seemed to please her. With an animal movement, contradicting the formality of her garments, she lay backward on the clover, looking up at the sky, undoubtedly as exhausted as I was. Moreover, she was only a girl. I felt tender toward her. "I ask your favor," she said.

"What do you want?" I asked.

"I'm hungry," she said.

"I am, too," I laughed, suddenly aware that I had not eaten anything since the night before. I was ravenous. "Over there," I said, "are some Ka-la-na trees. Wait here and I'll gather some fruit."

"No, I'll come with you—if you permit me," she said.

I was surprised at this deference on the part of the

daughter of the Ubar, but recalled that she had submitted herself.

"Surely," I said. "I would be pleased with your company."

I took her arm, but she drew back. "Having submitted myself," she said, "it is my part to follow."

"That's silly," I said. "Walk with me."

But she dropped her head shyly, shaking it. "I may not," she said.

"Do as you please," I laughed, and set out for the Ka-la-na trees. She followed, meekly, I thought.

We were near the Ka-la-na trees when I heard a slight rustle of brocade behind me. I turned, just in time to seize the wrist of the daughter of the Ubar as she struck savagely down at my back with a long, slender dagger. She howled with rage as I twisted the weapon from her hand.

"You animal!" I yelled, blind with fury. "You dirty, filthy, stinking, ungrateful animal!"

Wild with anger, I picked up the dagger and for an instant felt tempted to plunge it into the heart of the treacherous girl. Angrily I shoved it in my belt.

"You submitted," I said to her.

In spite of my hold on her wrist, which must have been tight and painful, the daughter of Marlenus straightened herself before me and said arrogantly, "You tharlarion! Do you think that the daughter of the Ubar of all Gor would submit to such as you?"

Cruelly I forced her to her knees before me, the filthy, proud wench.

"You submitted," I said.

She cursed me, her greenish eyes blazing with hatred. "Is this how you treat the daughter of a Ubar?" she cried.

"I will show you how I treat the most treacherous wench on all Gor," I exclaimed, releasing her wrist. With both hands I wrenched the veil back from her face, thrusting my hand under it to fasten my fist in her hair, and then, as if she were a common tavern girl or a camp slut, I dragged the daughter of the Ubar of all Gor to the shelter of the Ka-la-na trees. Among the trees, on the clover, I threw her to my feet. She tried frantically to readjust the folds of her veil, but with both hands I tore it fully away, and she lay at my feet, as it is said on Gor, face-stripped. A marvelous cascade of hair, as black as the wing of my tarn, loosened behind her, falling to the ground. I saw magnificent olive skin and those wild green eyes and features that were breathtakingly beautiful. The mouth, which might have been magnificent, was twisted with rage. "I like it better," I said, "being able to see the face of my enemy. Do not replace your veil."

In fury she glared up at me, shamed as my eyes boldly regarded the beauty of her face. She made no move to replace the veil.

As I looked upon her, incredibly perhaps, my rage dissipated and with it the vengeful desires that had filled me. In anger I had dragged her, helpless, mine by all the Codes of Gor, to the shelter of the trees. Yet now once again I saw her as a girl, this time as a beautiful girl, not to be abused.

"You will understand," I said, "that I can no longer trust you."

"Of course not," she said. "I am your enemy."

"Accordingly I can take no chances with you."

"I am not afraid to die," she said, her lip trembling slightly. "Be quick."

"Remove your clothing," I said.

"No!" she cried, shrinking back. She rose to her knees before me, putting her head to my feet. "With all my heart, Warrior," she pleaded, "the daughter of a Ubar, on her knees, begs your favor. Let it be only the blade and quickly."

I threw back my head and laughed. The daughter of

the Ubar feared that I would force her to serve my pleasure—I, a common soldier. But then, shamefacedly, I admitted to myself that I had, while dragging her to the trees, intended to take her and that it had only been the sudden spell of her beauty which, paradoxically enough, had claimed my respect, forced me to recognize that selfishly I was about to injure or dominate what Nar would have referred to as a rational creature. I felt ashamed and resolved that I would do no harm to this girl, though she was as wicked and faithless as a tharlarion.

"I do not intend to force you to serve my pleasure," I said, "nor do I intend to injure you."

She lifted her head and looked at me wonderingly.

Then, to my amazement, she stood up and regarded me contemptuously. "If you had been a true warrior," she said, "you would have taken me on the back of your tarn, above the clouds, even before we had passed the outermost ramparts of Ar, and you would have thrown my robes to the streets below to show my people what had been the fate of the daughter of their Ubar." Evidently she believed that I had been afraid to harm her and that she, the daughter of a Ubar, remained above the perils and obligations of the common captive. She looked at me insolently, angry that she had so demeaned herself as to kneel before a coward. She tossed her head back and snorted. "Well, Warrior," she said, "what would you have me do?"

"Remove your clothing," I said.

She looked at me in rage.

"I told you," I said, "I am not going to take any more chances with you. I have to find out if you have any more weapons."

"No man may look upon the daughter of the Ubar," she said.

"Either you will remove your robes," I said, "or I shall."

In fury the hands of the Ubar's daughter began to fumble with the hooks of her heavy robes.

She had scarcely removed a braided loop from its hook when her eyes suddenly lit with triumph and a sound of joy escaped her lips.

"Don't move," said a voice behind me. "You are covered with a crossbow."

"Well done, Men of Ar," exclaimed the daughter of the Ubar.

I turned slowly, my hands away from my body, and found myself facing two of the foot soldiers of Ar, one of them an officer, the other of common rank. The latter had trained his crossbow on my breast. At that distance he could not have missed, and if he had fired at that range, most probably the quarrel would have passed through my body and disappeared in the woods behind. The initial velocity of a quarrel is the better part of a pasang per second.

The officer, a swaggering fellow whose helmet, though polished, bore the marks of combat, approached me, holding his sword to me, and seized my weapon from its scabbard and the girl's dagger from my belt. He looked at the signet on the dagger hilt and seemed pleased. He placed it in his own belt and took from a pouch at his side a pair of manacles, which he snapped on my wrists. He then turned to the girl.

"You are Talena," he said, tapping the dagger, "daughter of Marlenus?"

"You see I wear the robes of the Ubar's daughter," said the girl, scarcely deigning to respond to the officer's question. She paid her rescuers no more attention, treating them as if they were no more worthy of her gratitude than the dust beneath her feet. She strode to face me, her eyes mocking and triumphant, seeing me shackled and in her power. She spat viciously in my face, which insult I accepted, unmoving. Then, with her right hand, she slapped me savagely with all the force and fury of her body. My cheek felt as though it had been branded.

"Are you Talena?" asked the officer, once again, patiently. "Daughter of Marlenus?"

"I am indeed, Heroes of Ar," replied the girl proudly, turning to the soldiers. "I am Talena, daughter of Marlenus, Ubar of all Gor."

"Good," said the officer, and then nodded to his subordinate. "Strip her and put her in slave bracelets."

8

I Acquire a Companion

I LUNGED FORWARD, BUT WAS checked by the point of the officer's sword. The common soldier, setting the crossbow on the ground, strode to the daughter of the Ubar, who stood as though stunned, her face drained of color. The soldier, beginning at the high, ornate collar of the girl's robes, began to break the braided loops, ripping them loose from their hooks; methodically he tore her robes apart and pulled them down and over her shoulders; in half a dozen tugs the heavy layers of her garments had been jerked downward until she stood naked, her robes in a filthy pile about her feet. Her body, though stained with the mire of the swamp, was exquisitely beautiful.

"Why are you doing this?" I demanded.

"Marlenus has fled," said the officer. "The city is in chaos. The Initiates have assumed command and have ordered that Marlenus and all members of his household and family are to be publicly impaled on the walls of Ar."

A moan escaped the girl.

The officer continued: "Marlenus lost the Home Stone, the Luck of Ar. He, with fifty tarnsmen, disloyal to the city, seized what they could of the treasury and escaped. In the streets there is civil war, fighting between the factions that would master Ar. There is looting and pillaging. The city is under martial law."

Unresisting, the girl extended her wrists, and the soldier snapped slave bracelets on them—light, restraining bracelets of gold and blue stones that might have served as jewelry if it had not been for their function. She seemed unable to speak. In a moment her world had crumbled. She was nothing now but the abominated daughter of the villain in whose reign the Home Stone, the Luck of Ar, had been stolen. Now she, like all other members of the household of Marlenus, slave or free, would be subjected to the vengeance of the outraged citizens, citizens who had marched in the processions of the Ubar in the days of his glory, carrying flasks of Ka-la-na wine and sheaves of Sa-Tarna grain, singing his praises in the melodious litanies of Gor.

"I am the one who stole the Home Stone," I said.

The officer prodded me with the sword. "We presumed so, finding you in the company of the offspring of Marlenus." He chuckled. "Do not fear—though there are many in Ar who rejoice in your deed, your death will not be pleasant or swift."

"Release the girl," I said. "She has done no harm. She did her best to save the Home Stone of your city."

Talena seemed startled that I had asked for her freedom.

"The Initiates have pronounced their sentence," said the officer. "They have decreed a sacrifice to the Priest-

Kings to ask them to have mercy and to restore the Home Stone."

In that moment I detested the Initiates of Ar, who, like other members of their caste throughout Gor, were only too eager to seize some particle of the political power they had supposedly renounced in choosing to wear the white robes of their calling. The real purpose of the "sacrifice to the Priest-Kings" was probably to remove possible claimants to the throne of Ar and thereby strengthen their own political position.

The officer's eyes narrowed. He jabbed me with his sword. "Where," he demanded, "is the Home Stone?"

"I don't know," I said.

The blade was at my throat.

Then, to my amazement, the daughter of the Ubar spoke. "He tells the truth."

The officer regarded her calmly, and she blushed, realizing her body was no longer sacred in his sight, no longer protected by the power of the Ubar.

She raised her head and said quietly, "The Home Stone was in the saddle pack of his tarn. The tarn escaped. The Stone is gone."

The officer cursed under his breath.

"Take me back to Ar," said Talena. "I am ready." She stepped from the pile of filthy garments at her feet and stood proudly among the trees, the wind slightly moving her long dark hair.

The officer looked her over, slowly, carefully, his eyes gleaming. Without glancing at the common soldier, he ordered him to leash me, to fasten around my throat the leading chain often used on Gor for slaves and prisoners.

The officer sheathed his sword, not taking his eyes from Talena, who drew back. "This one I'll leash myself," he said, drawing a leading chain from his pouch and approaching the girl. She stood still, not quivering.

"The leash will not be necessary," she said proudly.

"That is for me to decide," said the officer, and laughed

as he snapped the chain on the throat of the girl. It clicked shut. He gave it a playful tug. "I never thought that I would have my chain on Talena, the daughter of Marlenus," he said.

"You beast!" she hissed.

"I see that I must teach you to respect an officer," he said, putting his hand between her throat and the chain, drawing her to him. He suddenly, savagely, thrust his mouth on her throat, and she screamed, being pressed backward, down to the clover. The common soldier was watching with delight, perhaps expecting that he, too, might take his turn. With all the weight of the heavy manacles on my wrist, I struck him across the temple, and he sank to his knees.

The officer turned from Talena, scrambling to his feet and growling with rage, unsheathing his blade. It was only halfway from its sheath when I leaped upon him, my manacled hands seeking his throat. He struggled furiously, his hands trying to pry apart my fingers, his sword slipping from the sheath. My hands were on his throat like the talons of a tarn. His hand drew Talena's dagger from his belt, and, manacled as I was, I could not have prevented the blow.

Suddenly his eyes emitted a wordless scream, and I saw a bloody stump at the end of his arm. Talena had picked up his sword and struck off the hand that held the dagger. I released my grip. The officer shuddered convulsively on the grass and was dead. Talena, naked, still held the bloody sword, her eyes glassy with the horror of what she had done.

"Drop the sword," I commanded harshly, fearing it would occur to her to strike me with it. The girl dropped the weapon, sinking to her knees and covering her face with her hands. The daughter of the Ubar was apparently not as inhuman as I had supposed.

I took the sword and approached the other soldier, asking myself if I would kill him if he was still alive.

I suppose now that I would have spared him, but I was not given the opportunity. He lay on the grass, motionless. The heavy manacles had broken in the side of his skull. He hadn't bled much.

I fumbled through the officer's pouch and found the key to the manacles. It was hard to put the key in the lock, restrained as I was.

"Let me," said Talena, and took the key and opened the lock. I threw the manacles to the ground, rubbing my wrists.

"I ask your favor," said Talena, standing meekly by my side, her hands confined in front of her by the colorful slave bracelets, the leading chain still dangling from her throat.

"Of course," I said. "I'm sorry." I dug about in the pouch and found the tiny key to the slave bracelets, which I opened immediately. I then removed her leading chain, and she removed mine.

I examined with greater detail the pouches and equipment of the soldiers.

"What are you going to do?" she asked.

"Take what I can use," I said, sorting out the articles in the pouches. Most importantly, I found a compass-chronometer, some rations, two water flasks, bowstrings, binding fiber, and some oil for the mechanism of the crossbow. I decided to carry my own sword and the soldier's crossbow, which I unwound, relaxing the tension on the metal span. His quiver contained some ten quarrels. Neither soldier had carried a spear or shield. I didn't want to be burdened with a helmet. I tossed to one side the leading chains, manacles, and slave bracelets that Talena and I had worn. There was also a slave hood, which I similarly discarded. I then carried the two bodies down to the swamp and pitched them into the mire.

When I returned to the glade, Talena was sitting in the grass, near the garments that had been ripped from her. I was surprised that she had not tried to dress herself.

Her chin was on her knees, and when she saw me she asked—rather humbly, I thought, "May I clothe myself?"

"Surely," I said.

She smiled. "As you can see, I carry no weapons."

"You underestimate yourself," I said.

She seemed flattered, then bent to the task of poking about in that pile of heavy, filthy garments. They must have been as offensive to her nostrils as to mine. At last she took a relatively unsoiled undergarment, something blue and silk, bare at the shoulders, and drew it on, belting it with a strip of what had been her veil. It was all she wore. Surprisingly, she no longer seemed as concerned about her modesty. Perhaps she felt it would be foolish after her utter exposure. On the other hand, I think that Talena was actually pleased to be rid of the encumbering, ornate robes of the daughter of the Ubar. Her garment was, of course, too long, as it had originally reached to the ground, covering the absurd platformlike shoes she had worn. At her request I cut the garment until it hung a few inches above her ankles.

"Thank you," she said.

I smiled at her. It seemed so unlike Talena to express any consideration.

She walked about in the glade, pleased with herself, and twirled once or twice, delighted with the comparative freedom of movement she now enjoyed.

I picked some Ka-la-na fruit and opened one of the packages of rations. Talena returned and sat beside me on the grass. I shared the food with her.

"I'm sorry about your father," I said.

"He was a Ubar of Ubars," she said. She hesitated for a moment. "The life of a Ubar is uncertain." She gazed thoughtfully at the grass. "He must have known it would happen sometime."

"Did he speak to you about it?" I asked.

She tossed her head back and laughed. "Are you of Gor or not? I have never seen my father except on the days of public festivals. High Caste daughters in Ar are raised in the Walled Gardens, like flowers, until some highborn suitor, preferably a Ubar or Administrator, will pay the bride price set by their fathers."

"You mean you never knew your father?" I asked.

"Is it different in your city, Warrior?"

"Yes," I said, remembering that in Ko-ro-ba, primitive though it was, the family was respected and maintained. I then wondered if that might be due to the influence of my father, whose Earth ways sometimes seemed at variance with the rude customs of Gor.

"I think I might like that," she said. Then she looked at me closely. "What is your city, Warrior?"

"Not Ar," I replied.

"May I ask your name?" she asked tactfully.

"I am Tarl."

"Is that a use-name?"

"No," I said, "it is my true name."

"Talena is my true name," she said. Of High Caste, it was natural that she was above the common superstitions connected with revealing one's name. Then she asked suddenly, "You are Tarl Cabot of Ko-ro-ba, are you not?"

I failed to conceal my astonishment, and she laughed merrily. "I knew it," she said.

"How?" I asked.

"The ring," she said, pointing to the red metal band that encircled the second finger of my right hand. "It bears the crest of Cabot, Administrator of Ko-ro-ba, and you are the son, Tarl, whom the warriors of Ko-ro-ba were training in the arts of war."

"The spies of Ar are effective," I said.

"More effective than the Assassins of Ar," she said. "Pa-Kur, Ar's Master Assassin, was dispatched to kill you, but failed."

I recalled the attempt on my life in the cylinder of my father, an attempt that would have been successful except for the alertness of the Older Tarl.

"Ko-ro-ba is one of the few cities my father feared," said Talena, "because he realized it might someday be effective in organizing other cities against him. We of Ar thought they might be training you for this work, and so we decided to kill you." She stopped and looked at me, something of admiration in her eyes. "We never believed you would try for the Home Stone."

"How do you know all this?" I asked.

"The women of the Walled Gardens know whatever happens on Gor," she replied, and I sensed the intrigue, the spying and treachery that must ferment within the gardens. "I forced my slave girls to lie with soldiers, with merchants and builders, physicians and scribes," she said, "and I found out a great deal." I was dismayed at this—the cool, calculating exploitation of her girls by the daughter of the Ubar, merely to gain information.

"What if your slaves refused to do this for you?" I asked.

"I would whip them," said the daughter of the Ubar coldly.

I began to divide the rations I had taken from the pouches of the soldiers.

"What are you doing?" asked Talena.

"I am giving you half of the food," I said.

"But why?" she asked, her eyes apprehensive.

"Because I am leaving you," I said, shoving her share of the food toward her, also one of the water flasks. I then tossed her dagger on top of the pile. "You may want this," I said. "You may need it."

For the first time since she had learned of the fall of Marlenus, the daughter of the Ubar seemed stunned. Her eyes widened questioningly, but she read only resolve in my face.

I packed my gear and was ready to leave the glade. The girl rose and shouldered her small bag of rations. "I'm coming with you," she said. "And you cannot prevent me."

"Suppose I chain you to that tree," I suggested.

"And leave me for the soldiers?"

"Yes," I said.

"You will not do that," she said. "Why I do not know, but you will not do that."

"Perhaps I shall," I said.

"You are not like the other warriors of Ar," she said. "You are different."

"Do not follow me," I said.

"Alone," she said, "I will be eaten by animals or found by soldiers." She shuddered. "At best, I would be picked up by slavers and sold in the Street of Brands."

I knew that she spoke the truth or something much like it. A defenseless woman on the plains of Gor would not have much chance.

"How can I trust you?" I asked, weakening.

"You can't," she admitted. "For I am of Ar and must remain your enemy."

"Then it is to my best interest to abandon you," I said.

"I can force you to take me," she said.

"How?" I asked.

"Like this," she responded, kneeling before me, lowering her head and lifting her arms, the wrists crossed. She laughed. "Now you must take me with you or slay me," she said, "and I know you cannot slay me."

I cursed her, for she took unfair advantage of the Warrior Codes of Gor.

"What is the submission of Talena, the daughter of the Ubar, worth?" I taunted.

"Nothing," she said. "But you must accept it or slay me."

Furious beyond reason, I saw in the grass the discarded slave bracelets, the hood and leading chains.

To Talena's indignation, I snapped the slave bracelets on her wrists, hooded her, and put her on a leading chain.

"If you would be a captive," I said, "you will be

treated as a captive. I accept your submission, and I intend to enforce it."

I removed the dagger from her sash and placed it in my belt. Angrily I slung both bags of rations about her shoulders. Then I picked up the crossbow and left the glade, dragging after me, none too gently, the hooded, stumbling daughter of the Ubar. Beneath the hood, to my amazement, I heard her laugh.

9

Kazrak of Port Kar

WE TRAVELED TOGETHER THROUGH THE night, making our way through the silvery yellow fields of Sa-Tarna, fugitives under the three moons of Gor. Soon after we had left the glade, to Talena's amusement, I had removed her hood and, a few minutes later, her leading chain and slave bracelets. As we crossed the grain fields, she explained to me the dangers we would most likely face, primarily from the beasts of the plains and from passing strangers. It is interesting, incidentally, that in the Gorean language, the word for stranger is the same as the word for enemy.

Talena seemed to be animated, as if excited beyond comprehension at her escape from the seclusion of the Walled Gardens and the role of the Ubar's daughter.

She was now a free though submitted person, at large on the plains of the empire. The wind shook her hair and tore at her gown, and she would throw back her head, exposing her throat and shoulders to its rough caress, drinking it in as though it were Ka-la-na wine. I sensed that with me, nominal captive though she was, she was freer than she had ever been before; she was like a naturally wild bird which has been raised in a cage and at last escapes from the confining wire bars. Somehow her happiness was contagious, and, almost as though we were not mortal enemies, we talked to one another and joked as we made our way across the plains.

I was heading, as nearly as I could determine, in the general direction of Ko-ro-ba. Surely Ar was out of the question. It would be death for us both. And, I supposed, a similar fate would await us in most Gorean cities. Impaling the stranger is a not unusual form of hospitality on Gor. Moreover, owing to the almost universal hatred borne to the city of Ar by most Gorean cities, it would be imperative in any case to keep the identity of my fair companion a secret. Theoretically, given the seclusion of the High Caste women of Ar, their gilded confinement in the Walled Gardens, it should be reasonably easy to conceal her identity.

But I was troubled. What would happen to Talena if we did, by some outstanding stroke of fortune, reach Ko-ro-ba? Would she be publicly impaled, returned to the mercies of the Initiates of Ar, or would she perhaps spend the rest of her days in the dungeons beneath the cylinders? Perhaps she would be permitted to live as a slave?

If Talena was interested in these remote considerations, she gave no sign of her concern. She explained to me what, in her opinion, would give us our best chance to travel the plains of Gor in safety.

"I will be the daughter of a rich merchant whom

you have captured," she explained. "Your tarn was killed by my father's men, and you are taking me back to your city, to be your slave."

I grudgingly assented to this fabrication, or much of it. It was a plausible story on Gor and would be likely to provoke little skepticism. Indeed, some such account seemed to be in order. Free women on Gor do not travel attended by only a single warrior, not of their own free will. Both Talena and I agreed that there was little danger of being recognized for what we really were. It would be generally assumed that the mysterious tarnsman who had stolen the Home Stone and disappeared with the daughter of the Ubar must long ago have reached whatever unknown city it was to which he had pledged his sword.

Toward morning we ate some of the rations and refilled the water flasks at a secluded spring. I allowed Talena to bathe first, which seemed to surprise her. She was further surprised when I left her to herself.

"Aren't you going to watch?" she asked brazenly.

"No," I said.

"But I may escape," she laughed.

"That would be my good fortune," I remarked.

She laughed again and disappeared, and I soon heard the sounds of her splashing delightedly in the water. She emerged a few minutes later, having washed her hair and the blue silk gown she wore. Her skin was radiant, the dried mire of the swamp forest at last washed away. She knelt and spread her hair to dry, letting it fall forward over her head and shoulders.

I entered the pool and rejoiced in the invigorating, cleansing water. We slept afterward. To her annoyance, but as a safety measure I thought essential, I secured her a few feet from me, fastening her arms about a sapling by means of the slave bracelets. I had no wish to awake to a dagger being thrust into my breast.

In the afternoon we moved on again, this time daring

to use one of the wide paved highways that lead from Ar, highways built like walls in the earth, of solid, fitted stones intended to last a thousand years. Even so, the surface of the highway had been worn smooth, and the ruts of tharlarion carts were clearly visible, ruts worn deep by centuries of caravans. We met very little on the highway, perhaps because of the anarchy in the city of Ar. If there were refugees, they must have been behind us, and few merchants were approaching Ar. Who would risk his goods in a situation of chaos? When we did pass an occasional traveler, we passed warily. On Gor, as in my native England, one keeps to the left side of the road. This practice, as once in England, is more than a simple matter of convention. When one keeps to the left side of the road, one's sword arm faces the passing stranger.

It seemed we had little to fear, and we had passed several of the pasang stones that line the side of the highway without seeing anything more threatening than a line of peasants carrying brushwood on their backs, and a pair of hurrying Initiates. Once, however, Talena dragged me to the side of the road, and, scarcely able to conceal our horror, we watched while a sufferer from the incurable Dar-kosis disease, bent in his yellow shrouds, hobbled by, periodically clacking that wooden device which warns all within hearing to stand clear from his path. "An Afflicted One," said Talena, gravely, using the expression common for such plagued wretches on Gor. The name of the disease itself, Dar-kosis, is almost never mentioned. I glimpsed the face beneath the hood and felt sick. Its one bleared eye regarded us blankly for a moment, and then the thing moved on.

It gradually became clear that the road was becoming less traveled. Weeds were growing between cracks in the stone flooring of the highway, and the ruts of the tharlarion carts had all but disappeared. We passed several crossroads, but I kept moving generally in the direction of Ko-ro-ba. What I would do when we reached the Margin of Desolation and the broad Vosk River, I didn't know. The fields of Sa-Tarna were thinning out.

Late in the day we glimpsed a solitary tarnsman high above the road, a lonely image that depressed both myself and Talena.

"We will never reach Ko-ro-ba," she said.

That night we finished the rations and one of the water flasks. As I prepared to bracelet her for the night, she became practical once again, her optimism and good spirits apparently restored by the food.

"We must make a better arrangement than this," she said, pushing away the bracelets. "It's uncomfortable."

"What do you suggest?" I asked.

She looked about and suddenly smiled brightly.

"Here," she said, "I have it!" She took a lead chain from my pouch, wrapped it several times about her slim ankle and snapped it shut, placing the key in my hand. Then, carrying the chain, which was still attached to her ankle, she walked to a nearby tree, bent down, and looped the loose end of the chain around the trunk. "Give me the slave bracelets!" she ordered. I gave them to her, and she placed the bracelets through two links of the part of the chain that encircled the tree, snapping them shut and handing me the key. She stood up and jerked her foot against the chain, demonstrating that she was perfectly secured. "There, bold Tarnsman," she said, "I will teach you how to keep a prisoner. Now sleep in peace, and I promise I won't cut your throat tonight."

I laughed and held her briefly in my arms. I suddenly sensed the rush of blood in her and in myself. I wanted never to release her. I wanted her always thus, so locked in my arms, mine to hold and love. Summoning all my strength, I put her from me.

"So," she said contemptuously, "that is how a Warrior tarnsman treats the daughter of a rich merchant?"

I rolled onto the ground, turning away from her, unable to sleep.

In the morning we left our camp early. A swallow of water from the flask and small, dry berries gathered from the nearby shrubbery were our only sustenance. We had not been on the road long when Talena clutched my arm. I listened carefully, hearing the distant clank of a shod tharlarion on the road. "A warrior," I guessed.

"Quick," she commanded. "Hood me."

I hooded her and snapped her wrists together in the slave bracelets.

The ringing of the tharlarion's shod claws on the road grew louder.

In a minute the rider appeared in view—a fine, bearded warrior with a golden helmet and a tharlarion lance. He drew the riding lizard to a halt a few paces from me. He rode the species of tharlarion called the high tharlarion, which ran on its two back feet in great bounding strides. Its cavernous mouth was lined with long, gleaming teeth. Its two small, ridiculously disproportionate forelegs dangled absurdly in front of its body.

"Who are you?" demanded the warrior.

"I am Tarl of Bristol," I said.

"Bristol?" asked the warrior, puzzled.

"Have you never heard of it?" I challenged, as if insulted.

"No," admitted the warrior. "I am Kazrak of Port Kar," he said, "in the service of Mintar, of the Merchant Caste."

I did not need to ask about Port Kar. It is a city in the delta of the Vosk and as much a den of pirates as anything else.

The warrior gestured at Talena with his lance. "Who is she?" he asked.

"You need not know her name or lineage," I said.

The warrior laughed and slapped his thigh. "You

would have me believe that she is of High Caste," he said. "She is probably the daughter of a goat keeper."

I could see Talena move under the hood, her fists clenched in the slave bracelets.

"What news of Ar?" I asked.

"War," said the mounted spearman approvingly. "Now, while the men of Ar fight among themselves for the cylinders, an army is gathering from fifty cities, massing on the banks of the Vosk to invade Ar. There is a camp there such as you have never seen—a city of tents, pasangs of tharlarion corrals; the wings of the tarns sound like thunder overhead. The cooking fires of the soldiers can be seen two days' ride from the river."

Talena spoke, her voice muffled in the hood. "Scavengers come to feast on the bodies of wounded tarnsmen." It was a Gorean proverb, which seemed to be singularly inappropriate, coming from a hooded captive.

"I did not speak to the girl," said the warrior.

I excused Talena. "She has not worn her bracelets long," I said.

"She has spirit," said the warrior.

"Where are you bound for?" I asked.

"To the banks of the Vosk, to the City of Tents," said the warrior.

"What news of Marlenus, the Ubar?" demanded Talena.

"You should beat her," said the warrior, but responded to the girl. "None. He has fled."

"What news of the Home Stone of Ar and the daughter of Marlenus?" I asked, feeling it would be the sort of thing the warrior would expect me to be interested in.

"The Home Stone is rumored to be in a hundred cities," he said. "Some say it has been destroyed. Only the Priest-Kings know."

"And the daughter of Marlenus?" I insisted.

"She is undoubtedly in the Pleasure Gardens of the boldest tarnsman on Gor," laughed the warrior. "I hope he has as much luck with her as the Home Stone. I have heard she has the temper of a tharlarion and a face to match!"

Talena stiffened, her pride offended.

"I have heard," she said imperiously, "that the daughter of the Ubar is the most beautiful woman on all Gor."

"I like this girl," said the warrior. "Yield her to me!"

"No," I said.

"Yield her or I will have my tharlarion trample you," he snapped, "or would you prefer to be spitted on my lance?"

"You know the codes," I said evenly. "If you want her, you must challenge for her and meet me with the weapon of my choice."

The warrior's face clouded, but only for an instant. He threw back his fine head and laughed, his teeth white in his bushy beard.

"Done!" he cried, fastening his lance in its saddle sheath and slipping from the back of the tharlarion. "I challenge you for her!"

"The sword," I said.

"Agreed," he said.

We shoved Talena, who was now frightened, to the side of the road. Hooded, she cowered there, the prize, her ears filled with the sudden violent ringing of blade on blade as two warriors fought to the death to possess her. Kazrak of Port Kar was a superb swordsman, but in the first moments we both knew that I was his master. His face was white beneath his helmet as he wildly attempted to parry my devastating attack. Once I stepped back, gesturing to the ground with my sword, the symbolic granting of quarter should it be desired. But Kazrak would not lay his sword on the stones at my feet. Rather, he suddenly launched a vicious attack, forcing me to defend myself as best I could. He seemed to fight with new fury, perhaps enraged that he had been offered quarter.

At last, terminating a frenzied exchange, I managed

to drive my blade into his shoulder, and as his sword arm dropped, I kicked the weapon from his grasp. He stood proudly in the road, waiting for me to kill him.

I turned and went to Talena, who was standing piteously by the side of the road, waiting to see who it was that would unhood her.

As I lifted the hood, she uttered a small, joyful sound, her green eyes bright with pleasure. Then she saw the wounded warrior. She shuddered slightly. "Kill him," she commanded.

"No," I replied.

The warrior, who held his shoulder, blood streaming down from his hand, smiled bitterly. "It was worth it," he said, his gaze sweeping over Talena. "I'd challenge you again."

Talena seized her dagger from my belt and raced to the warrior. I caught her braceleted hands as she was going to drive the dagger into his breast. He had not moved. "You must kill him," said Talena, struggling. Angrily I removed her bracelets and replaced them so that her wrists were bound behind her back.

"You should use the whip on her," said the warrior matter-of-factly.

I tore some inches from the bottom of Talena's gown to make a bandage for Kazrak's shoulder. She endured this in fury, her head in the air, not watching me. I had scarcely finished bandaging his wound when I was aware of a ringing on metal, and, lifting my head, I saw myself surrounded by mounted spearmen, who wore the same livery as Kazrak. Behind them, stretching into the distance, came a long line of broad tharlarions, or the four-footed draft monsters of Gor. These beasts, yoked in braces, were drawing mighty wagons, filled with merchandise protected under the lashings of its red rain-canvas.

"It is the caravan of Mintar, of the Merchant Caste," said Kazrak.

10

The Caravan

"Do not harm him," said Kazrak. "He is my sword brother, Tarl of Bristol." Kazrak's remark was in accord with the strange warrior codes of Gor, codes which were as natural to him as the air he breathed, and codes which I, in the Chamber of the Council of Ko-ro-ba, had sworn to uphold. One who has shed your blood, or whose blood you have shed, becomes your sword brother, unless you formally repudiate the blood on your weapons. It is a part of the kinship of Gorean warriors regardless of what city it is to which they owe their allegiance. It is a matter of caste, an expression of respect for those who share their station and profession, having nothing to do with cities or Home Stones.

As I stood tensely, ringed by the lances of the caravan guards, the wall of tharlarions parted to allow the approach of Mintar, of the Merchant Caste. A bejeweled, curtained platform slung between the slow, swaying bodies of two of the broad tharlarions appeared. The beasts were halted by their strap-master, and after some seconds the curtains parted. Seated inside on several pillows of tasseled silk was a mammoth toad of a man, whose head was as round as a tarn's egg, the eyes nearly lost in the folds of fat, pocked skin. A slender straggling wisp of hair dropped languidly from the fat chin. The little eyes of the merchant swept the scene quickly, like a bird's, startling in their contrast with the plethoric giganticism of his frame.

"So," said the merchant, "Kazrak of Port Kar has met his match?"

"It is the first challenge I have ever lost," replied Kazrak proudly.

"Who are you?" asked Mintar, leaning forward a bit, inspecting first me and then Talena, whom he regarded with small interest.

"Tarl of Bristol," I said. "And this is my woman, whom I claim by sword-right."

Mintar closed his eyes and opened them and pulled on his beard. He had, of course, never heard of Bristol, but did not wish to admit it, at least before his men. Moreover, he was far too shrewd to pretend that he had heard of the city. After all, what if there was no such city?

Mintar looked at the ring of mounted spearmen encircling me. "Does any man in my service challenge for the woman of Tarl of Bristol?" he asked.

The warriors shifted nervously. Kazrak laughed, a derisive snort. One of the mounted warriors said, "Kazrak of Port Kar is the best sword in the caravan."

Mintar's face clouded. "Tarl of Bristol," he said, "you have disabled my finest sword."

One or two of the mounted warriors readjusted their grip on their lances. I became acutely conscious of the proximity of the several points.

"You owe me a debt," said Mintar. "Can you pay the hiring price of such a sword?"

"I have no goods other than this girl," I said, "and I will not give her up."

Mintar sniffed. "In the wagons I have four hundred fully as beautiful, destined for the City of Tents." He looked at Talena carefully, but his appraisal was remote, detached. "Her sale price would not bring half the hiring price of a sword such as that of Kazrak of Port Kar." Talena reacted as if slapped.

"Then I cannot pay the debt I owe you," I said.

"I am a merchant," said Mintar, "and it is in my code to see that I am paid."

I set myself to sell my life dearly. Oddly enough, my only fear was what would happen to the girl.

"Kazrak of Port Kar," said Mintar, "do you agree to surrender the balance of your hiring price to Tarl of Bristol if he takes your place in my service?"

"Yes," responded Kazrak. "He has done me honor and is my sword brother."

Mintar seemed satisfied. He looked at me. "Tarl of Bristol," he said, "do you take service with Mintar, of the Merchant Caste?"

"If I do not?" I asked.

"Then I shall order my men to kill you," sighed Mintar, "and we shall both suffer a loss."

"Oh, Ubar of Merchants," I said, "I would not willingly see your profits jeopardized."

Mintar relaxed on the cushions and seemed pleased. I realized, to my amusement, that he had been afraid that some particle of his investment might have been sacrificed. He would have had a man killed rather than risk the loss of a tenth of a tarn disk, so well he knew the codes of his caste.

"What about the girl?" asked Mintar.

"She must accompany me," I said.

"If you wish," he said, "I will buy her."

"She is not for sale."

"Twenty tarn disks," Mintar proposed.

I laughed.

Mintar smiled, too. "Forty," he said.

"No," I said.

He seemed less pleased.

"Forty-five," he said, his voice flat.

"No," I said.

"Is she of High Caste?" asked Mintar, apparently puzzled at my lack of interest in his bargaining. Perhaps his price was too low for a girl of High Caste.

"I am," announced Talena proudly, "the daughter of a rich merchant, the richest on Gor, stolen from her father by this tarnsman. His tarn was killed, and he is taking me to—to Bristol—to be his slave."

"I am the richest merchant on Gor," said Mintar calmly.

Talena gulped.

"If your father is a merchant, tell me his name," he said. "I will know of him."

"Great Mintar," I spoke up, "forgive this she-tharlarion. Her father was a goat keeper by the swamp forests of Ar, and I did steal her, but she begged me to take her from the village. She foolishly ran away with me, thinking I would take her to Ar, to dress her in jewels and silks and give her quarters in the high cylinders. As soon as we left her village, I put the bracelets on her and am taking her to Bristol, where she will tend my goats."

The soldiers laughed uproariously, Kazrak loudest of all. For a moment I was afraid Talena was going to announce that she was the daughter of the Ubar Marlenus, preferring possible impalement to the insult of being considered the offspring of a goat keeper.

Mintar seemed amused. "While in my service, you may keep her on my chain if you wish," he said.

"Mintar is generous," I granted.

"No," said Talena. "I will share the tent of my warrior."

"If you like," said Mintar, paying no attention to Talena, "I will arrange her sale in the City of Tents and add her price to your wages."

"If I sell her, I will sell her myself," I said.

"I am an honest merchant," said Mintar, "and I would not cheat you, but you do well to handle your own affairs."

Mintar eased his great frame deeper into the silken pillows and motioned the strap-master of his tharlarions to close the curtains. Before they swept shut, he said, "You will never get forty-five tarn disks."

I suspected he was right. He undoubtedly had better merchandise, more reasonably priced.

Led by Kazrak, I went with Talena, walking back along the line of wagons to see where she would be placed. Beside one of several long wagons of the sort covered with yellow and blue silk, I removed the bracelets from her wrists and turned her over to an attendant.

"I have a spare ankle ring," he said, and took Talena by the arm, thrusting her inside the wagon. In the wagon there were some twenty girls, dressed in the slave livery of Gor, perhaps ten on a side, chained to a metal bar which ran the length of the wagon. Talena would not like that. Before she disappeared, she called over her shoulder saucily, "You're not rid of me as easily as this, Tarl of Bristol."

"See if you can slip the ankle ring," laughed Kazrak, and led me back among the supply wagons.

We had gone scarcely ten paces and Talena could hardly have been fastened in the wagon before we heard a female scream of pain and a bevy of howls and shrieks. From the wagon came the sound of rolling bodies, slamming and cracking against the sides, and the rattle of chains on wood, pierced by squeals of pain and anger. The attendant leaped into the back of the wagon with his strap, and there was added to the din the sound of his curses and the crack of the strap as he smartly laid about him. As Kazrak and I watched, the attendant, puffing and furious, emerged from the wagon, dragging Talena by the hair. As Talena struggled and kicked and the girls in the wagon shouted their approval and encouragement to the attendant, he angrily hurled Talena into my arms. Her hair was in wild disarray; there were nail marks on her shoulder and four strap welts on her back. Her arm was bruised. Her dress had been half torn from her.

"Keep her in your tent," snarled the attendant.

"Let the Priest-Kings blast me if she didn't do it," said Kazrak with admiration, "A true she-tharlarion."

Talena lifted a bloody nose to me and smiled brightly.

The next few days were among the happiest of my life, as Talena and I became a part of Mintar's slow, ample caravan, members of its graceful, interminable, colorful procession. It seemed the routine of the journey would never end, and I grew enamored of the long line of wagons, each filled with its various goods, those mysterious metals and gems, rolls of cloth, foodstuffs, wines and Paga, weapons and harness, cosmetics and perfumes, medicines and slaves.

Mintar's caravan, like most, was harnessed long before dawn and traveled until the heat of the day. Camp would be made early in the afternoon. The beasts would be watered and fed, the guards set, the wagons secured, and the members of the caravan would turn to their cooking fires. In the evening the strap-masters and warriors would amuse themselves with stories and songs, recounting their exploits, fictitious and otherwise, and bawling out their raucous harmonies under the influence of Paga.

In those days I learned to master the high tharlarion, one of which had been assigned to me by the caravan's tharlarion master. These gigantic lizards had been bred on Gor for a thousand generations before the first tarn was tamed, and were raised from the leathery shell to carry warriors. They responded to voice signals, conditioned into their tiny brains in the training years. Nonetheless, the butt of one's lance, striking about the eye or ear openings, for there are few other sensitive areas in their scaled hides, is occasionally necessary to impress your will on the monster.

The high tharlarions, unlike their draft brethren, the slow-moving, four-footed broad tharlarions, were carnivorous. However, their metabolism was slower than that of a tarn, whose mind never seemed far from food and, if it was available, could consume half its weight in a single day. Moreover, they needed far less water than tarns. To me, the most puzzling thing about the domesticated tharlarions, and the way in which they differed most obviously from wild tharlarions and the lizards of my native planet, was their stamina, their capacity for sustained movement. When the high tharlarion moves slowly, its stride is best described as a proud, stalking movement, each great clawed foot striking the earth with a measured rhythm. When urged to speed, however, the high tharlarion bounds, in great leaping movements that carry it twenty paces at a time.

The tharlarion saddle, unlike the tarn saddle, is constructed to absorb shock. Primarily, this is done by constructing the tree of the saddle in such a way that the leather seat is mounted on a hydraulic fitting which actually floats in a thick lubricant. Not only does this lubricant absorb much of the shock involved, but it tends, except under abnormal stress, to keep the seat of the saddle parallel to the ground. In spite of this invention, the mounted warriors always wear, as an essential portion of their equipment, a thick leather belt, tightly buckled about their abdomen. In addition, the mounted warriors inevitably wear a high, soft pair of boots called tharlarion boots. These protect their legs from the abrasive hides of their mounts. When a tharlarion runs, its hide could tear the unprotected flesh from a man's bones.

Kazrak, as he had promised, turned over the balance of his hiring price to me—a very respectable eighty tarn disks. I argued with him to accept forty, on the ground that he was a sword brother, and at last convinced him to accept half of his own wages back. I felt better about this arrangement. Also, I didn't want Kazrak, when his wound was healed, to be reduced to challenging some luckless warrior for a bottle of Ka-la-na wine. We, with Talena, shared a tent, and, to Kazrak's amusement, I set aside a portion of the tent for the girl's private use, protecting it with a silk hanging.

Because of the miserable condition of Talena's single garment, Kazrak and I procured from the supply master some changes of slave livery for the girl. This seemed to me the most appropriate way to diminish any possible suspicion as to her true identity. From his own tarn disks, Kazrak purchased two additional articles which he regarded as essential—a collar, which he had properly engraved, and a slave whip.

We returned to the tent, handing the new livery to Talena, who, in fury, regarded the brief, diagonally striped garments. She bit her lower lip, and, if Kazrak had not been present, would undoubtedly have roundly informed me of her displeasure.

"Did you expect to be dressed as a free woman?" I snapped.

She glared at me, knowing that she must play her role, at least in the presence of Kazrak. She tossed her head haughtily. "Of course not," she said, adding ironically, "Master." Her back straight as a tarn-goad, she disappeared behind the silk hanging. A moment later the torn rag of blue silk flew out from behind the hanging.

A moment or two after, Talena stepped forth for our inspection, brazen and insolent. She wore the diagonally striped slave livery of Gor, as had Sana—that briefly skirted, simple, sleeveless garment.

She turned before us.

"Do I please you?" she asked.

It was obvious she did. Talena was a most beautiful girl.

"Kneel," I said, drawing out the collar.

Talena blanched, but, as Kazrak chuckled, she knelt before me, her fists clenched.

"Read it," I ordered.

Talena looked at the engraved collar and shook with rage.

"Read it," I said. "Out loud."

She read the simple legend aloud: "I AM THE PROPERTY OF TARL OF BRISTOL."

I snapped the slender steel collar on her throat, placing the key in my pouch.

"Shall I call for the iron?" asked Kazrak.

"No," begged Talena, now, for the first time, frightened.

"I shall not brand her today," I said, keeping a straight face.

"By the Priest-Kings," laughed Kazrak, "I believe you care for the she-tharlarion."

"Leave us, Warrior," I said.

Kazrak laughed again, winked at me, and backed with mock ceremony from the tent.

Talena sprang to her feet, her two fists flying for my face. I caught her wrists.

"How dare you?" she raged. "Take this thing off," she commanded.

She struggled fiercely, futilely. When in sheer frustration she stopped squirming, I released her. She pulled at the circle of steel on her throat. "Remove this degrading object," she commanded, "now!" She faced me, her mouth trembling with rage. "The daughter of the Ubar of Ar wears no man's collar."

"The daughter of the Ubar of Ar," I said, "wears the collar of Tarl of Bristol."

There was a long pause.

"I suppose," she said, attempting to save face, "it

would perhaps be appropriate for a tarnsman to place his collar on the captive daughter of a rich merchant."

"Or the daughter of a goat keeper," I added.

Her eyes snapped. "Yes, perhaps," she said. "Very well. I concede the reasonableness of your plan." Then she held out her small hand imperiously. "Give me the key," she said, "so that I may remove this when I please."

"I will keep the key," I said. "And it will be removed, if at all, when I please."

She straightened and turned away, enraged but helpless. "Very well," she said. Then, her eyes lit on the second object Kazrak had donated to the project of taming what he called the she-tharlarion—the slave whip. "What is the meaning of that?"

"Surely you are familiar with a slave whip?" I asked, picking it up and, with amusement, slapping it once or twice in my palm.

"Yes," she said, regarding me evenly. "I have often used it on my own slaves. Is it now to be used on me?"

"If necessary," I said.

"You wouldn't have the nerve," she said.

"More likely the inclination," I said.

She smiled.

Her next remark astonished me. "Use it on me if I do not please you, Tarl of Bristol," she said. I pondered this, but she had turned away.

In the next few days, to my surprise, Talena was buoyant, cheerful, and excited. She became interested in the caravan and would spend hours walking alongside the colored wagons, sometimes hitching rides with the strapmasters, wheedling from them a piece of fruit or a sweetmeat. She even conversed delightedly with the inmates of the blue and yellow wagons, bringing them precious tidbits of camp news, teasing them as to how handsome their new masters would be.

She became a favorite of the caravan. Once or twice mounted warriors of the caravan had accosted her, but on reading her collar had backed grumblingly away, enduring with good humor her jibes and taunts. In the early afternoon, when the caravan halted, she would help Kazrak and me set up our tent and would then gather wood for a fire. She cooked for us, kneeling by the fire, her hair bound back so as not to catch the sparks, her face sweaty and intent on the piece of meat she was most likely burning. After the meal she would clean and polish our gear, sitting on the tent carpet between us, chatting about the small, pleasant inconsequentialities of her day.

"Slavery apparently agrees with her," I remarked to Kazrak.

"Not slavery," he smiled. And I puzzled as to the meaning of his remark. Talena blushed and lowered her face, rubbing vigorously on the leather of my tharlarion boots.

11

The City of Tents

FOR SEVERAL DAYS, TO THE sound of the caravan bells, we made our way through the Margin of Desolation, that wild, barren strip of soil with which the Empire of Ar had girded its borders. Now, in the distance, we could hear the muffled roar of the mighty Vosk. As the caravan mounted a rise, we saw spread far below us, on the banks of the Vosk, a sight of incredible barbaric splendor—pasangs of brightly colored tents stretching as far as the eye could see, a vast assemblage of tents housing one of the greatest armies ever gathered on the plains of Gor. The flags of a hundred cities flew above the tents, and, against the steady roar of the river, the sound of the great tarn drums reached us, those huge drums whose signals control the complex war formations of Gor's flying cavalries. Talena ran to the foot of my tharlarion, and with my lance I hoisted her to the saddle so that she could see. For the first time in days her eyes filled with anger. "Scavengers," she said, "come to feast on the bodies of wounded tarnsmen."

I said nothing, knowing in my heart that I, in my way, had been responsible for this vast martial array on the banks of the Vosk. It was I who had stolen the Home Stone of Ar, who had brought about the downfall of Marlenus, the Ubar, who had set the spark that had brought Ar to anarchy and the vultures below to feed on the divided carcass of what had been Gor's greatest city.

Talena leaned back against my shoulder. Without looking at me, her shoulders shook, and I knew she was weeping.

If I could have, I would in that moment have rewritten the past, would have selfishly abandoned the quest for the Home Stone—yes, willingly would have left the scattered hostile cities of Gor to face, one by one, the imperialistic depredations of Ar, if it were not for one thing—the girl I held in my arms.

The caravan of Mintar did not camp as usual in the heat of the day but moved on, attempting to reach the City of Tents before darkness. As it was, my fellow guards and I earned our pay those last few pasangs to the banks of the Vosk. We fought off three groups of raiders from the camp on the river, two of them small, undisciplined contingents of mounted warriors, but the other a lightning strike of a dozen tarnsmen on the weapons wagon. They withdrew in good order, driven off by our crossbows, and couldn't have gotten much.

I saw Mintar again, the first time since I had joined the caravan. His palanquin swayed past. His face was sweating, and he fumbled in his heavy wallet, taking out tarn disks and tossing them to the warriors for their work. I snapped a tarn disk from the air and put it in my pouch.

That night we brought the caravan into the palisaded keep prepared for Mintar by Pa-Kur, the Master Assassin, who was the Ubar of this vast, scarcely organized, predatory horde. The caravan was secured, and in a few hours trade would begin. The caravan, with its varied goods, was needed by the camp, and its merchandise would command the highest prices. I noted with satisfaction that Pa-Kur, Master Assassin, proud leader of perhaps the greatest horde ever assembled on the plains of Gor, had need of Mintar, who was only of the Merchant Caste.

My plan, as I explained to Talena, was simple. It amounted to little more than buying a tarn, if I could afford it, or stealing one if I could not, and making a run for Ko-ro-ba. The venture might be risky, particularly if I had to steal the tarn and elude pursuit, but, all things considered, an escape on tarnback seemed to me far safer than trying to cross the Vosk and make our way on foot or tharlarion through the hills and wilderness to the distant cylinders of Ko-ro-ba.

Talena seemed depressed, in odd contrast to her liveliness of the caravan days. "What will become of me in Ko-ro-ba?" she asked.

"I don't know," I said, smiling. "Perhaps you could be a tavern slave."

She smiled wryly. "No, Tarl of Bristol," she said. "More likely I would be impaled, for I am still the daughter of Marlenus."

I did not tell her, but if that was decreed to be her

fate and I could not prevent it, I knew she would not be impaled alone. There would be two bodies on the walls of Ko-ro-ba. I would not live without her.

Talena stood up. "Tonight," she said, "let us drink wine." It was a Gorean expression, a fatalistic maxim in which the events of the morrow were cast into the laps of the Priest-Kings.

"Let us drink wine," I agreed.

That night I took Talena into the City of Tents, and by the light of torches set on lances we walked arm in arm through the crowded streets, among the colorful tents and market stalls.

Not only warriors were in evidence, but tradesmen and artisans, peddlers and peasants, camp women and slaves. Talena clung to my arm, fascinated. We watched in one stall a bronzed giant apparently swallowing balls of fire, in the next a silk merchant crying the glories of his cloth, in another a hawker of Paga; in still another we watched the swaying bodies of dancing slave girls as their master proclaimed their rent price.

"I want to see the market," Talena said eagerly, and I knew the market she meant. This vast city of silk would surely have its Street of Brands. Reluctantly I took Talena to the great tent of blue and yellow silk, and we pressed in among the hot, smelling bodies of the buyers, forcing our way toward the front. There Talena watched, thrilled, as girls, several of whom she had known in the caravan, were placed on the large, rounded wooden block and sold, one by one, to the highest bidder.

"She's beautiful," Talena would say of one as the auctioneer would tug the single loop on the right shoulder of the slave livery, dropping it to the girl's ankles. Of another, Talena would sniff scornfully. She seemed to be pleased when her friends were bought by handsome tarnsmen, and laughed delightedly when one girl, to whom she had taken a dislike, was purchased by a fat, odious fellow, of the Caste of Tarn Keepers.

To my surprise, most of the girls seemed excited by their sale and displayed their charms with brazen gusto, each seeming to compete with the one before to bring a higher price. It was, of course, far more desirable to bring a high price, thereby guaranteeing that one's master would be well-fixed. Accordingly, the girls did their best to move the interest of the buyers. I noted that Talena, like others in the room, did not seem in the least to feel that there was anything objectionable or untoward in this commerce in beauty. It was an accepted, ordinary part of the life of Gor.

I wondered if, on my own planet, there was not a similar market, invisible but present, and just as much accepted, a market in which women were sold, except that they sold themselves, were themselves both merchandise and merchant. How many of the women of my native planet, I wondered, did not with care consider the finances, the property of their prospective mates? How many of them did not, for all practical purposes, sell themselves, bartering their bodies for the goods of the world? Here on Gor, however, I observed ironically, bitterly, there was a clear division between merchandise and merchant. The girls would not collect their own profit, not on Gor.

I had noticed that there was among the crowd one tall, somber figure who sat alone on a high, wooden throne, surrounded by tarnsmen. He wore the black helmet of a member of the Caste of Assassins. I took Talena by the elbow and, though she protested, moved her gently through the crowd and out into the air.

We purchased a bottle of Ka-la-na wine and shared it as we walked through the streets. She begged a tenth of a tarn disk from me, and I gave it to her. Like a child she went to one or two stalls, making me look the other way. In a few minutes she returned, carrying a small package. She gave me the change and leaned against my shoulder, claiming that she was weary. We returned to our tent. Kazrak was gone, and my suspicion was that he was gone for the night, that he was even now tangled in the sleeping robes of one of the torchlit booths of the City of Tents.

Talena retired behind the silk partition, and I built up the fire in the center of the tent, not wishing to retire as yet. I could not forget the figure on the throne, he of the black helmet, and I thought perhaps that he had noticed me and had reacted. It had been, perhaps, my imagination. I sat on the tent carpet, poking at the small fire in the cooking hole. I could hear from a tent nearby the sound of a flute, some soft drums, and the rhythmic jangle of some tiny cymbals.

As I mused, Talena stepped forth from behind the silk curtain. I had thought she had retired. Instead, she stood before me in the diaphanous, scarlet dancing silks of Gor. She had rouged her lips. My head swam at the sudden intoxicating scent of a wild perfume. Her olive ankles bore dancing bangles with tiny bells. Attached to the thumb and index finger of each hand were tiny finger cymbals. She bent her knees ever so slightly and raised her arms gracefully above her head. There was a sudden bright clash of the finger cymbals, and, to the music of the nearby tent, Talena, daughter of the Ubar of Ar, began to dance for me.

As she moved slowly before me, she asked softly, "Do I please you, Master?" There had been no scorn, no irony in her voice.

"Yes," I said, not thinking to repudiate the title by which she had addressed me.

She paused for a moment and walked lightly to the side of the tent. She seemed to hesitate for an instant, then quickly gathered up the slave whip and a leading chain. She placed them firmly in my hands and knelt on the tent carpet before me, her eyes filled with a strange light, her knees not in the position of a Tower Slave but of a Pleasure Slave.

"If you wish," she said, "I will dance the Whip Dance for you, or the Chain Dance."

I threw the whip and chain to the wall of the tent. "No," I said angrily. I would not have Talena dance those cruel dances of Gor, which so humbled a woman.

"Then I will show you a love dance," she said happily, "a dance I learned in the Walled Gardens of Ar."

"I should like that," I said, and, as I watched, Talena performed Ar's strangely beautiful dance of passion.

She danced before me for several minutes, her scarlet dancing silks flashing in the firelight, her bare feet, with their belled ankles, striking softly on the carpet. With a last flash of the finger cymbals, she fell to the carpet before me, her breath hot and quick, her eyes blazing with desire. I was at her side, and she was in my arms. Her heart beat wildly against my breast. She looked into my eyes, her lips trembling, the words stumbling but audible.

"Call for the iron," she said. "Brand me, Master."

"No, Talena," I said, kissing her mouth. "No."

"I want to be owned," she whimpered. "I want to belong to you, fully, completely in every way. I want your brand, Tarl of Bristol, don't you understand? I want to be your branded slave."

I fumbled with the collar at her throat, unlocked it, threw it aside.

"You're free, my love," I whispered. "Always free."

She sobbed, shaking her head, her lashes wet with tears. "No," she wept. "I am your slave." She clenched her body against mine, the buckles of the wide tharlarion belt cutting into her belly. "You own me," she whispered. "Use me."

There was a sudden rush of men behind me as tarnsmen broke into the tent. I remember turning swiftly and seeing for the fraction of a second the butt of a spear crashing toward my face. I heard Talena scream. There was a sudden flash of light, and then darkness.

12

In the Tarn's Nest

MY WRISTS AND ANKLES WERE bound to a hollow, floating frame. The ropes sawed into my flesh as the weight of my body drew on them. I turned my head, sick to my stomach, and threw up into the turbid waters of the Vosk. I blinked my eyes against the hot sun and tried to move my wrists and ankles.

A voice said, "He's awake."

Dimly I felt spear butts thrust against the side of the hollow frame, ready to edge it out into the current.

I cleared my head as best I could, and into my uncertain field of vision moved a dark object, which became the black helmet of a member of the Caste of Assassins. Slowly, with a stylized movement, the helmet was lifted, and I found myself staring up into a gray, lean, cruel face, a face that might have been made of metal. The eyes were inscrutable, as if they had been made of glass or stone and set artificially in that metallic mask of a countenance.

"I am Pa-Kur," said the man.

It was he, the Master Assassin of Ar, leader of the assembled horde.

"We meet again," I said.

The eyes, like glass or stone, revealed nothing.

"The cylinder at Ko-ro-ba," I said. "The crossbow."

He said nothing.

"You failed to kill me that time," I taunted. "Perhaps you would care to risk another shot now. Perhaps the mark would be more suited to your skills."

The men behind Pa-Kur muttered at my impudence. He himself showed no impatience.

"My weapon," he said, simply extending his hand. A crossbow was immediately placed in his grip. It was a large steel bow, wound and set, the iron quarrel placed in the guide.

I prepared to welcome the bolt flashing through my body. I was curious to know if I would be conscious of its strike. Pa-Kur raised his hand with an imperious gesture. From somewhere I saw a small, round object sailing high into the air, out over the river. It was a tarn disk hurled by one of Pa-Kur's men. Just as the tiny object, black against the blue sky, reached its apogee, I heard the click of the trigger, the vibration of the string, and the swift hiss of the quarrel. Before the tarn disk could begin its fall, the quarrel pierced it, carrying it, I would judge, some two hundred and fifty yards out into the river. The men of Pa-Kur stamped their feet in the sand and clanged their spears on their shields.

"I spoke as a fool," I said to Pa-Kur.

"And you will die the death of a fool," he said. He spoke with no trace of anger or emotion of any kind.

He motioned to the men to thrust the frame out into the river, where it would be swept away.

"Wait," I said, "I ask your favor." The words came hard.

Pa-Kur gestured to the men to desist.

"What have you done with the girl?"

"She is Talena, daughter of the Ubar Marlenus," said Pa-Kur. "She will rule in Ar as my queen."

"She would die first," I said.

"She has accepted me," said Pa-Kur, "and will rule by my side." The stone eyes regarded me, expressionless.

"It was her wish that you die the death of a villain," he said, "on the Frame of Humiliation, unworthy to stain our weapons."

I closed my eyes. I should have known that the proud Talena, daughter of a Ubar, would leap at the first chance to return to power in Ar, even though it be at the head of a plundering host of brigands. And I, her protector, was now to be discarded. Indeed, the Frame of Humiliation would be ample vengeance to satisfy even Talena for the indignities she had suffered at my hands. It, if anything, would wipe out forever from her mind the offensive memory that she had once needed my help and had pretended to love me.

Then, each of the men of Pa-Kur, as is the custom before a frame is surrendered to the waters of the Vosk, spit on my body. Lastly, Pa-Kur spit in his hand and then placed his hand on my chest. "Were it not for the daughter of Marlenus," said Pa-Kur, his metallic face as placid as the quicksilver behind a mirror, "I would have slain you honorably. That I swear by the black helmet of my caste."

"I believe you," I said, my voice choked, no longer caring if I lived or died.

The spear butts pressed against the frame, shoving it away from the bank. The current soon caught it, and it began to spin in slow circles farther and farther out into the midst of that vast force of nature called the Vosk.

The death would not be a pleasant one. Bound helplessly, without food or water, my own body would torture me by its weight dragging on the hand and ankle ropes, suspended a few inches above the roiling, muddy surface under the fiery sun. I knew that I would not, some days hence, reach the delta of the Vosk and the cities in the delta except perhaps as a bound corpse, withered by exposure and the lack of water. Indeed, it was unlikely my body would reach the delta at all. It was far more likely that one of the water lizards of the Vosk or one of the great hook-beaked turtles of the river would seize my body and drag it and the frame under the water, destroying me in the mud below. There was also the chance that a wild tarn might swoop down and feed on the helpless living morsel fastened to that degrading frame. Of one thing I was certain—there would be no human assistance or even pity, for the poor wretches on the frames are none but villains, betrayers, and blasphemers against the Priest-Kings, and it is a sacrilegious act even to consider terminating their sufferings.

My wrists and ankles had turned white and were numb. The oppressive, blinding glare of the sun, the heavy weight of its heat bore down on me. My throat was parched, and, hanging only an inch or so above the Vosk, I burned with thirst. Thoughts, like prodding needles, vexed my brain. The image of the treacherous, beautiful Talena, in her dancing silks, as she had lain in my arms, tormented me—she who would glady give her kisses to the cold Pa-Kur for a place on the throne of Ar, she whose implacable hatred had sent me to this terrible death, not even permitting me the honor of a warrior's end. I wanted to hate her—so much I wanted to hate her—but I found that I could not. I had come to love her. In the glade by the swamp forests, in the grain fields of the empire, on the great highway of Ar, in the regal, exotic caravan of Mintar, I had found the woman I loved, a scion of a barbaric race on a remote and unknown world.

The night came with infinite slowness, but at last the blinding sun was gone and I welcomed the chill, windy darkness. The water lapped against the side of the frame, the stars sparkled above in frosty detachment. Once, to my horror, a scaled body crested under the frame, its glistening hide rubbing my body as it snapped its tail and suddenly darted beneath the water. It apparently was not carnivorous. Oddly enough, I cried out to the stars in joy, still clinging to life, unwilling to lament the fact that my miseries must now be prolonged.

The sun swept into the sky again, and my second day on the Vosk began. I remember being afraid that I would never be able to use my hands and feet again, that they would never withstand the punishment of the ropes. Then I remember laughing foolishly, like a madman, when I considered that it wouldn't matter, that I would never have any further use for them.

Perhaps it was my wild, almost demented laughter that attracted the tarn. I saw him coming, making his silent strike with the sun at his back, his talons extended like hooks. Savagely those vast talons struck and closed on my body, forcing the frame for an instant beneath the water, then the tarn was beating the air angrily with his wings, struggling to lift his prey, and suddenly both myself and the heavy frame were pulled free from the water. The sudden weight of the frame swinging against my roped wrists and ankles, while the talons of the bird gripped my body, almost tore me apart. Then, mercifully, the ropes, not meant to sustain the weight of the heavy frame, broke loose, and the tarn triumphantly climbed skyward, still clutching me in his wild talons.

I would have a few moments more of life, the same brief reprieve nature grants the mouse carried by the hawk to its nest; then on some barren crag my body would be torn to pieces by the beast whose prey I was. The tarn, a brown tarn with a black crest like most wild tarns, streaked for that vague, distant smudge I knew marked the escarpments of some mountain wilderness. The Vosk became a broad, glimmering ribbon in the distance.

Far below, I could see that the burned, dead Margin of Desolation was dotted here and there with patches of green, where some handfuls of seed had blindly asserted themselves, reclaiming something of that devastated country for life and growth. Near one of the green stretches I saw what I first thought was a shadow, but as the tarn passed, it scattered into a scampering flock of tiny creatures, probably the small, three-toed mammals called qualae, dun-colored and with a stiff brushy mane of black hair.

As nearly as I could determine, we did not pass over or near the great highway that ran to the Vosk. Had we done so, I might have seen the war horde of Pa-Kur on its way to Ar, with its marching columns, its lines of tharlarion riders, its foraging cavalries of tarnsmen, its supply wagons and pack animals. And somewhere in that vast array, among the flags and the booming of tarn drums, would have been the girl who had betrayed me.

As well as I could, I opened and closed my hands and moved my feet, trying to restore in them some semblance of feeling. The flight of the tarn was serene, and I, grateful to be free at last of the painful Frame of Humiliation, found myself, strangely enough, almost reconciled to the savage but swift fate I knew awaited me.

But suddenly the flight of the tarn became much more rapid and then in another minute almost erratic and frenzied. He was fleeing! I twisted about in his claws, and my heart seemed to jerk spasmodically in my breast. My hair froze as I heard the shrill, angry cry of another tarn; he was an enormous creature as sable as the helmet of Pa-Kur, his wings beating like whips, bearing down relentlessly on my captor. My bird swerved dizzily, and the great assailant's talons passed harmlessly. Then he attacked again, and my bird swerved again, but the attacking tarn had allowed for the maneuver, compensating for it an instant before my own bird turned, with the result that it met my bird in full collision.

I was conscious in that mad, terrible instant of the flash of steel-shod talons at the breast of my bird, and then my bird shook as though seized with a convulsion and opened his talons. I began to drop toward the wastes below. In that wild instant I saw my bird beginning to fall, flopping downward, and saw his attacker wheeling in my direction. Falling, I twisted madly, unsupported in the air, a wordless cry of anguish in my throat, and watched in horror as the ground seemed to rush upward to meet me. But I never reached it, for the attacking bird had swooped to intercept me and seized me in his beak much as one gull might seize a fish dropped by another. The beak, curved like an instrument of war, slit with its narrow nostrils, closed on my body, and I was once more the prize of a tarn.

Soon my swift captor had reached his mountains, and the vague, distant smudge that I had seen had become a lonely, frightening, inaccessible wilderness of reddish cliffs. High on a sunlit mountain ledge, the sable tarn dropped me to the sticks and brush of its nest and set one steel-shod taloned foot across my body, to hold me steady as the great beak did its work. As the beak reached down for me, I managed to get one leg between it and my body and kicked it back, cursing wildly.

The sound of my voice had an unusual effect on the bird. He tilted his head to one side quizzically. I shouted at him again and again. And then, fool that I was, half demented with hunger and terror, I only then realized that the tarn was none other than my own! I shoved on the steel-shod foot that pressed me into the sticks of the nest, uttering my command with ringing authority. The bird lifted his foot and backed away, still uncertain as to what to do. I sprang to my feet, standing well within the reach of his beak, showing no fear. I slapped his beak affectionately, as if we were in a tarn cot, and shoved my hands into his neck feathers, the area where the tarn can't preen, as the tarn keepers do when searching for parasites.

I withdrew some of the lice, the size of marbles, which tend to infest wild tarns, and slapped them roughly into the mouth of the tarn, wiping them off on his tongue. I did this again and again, and the tarn stretched out his neck. The saddle and reins of the tarn were no longer on the bird and had undoubtedly rotted off or had been rubbed from his back by scraping against the rock escarpment backing its nest ledge. After a few minutes of my ministrations the tarn, satisfied, spread his wings and took flight, to continue the search for food which had been interrupted. Apparently, in his limited fashion, he no longer conceived of me as being in the immediate category of the edible. That he might soon change his mind, particularly if he found nothing on the plains below, was only too obvious. I cursed because I had lost the tarn-goad in the quicksands of Ar's swamp forest. I examined the ledge for some means of escape, but the cliffs above and below were almost smooth.

Suddenly a great shadow covered the ledge. My tarn had returned. I looked up and, to my horror, saw that it was not my tarn. It was another tarn, a wild tarn. He lit on the ledge, snapping his beak. This time I had none of the careful conditioning of the tarn keepers working in my favor.

I frantically looked about for a weapon, and then, hardly believing my eyes, I saw, woven roughly into the nest sticks, the remains of my harness and saddle. I seized my spear from the saddle sheath and turned. The beast had waited a moment too long; he had been too confident of his trapped quarry. As he stalked forward, oblivious of the spear, I hurled the broad-headed weapon deep into his breast. His legs gave way, and his body, wings outspread, sank to the granite flooring of the ledge. Head jerking and eyes glassy, the bird twitched and trembled uncontrollably—a cluster of spasmodic reflexes. He had died the instant the spear had entered his heart. I withdrew the weapon and, using it as a lever, rolled the twitching body to the brink of the ledge and sent it flopping to the depths below.

I returned to the nest and salvaged what I could of the tarn harness and saddle. The crossbow and longbow, with their respective missiles, were nowhere in evidence. The shield was also gone. With the spear blade I cut into the locked saddle pack. It contained, as I'd known it would, the Home Stone of Ar. It was unimpressive, small, flat, and of a dull brown color. Carved on it, crudely, was a single letter in an archaic Gorean script, that single letter which, in the old spelling, would have been the name of the city. At the time the stone was carved, Ar, in all probability, had been one of dozens of inconspicuous villages on the plains of Gor.

Impatiently I set the stone aside. The pack also contained, and more importantly from my point of view, the balance of my supplies, intended for the home flight to Ko-ro-ba. The first thing I did was unseal one of the two water flasks and open the dried rations. And there on that windy ledge, in that abode of the tarn, I ate the meal that satisfied me as no other had ever done, though it consisted only of some mouthfuls of water, some stale biscuits, and a wrapper of dried meat.

I poked through the other contents of the saddle pack, delighted to find my old maps and that device that serves Goreans as both compass and chronometer. As nearly as I could determine from the map and my memory of the location of the Vosk and the direction I had been carried, I was somewhere in the Voltai Range, sometimes called the Red Mountains, south of the river and to the east of Ar. That would mean that I had unknowingly passed over the great highway, but whether ahead of or behind Pa-Kur's horde I had no idea. My calculations as to my locale tended to be confirmed by the dull reddish color of the cliffs, due to the presence of large deposits of iron oxide.

I then took the binding fiber and extra bowstrings from the pack. I would use them in repairing the saddle and harness. I cursed myself for not having carried an extra tarn-goad somewhere in the saddle gear. Also, I should have carried an extra tarn whistle. Mine had been lost when Talena had thrown me from the back of the tarn, shortly after we had fled the walls of Ar.

I wasn't sure I could control the tarn without a tarn-goad. I had used it sparingly in my flights with him, even more sparingly than is recommended, but it had always been there, ready to be used if needed. Now it was no longer there. Whether I could control the tarn or not would probably, at least for a time, depend on whether or not he had been successful in his hunt and on how well the tarn keepers had done their work with the young bird. And would it not also depend on how deep the bite of freedom had been felt by the bird, how ready he would be to be controlled once more by man? With my spear I could kill him, but that would not rescue me from the ledge. I had no desire to die eventually of starvation in the lonely aerie of my tarn. I would leave on his back or die.

In the hours that remained before the tarn returned to his nest, I used the binding fiber and bowstrings to repair, as well as I could, the harness and saddle. By the time my great mount had settled again on his ledge, I had finished my work, even to restoring the gear in my saddle pack. Almost as an afterthought I had included the Home Stone of Ar, that simple, uncomely piece of rock that had so transformed my destiny and that of an empire.

Gripped in the talons of the tarn was the dead body of an antelope, one of the one-horned, yellow antelopes called tabuks that frequent the bright Ka-la-na thickets of Gor. The antelope's back had been broken, apparently in the tarn's strike, and its neck and head lolled aimlessly to one side.

When the tarn had fed, I walked over to him, speaking familiarly, as if I might be doing the most customary thing on Gor. Letting him see the harness fully, I slowly and with measured care fastened it around his neck. I then threw the saddle over the bird's back and crawled under its stomach to fasten the girth straps. Then I calmly climbed the newly repaired mounting ladder, drew it up, and fastened it to the side of the saddle. I sat still for a moment and then decisively drew back on the one-strap. I breathed a sigh of relief as the black monster lifted himself in flight.

13

Marlenus, Ubar of Ar

I SET MY COURSE FOR Ko-ro-ba, carrying in my saddle pack the trophy that was now, at least to me, worthless. It had done its work. Its loss to Ar had already riven an empire and, for the time at least, had guaranteed the independence of Ko-ro-ba and her hostile sister cities. Yet my victory, if victory it was, brought me no satisfaction. My mission might have been concluded, but I did not rejoice. I had lost the girl I had loved, cruel and treacherous though she might have been.

I took the tarn high, to bring a circle of some two hundred pasangs or so under my view. In the far distance I could see the silver wire I knew must be the great Vosk, could see the abrupt shift from the grassy plains to the Margin of Desolation. From the height I could look down on a portion of the Voltai Range, with its arrogant reddish heights, as it faded away to the east. To the southwest I could see dimly the evening light reflected from the spires of Ar, and to the north, approaching from the Vosk, I could see the glow from what must be thousands of cooking fires, the night's camp of Pa-Kur.

As I was drawing on the two-strap, to guide the tarn to Ko-ro-ba, I saw something I did not expect to see, something directly below, which startled me. Shielded among the crags of the Voltai, invisible except from directly above, I saw four or five small cooking fires, such as might mark the camp of a mountain patrol or a small company of hunters, perhaps after the agile and bellicose Gorean mountain goat, the long-haired, spiral-horned verr, or, more dangerously, the larl, a tawny leopardlike beast indigenous to the Voltai and several of Gor's ranges, standing an incredible seven feet high at the shoulder and feared for its occasional hunger-driven visitations to the civilized plains below. Curious, I dropped the tarn lower, not willing to believe the fires belonged to either a patrol or to hunters. It did not seem likely that one of Ar's patrols would be presently bivouacked in the Voltai, nor did it seem likely the fires below would be those of hunters.

As I dropped lower, my suspicions were confirmed. Perhaps the men of the mysterious camp heard the beating of the tarn's wings, perhaps I had been outlined for an instant against one of Gor's three circling moons, but suddenly the fires disappeared, kicked apart in a flash of sparks, and the glowing embers were smothered almost immediately. Outlaws, I supposed, or perhaps deserters from Ar. There would be many who would leave the city to seek the comparative safety of the mountains. Feeling that I had satisfied my curiosity and not wanting to risk a landing in the darkness, where a spear might dart from any shadow, I drew back on the one-strap and prepared to return at last to Ko-ro-ba, whence I had departed several days—an eternity—before.

As the tarn wheeled upward, I heard the wild, uncanny hunting cry of the larl, piercing the dusk from somewhere in the peaks below. Even the tarn seemed to shiver in its flight. The hunting cry was answered from elsewhere in the peaks and then again from a farther distance. When the larl hunts alone, it hunts silently, never uttering a sound until the sudden roar that momentarily precedes its charge, the roar calculated to terrify the quarry into a fatal instant of immobility. But tonight a pride of larls was hunting, and the cries of the three beasts were driving cries, herding the prey, usually several animals, toward the region of silence, herding them in the direction from which no cries would come, the direction in which the remainder of the pride waited.

The light of the three moons was bright that night, and in the resultant exotic patchwork of shadows below, I caught sight of one of the larls, padding softly along, its body almost white in the moonlight. It paused, lifted its wide, fierce head, some two or three feet in diameter, and uttered the hunting scream once more. Momentarily it was answered, once from about two pasangs to the west and once from about the same distance to the southwest. It appeared ready to resume its pace when suddenly it stopped, its head absolutely motionless, its sharp, pointed ears tense and lifted. I thought perhaps he had heard the tarn, but he seemed to show no awareness of us.

I brought the bird somewhat lower, in long, slow circles, keeping the larl in view. The tail of the animal began to lash angrily. It crouched, holding its long, terrible body close to the ground. It then began to move forward, swiftly but stealthily, its shoulders hunched forward, its hind quarters almost touching the ground. Its ears were lying back, flat against the sides of its wide head. As it moved, for all its speed, it placed each paw carefully on the ground, first the toes and then the ball of the foot, as silently as the wind might bend grass, in a motion that was as beautiful as it was terrifying.

Something unusual was apparently happening. Some animal must be trying to break the hunting circle. One would suppose that the larl might be unconcerned with a single animal escaping its net of noise and fear and would neglect an isolated kill in order to keep the hunting circle closed, but that is not true. For whatever reason, the larl will always prefer ruining a hunt, even one involving a quarry of several animals, to allowing a given animal to move past it to freedom. Though I suppose this is purely instinctive on the larl's part, it does have the effect, over a series of generations, of weeding out animals which, if they survived, might transmit their intelligence, or perhaps their erratic running patterns, to their offspring. As it is, when the larl loses its hunt, the animals which escape are those which haven't tried to break the circle, those which allow themselves to be herded easily.

Suddenly, to my horror, I saw the quarry of the larl. It was a human being, moving with surprising alacrity over the rough ground. To my astonishment, I saw it wore the yellow cerements of the sufferer of Dar-Kosis, that virulent, incurable, wasting disease of Gor.

Without bothering to think, I seized my spear and, dragging harshly on the four-strap, brought the tarn into a sharp, abrupt descent. The bird struck the ground between the diseased victim and the approaching larl.

Rather than risk casting my spear from the safe but unsteady saddle of the tarn, I leaped to the ground, just as the larl, furious that it had been discovered, uttered the paralyzing hunting roar and charged. For an instant I could not move, literally. Somehow the shock of that great, wild cry gripped me in a steel fist of terror. It was uncontrollable, an immobility as much a physiological reflex as the jerking of a knee or the blinking of an eye.

Then, as swiftly as it had come, that nightmarish instant of immobility passed and I set my spear to take the jolt of the larl's attack. Perhaps my sudden appearance had disoriented the beast or shaken its marvelous instincts, because it must have uttered its killing cry an instant too soon, or perhaps my muscles and nerves responded to my will more rapidly than it had anticipated. When, twenty feet away, the great, bounding beast, fangs bared, leaped for its prey, it encountered instead only the slender needle of my spear, set like a stake in the ground, braced by the half-naked body of a warrior of Ko-ro-ba. The spearhead disappeared from sight in the furry breast of the larl, and the shaft of the spear began to sink into it as the weight of the animal forced it deeper into its body. I leaped from under the tawny, monstrous body, narrowly escaping the slashings of its clawed forefeet. The spear shaft snapped and the beast fell to the earth, rolling on its back, pawing at the air, uttering piercing, enraged shrieks, trying to bite the toothpick-like object from its body. With a convulsive shudder, the great head rolled to one side and the eyes half closed, leaving a milky slit of death between the lids.

I turned to regard the individual whose life I had saved. He was now bent and crooked, like a broken, blasted shrub in his yellow shroudlike robe. The hood concealed his face.

"There are more of these things about," I said. "You'd better come with me. It won't be safe here."

The figure seemed to shrink backward and grow smaller in its yellow rags. Pointing to its shadowed, concealed face, it whispered, "The Holy Disease."

That was the literal translation of Dar-Kosis—the Holy Disease—or, equivalently, the Sacred Affliction. The disease is named that because it is regarded as being holy to the Priest-Kings, and those who suffer from it are regarded as consecrated to the Priest-Kings. Accordingly, it is regarded as heresy to shed their blood. On the other hand, the Afflicted, as they are called, have little to fear from their fellow men. Their disease is so highly contagious, so invariably devastating in its effect, and so feared on the planet that even the boldest of outlaws gives them a wide berth. Accordingly, the Afflicted enjoy a large amount of freedom of movement on Gor. They are, of course, warned to stay away from the habitations of men, and, if they approach too closely, they are sometimes stoned. Oddly enough, casuistically, stoning the Afflicted is not regarded as a violation of the Priest-Kings' supposed injunction against shedding their blood.

As an act of charity, Initiates have arranged at various places Dar-Kosis Pits where the Afflicted may voluntarily imprison themselves, to be fed with food hurled downward from the backs of passing tarns. Once in a Dar-Kosis Pit, the Afflicted are not allowed to depart. Finding this poor fellow in the Voltai, so far from the natural routes and fertile areas of Gor, I suspected he might have escaped, if that was possible, from one of the Pits.

"What is your name?" I asked.

"I am of the Afflicted," said the weird, cringing figure. "The Afflicted are dead. The dead are nameless." The voice was little more than a hoarse whisper.

I was glad that it was night and that the hood of the man was drawn, for I had no desire to look on what pieces of flesh might still cling to his skull.

"Did you escape from one of the Dar-Kosis Pits?" I asked.

The man seemed to cringe even more.

"You are safe with me," I said. I gestured to the tarn, which was impatiently opening and closing his wings. "Hurry. There are more larls about."

"The Holy Disease," the man protested, pointing into the hideously dark recesses of his drawn hood.

"I can't leave you here to die," I said. I shivered at the thought of taking this dread creature, this whispering corpse, with me. I feared the disease as I had not feared the larl, but I could not leave him here in the mountains to fall prey to one beast or another.

The man cackled—a thin, whining noise. "I am already dead," he laughed insanely. "I am of the Afflicted." Again the weird cackle came from the folds of the yellow shroud. "Would you like the Holy Disease?" he asked, stretching out one hand in the darkness, as if trying to clutch my hand.

I drew back my hand in horror.

The thing stumbled forward, reaching for me, and fell to the ground with a tiny, moaning sound. It sat on the ground, wrapped in its yellow cerements—a mound of decay and desolation under the three Gorean moons. It rocked back and forth, uttering mad little noises, as if grieving or whimpering.

From perhaps a pasang away I heard the frustrated roar of a larl, probably one of the companions of the beast I had killed, puzzled about the failure of the hunt.

"Get up," I said. "There isn't much time."

"Help me," whined the yellow mound.

I stilled a shiver of disgust and extended my hand to the object.

"Take my hand," I said. "I'll help you."

From the bent heap of rags that was a fellow human being, a hand reached up to me, the fingers crooked, as though they might have been the claws of a chicken. Disregarding my misgivings, I took the hand, to draw the unfortunate creature to its feet.

To my amazement, the hand that clasped mine firmly was as solid and hardened as saddle leather. Before I realized what was happening, my arm had been jerked downward and twisted, and I had been thrown on my back at the feet of the man, who leaped up and set his boot on my throat. In his hand was a warrior's sword, and the point was at my breast. He laughed a mighty, roaring laugh and threw his head back, causing the hood to fall to his shoulders. I saw a massive, lionlike head, with wild long hair and a beard as unkempt and magnificent as the crags of the Voltai itself. The man, who seemed to leap into gigantic stature as he lifted himself into full height, took from under his yellow robes a tarn whistle and blew a long, shrill note. Almost instantly the whistle had been answered by other whistles, responding from a dozen places in the nearby mountains. Within a minute the air was filled with the beating of wings, as some half a hundred wild tarnsmen brought their birds down about us.

"I am Marlenus, Ubar of Ar," said the man.

14

The Tarn Death

SHACKLED IN A KNEELING POSITION, my back open and bleeding from the lash, I was thrown before the Ubar. Nine days I had been a prisoner in his camp, subjected to torture and abuse. Yet this was the first time since I had saved his life that I had seen him. I gathered that he had finally seen fit to terminate the sufferings of the warrior who had stolen the Home Stone of his city.

One of the tarnsmen of Marlenus thrust his hand in my hair and forced my lips down to his sandal. I forced my head up and kept my back straight, my eyes granting my captor no satisfaction. I knelt on the granite floor of a shallow cave in one of the Voltai peaks, a sheltered fire on each side of me. Before me, on a rough throne of piled rocks, sat Marlenus, his long hair over his shouders, his great beard reaching almost to his sword belt. He was a gigantic man, larger even than the Older Tarl, and in his eyes, wild and green, I saw the masterful flame which had, in its way, also burned in the eyes of Talena, his daughter. Die though I must at the hands of this magnificent barbarian, I could feel no ill will toward him. If I had had to kill him, I would have done so not with hatred or rancor, but rather with respect.

Around his neck he wore the golden chain of the Ubar, carrying the medallionlike replica of the Home Stone of Ar. In his hands he held the Stone itself, that humble source of so much strife, bloodshed and honor. He held it gently, as though it might have been a child.

At the entrance of the cave two of his men had set a tharlarion lance, of the sort carried by Kazrak and his men, in a crevice obviously prepared to receive it. I supposed it was to serve for my impalement. There are various ways in which this cruel mode of execution can be accomplished, and, needless to say, some are more merciful than others. I did not expect that I would be granted a swift death.

"You are he who stole the Home Stone of Ar," said Marlenus.

"Yes," I said.

"It was well done," said Marlenus, looking at the Stone, holding it so the light reflected variously from its worn surface.

I waited, kneeling at his feet, puzzled that he, like the others in his camp, evinced no interest in the fate of his daughter.

"You realize clearly that you must die," said Marlenus, not looking at me.

"Yes," I said.

Holding the Home Stone in both hands, Marlenus leaned forward.

"You are a young and brave and foolish warrior," he said. He looked into my eyes for a long time, then leaned back against his rough throne. "I was once as young and brave as you," he said, "and perhaps as foolish—yes, perhaps as foolish." The eyes of Marlenus stared over my head, into the darkness outside. "I risked my life a thousand times and gave the years of my youth to the vison of Ar and its empire, that there might be on all Gor but one language, but one commerce, but one set of codes, that the highways and passes might be safe, that the peasants might cultivate their fields in peace, that there might be but one Council to decide matters of policy, that there might be but one supreme city to unite the cylinders of a hundred severed, hostile cities—and all this you have destroyed." Marlenus looked down at me. "What can you, a simple tarnsman, know of these things?" he asked. "But I, Marlenus, though a warrior, was more than a warrior, always more than a warrior. Where others could see no more than the codes of their castes, where others could sense no call of duty beyond that of their Home Stone, I dared to dream the dream of Ar—that there might be an end to meaningless warfare, bloodshed, and terror, an end to the anxiety and peril, the retribution and cruelty that cloud our lives —I dreamed that there might arise from the ashes of the conquests of Ar a new world, a world of honor and law, of power and justice."

"Your justice," I said.

"Mine, if you like," he agreed.

Marlenus set the Home Stone on the ground before him and drew his sword, which he laid across his knees; he looked like some remote and terrible god of war.

"Do you know, Tarnsman," he asked, "that there is no justice without the sword?" He smiled down on me grimly. "This is a terrible truth," he said, "and so consider it carefully." He paused. "Without this," he said, touching the blade, "there is nothing—no justice, no civilization, no society, no community, no peace. Without the sword there is nothing."

"By what right," I challenged, "is it the sword of Marlenus that must bring justice to Gor?"

"You do not understand," said Marlenus. "Right itself—that right of which you speak so reverently—owes its very existence to the sword."

"I think that is false," I said. "I hope it is false." I shifted, even that small movement irritating the whip cuts on my back.

Marlenus was patient. "Before the sword," he said, "there is no right, no wrong, only fact—a world of what is and what is not, rather than a world of what should be and what should not be. There is no justice until the sword creates it, establishes it, guarantees it, gives it substance and significance." He lifted the weapon, wielding the heavy metal blade as though it were a straw. "First the sword—" he said, "then government—then law—then justice."

"But," I asked, "what of the dream of Ar, that dream of which you spoke, that dream that you believed it right to bring about?"

"Yes?" said Marlenus.

"Is that a right dream?" I asked.

"It is a right dream," he said.

"And yet," I said, "your sword has not yet found the strength to bring it into being."

Marlenus looked at me thoughtfully, then laughed. "By the Priest-Kings," he said, "I think I have lost the exchange."

I shrugged, somewhat incongruously in the chains; it hurt.

"But," went on Marlenus, "if what you say is true, how shall we separate the right dreams from the wrong dreams?"

It seemed to me a difficult question.

"I will tell you," laughed Marlenus. He slapped the blade fondly. "With this!"

The Ubar then rose and sheathed his sword. As if this

were a signal, some of his tarnsmen entered the cave and seized me.

"Impale him," said Marlenus.

The tarnsmen began to unlock the shackles, that I might be impaled freely on the lance, perhaps so that my struggles might provide a more interesting spectacle to the onlookers.

I felt numb, even my back, which presumably would have been a riot of pain if I had not felt myself near death.

"Your daughter, Talena, is alive," I said to Marlenus. He had not asked and did not now appear to have much interest in the matter. Still, if he was human at all, I assumed this remote, kingly, dream-obsessed man would want to know.

"She would have brought a thousand tarns," said Marlenus. "Proceed with the impalement."

The tarnsmen grasped my arms more securely. Two others removed the tharlarion lance from its crevice and brought it forward. It would be forced into my body, and I would then be lifted, with it, into place.

"She's your daughter," I said to Marlenus. "She's alive."

"Did she submit to you?" asked Marlenus.

"Yes," I said.

"Then she valued her life more than my honor."

Suddenly my feeling of numbness, of incapacity, departed as if in a lightning flash of fury. "Damn your honor!" I shouted. "Damn your precious stinking honor!"

Without realizing what I was doing, I had shaken the two restraining tarnsmen from my arms as if they had been children, and I rushed on Marlenus and struck him violently in the face with my fist, causing him to reel backward, his face contorted with astonishment and pain. I turned just in time to knock the impaling lance aside as, carried by two men, it plunged toward my back. I seized it, twisting it, and, using it like a bar held by the men, leaped into the air, kicking at them. I heard two screams of pain and found that I held the lance. Some five or six tarnsmen ran toward the wide opening of the shallow cave, but I rushed forward, holding the lance parallel to my body, striking them with almost superhuman strength and forcing them over the ledge near the mouth of the cave. Their screams mingled with shouts of rage as the other tarnsmen rushed forward to capture me.

One tarnsman leveled a crossbow, and in that instant I hurled the lance and he toppled backward, the shaft of the weapon protruding from his chest, the bolt from his crossbow ricocheting from the rock above my head with a flash of sparks. One of the men I had kicked lay writhing at my feet. I seized the sword from his scabbard. I engaged and dropped the first of the tarnsmen to reach me and wounded the second, but was pressed back toward the rear of the cave. I was doomed, but resolved to die well.

As I fought, I could hear the lion laughter of Marlenus behind me, as what had been a simple impalement turned into a fight of the sort after his own heart. As I found a moment's respite, I spun to face him, hoping to have it out with the Ubar himself, but as I did so, the shackles that I had worn struck me forcibly in the face and throat, thrown like a bolo by Marlenus. I choked, and shook my head to clear the blood from my eyes, and in that instant was seized by three or four of the Ubar's tarnsmen.

"Well done, young warrior," acclaimed Marlenus. "I thought I would see if you would die like a slave." He addressed his men, pointing to me. "What say you?" he laughed. "Has this warrior not earned his right to the tarn death?"

"He has indeed," said one of the tarnsmen, who held a wadded lump of tunic over his slashed rib cage.

I was dragged outside, and binding fiber was fastened

to my wrists and ankles. The loose ends of the fiber were then attached by broad leather straps to two tarns, one of them my own sable giant.

"You will be torn to pieces," said Marlenus. "Not pleasant, but better than impalement."

I was fastened securely. A tarnsman mounted one tarn; another tarnsman mounted the other tarn.

"I'm not dead yet," I said. It was a stupid thing to say, but I felt that it was not yet my time to die.

Marlenus did not deride me. "You it was who stole the Home Stone of Ar," he said. "You have luck."

"No man can escape the tarn death," said one of the men.

The warriors of the Ubar moved back, to give the tarns room.

Marlenus himself knelt in the darkness to check the knots in the binding fiber, tightening them carefully. As he checked the knots at my wrists, he spoke to me.

"Do you wish me to kill you now?" he asked softly. "The tarn death is an ugly death." His hand, shielded from his men by his body, was on my throat. I felt it could have crushed it easily.

"Why this kindness?" I asked.

"For the sake of a girl," he said.

"But why?" I asked.

"For the love she has for you," he said.

"Your daughter hates me," I said.

"She agreed to be the mate of Pa-Kur, the Assassin," he said, "in order that you might have one small chance of life, on the Frame of Humiliation."

"How do you know this?" I asked.

"It is common knowledge in the camp of Pa-Kur," replied Marlenus. I could sense him smiling in the darkness. "I myself, as one of the Afflicted, learned it from Mintar, of the Merchant Caste. Merchants must keep their friends on both sides of the fence, for who knows if Marlenus may not once more sit upon the throne of Ar?"

I must have uttered a sound of joy, for Marlenus quickly placed his hand over my mouth.

He asked no more if he should kill me, but rose to his feet and walked away, under the snapping wing of one of the tarns, and waved farewell. "Good-bye, Warrior," he called.

With a sickening lurch and sharp jolt of pain the two tarnsmen brought their birds into the air. For a moment I swung between the birds, and then, perhaps a hundred feet in the air, the tarnsmen, at a prearranged signal—a sharp blast of a tarn whistle from the ground—turned their birds in opposite directions. The sudden wrenching pain seemed to rip my body. I think I inadvertently screamed. The birds were pulling against one another, stabilized in their flight, each trying to pull away from the other. Now and again there would be a moment's giddy respite from the pain as one or the other of the birds failed to keep the ropes taut. I could hear the curses of the tarnsmen above me and saw once or twice the flash of the striking tarn-goad. Then the birds would throw their weight again on the ropes, bringing another flashing wrench of agony.

Then, suddenly, there was a ripping sound as one of the wrist ropes broke. Without thinking, but responding blindly, with a surge of joy, I seized the other wrist rope and tried to force it over the wrist. When the bird drew again, there was a sharp pain as flesh was torn from my hand, but the rope darted off into the darkness, and I was swinging by my ankles from the other ropes. It might take a moment for the tarnsmen to realize what had happened. The first guess would be that my body had torn in two, and the darkness would conceal the truth for a moment, until the tarnsman himself would try the ropes, to test the weight of their burden.

I swung myself up and began to climb one of the two ropes leading to the great bird above me. In a few wild moments I had gained the saddle straps of the bird and hauled myself nearly to the weapon rings.

Then the tarnsman saw me and shouted in rage, drawing his sword. He slashed downward, and I slipped down one talon of the bird, which screamed and became unmanageable. Then, with one hand, while clinging to the talon, I loosened the girth straps. In a moment, given the wild motion of the bird, the entire saddle, to which the tarnsman was fixed by the saddle straps, slid from the bird's back and flew wildly into the depths below.

I heard the scream of the tarnsman and then the sudden silence.

The other tarnsman would be alerted now. Each moment was precious. Daring everything, I leaped in the darkness for the reins of the bird and with one scrambling hand managed to seize the guiding collar. The sudden tug downward caused the bird to respond as I had hoped it would, as if pressure had been exerted on the four-strap. It immediately descended, and a minute later I was on the ground, on a sort of rough plateau. There was a rim of red light over the mountains, and I knew it was nearly dawn. My ankles were still fastened to the bird, and I quickly untied the ropes.

In the first streak of the early light I saw a few hundred yards away what I had hoped to find—the saddle and twisted body of the tarnsman. I released the bird, ran to the saddle, and removed the crossbow which, to my joy, was intact. None of the bolts had escaped from the specially constructed quiver. I set the bow and fitted one of them on the guide. I could hear the flight of another tarn above me. As it swept in for the kill, its tarnsman, too late, saw my leveled bow. The missile left him sagging lifeless in the saddle.

The tarn, my sable giant from Ko-ro-ba, landed and stalked majestically forward. I waited uneasily until he thrust his head past me, over my shoulder, extending his neck for preening. Good-naturedly, I scratched out a handful or two of lice which I slopped on his tongue like candy. Then I slapped his leg with affection, climbed to the saddle, dropped the dead tarnsman to the ground, and fastened myself in the saddle straps.

I felt ebullient. I had weapons again, and my tarn. There was even a tarn-goad and saddle gear. I rose into flight, not thinking about Ko-ro-ba again or the Home Stone. Foolishly perhaps, but with invincible optimism, I lifted the tarn above the Voltai and turned it toward Ar.

15

In Mintar's Compound

AR, BELEAGUERED AND DAUNTLESS, WAS a magnificent sight. Its splendid, defiant shimmering cylinders loomed proudly behind the snowy marble ramparts, its double walls—the first three hundred feet high; the second, separated from the first by twenty yards, four hundred feet high—walls wide enough to drive six tharlarion wagons abreast on their summits. Every fifty yards along the walls rose towers, jutting forth so as to expose any attempt at scaling to the fire of their numerous archer ports. Across the city, from the walls to the cylinders and among the cylinders, I could occasionally see the slight flash of sunlight on the swaying tarn wires, literally hundreds of thousands of slender, almost invisible wires stretched in a protective net across the city. Dropping the tarn through such a maze of wire would be an almost impossible task. The wings of a striking tarn would be cut from its body by such wires.

Within the city the Initiates, who had seized control shortly after the flight of Marlenus, would have already tapped the siege reservoirs and begun to ration the stores of the huge grain cylinders. A city such as Ar, properly commanded, might withstand a siege for a generation.

Beyond the walls were Pa-Kur's lines of investment, set forth with all the skill of Gor's most experienced siege engineers. Some hundreds of yards from the wall, just beyond crossbow range, a gigantic ditch was being dug by thousands of siege slaves and prisoners. When completed, it would be fifty or sixty feet wide, and seventy or eighty feet deep. In back of the ditch slaves were piling up the earth which had been removed from the ditch, packing and hardening it into a rampart. On the summit of the rampart, where it was completed, were numerous archer blinds, movable wooden screens to shield archers and light missile equipment.

Between the ditch and the walls of the city, under the cover of darkness, thousands of sharpened stakes had been set, inclined toward the walls. I knew that the worst of such devices would be invisible. Indeed, several of the spaces between the stakes were probably occupied by covered pits, more sharpened stakes being fixed in the bottom. Also, half buried in the sands among the stakes and set in wooden blocks would be iron hooks, much like those used in ancient times on Earth and sometimes called spurs. Behind the great ditch, separated from it by some hundred yards, there was a smaller ditch, perhaps twenty feet wide and twenty feet deep, also with a rampart formed from the excavated earth. Surmounting this rampart was a palisade of logs, sharpened at the tips. In the walls, every hundred yards or so, was a log gate. Behind this wall were the innumerable tents of Pa-Kur's horde.

Here and there among the tents siege towers were being constructed. Nine towers were in evidence. It was unthinkable that they should top the walls of Ar, but with their battering rams they would attempt to break through at the lower levels. Tarnsmen would make the attack at the summit of the walls. When it came time for Pa-Kur to attack, bridges would be constructed over the ditches. Over these bridges the siege towers would be rolled to the walls of Ar; over them his tharlarion cavalry would march; over them his horde would flow. Light engines, mostly catapults and ballistae, would be transported over the ditches by harnessed tarn teams.

One aspect of the siege which I knew would exist but which I obviously could not witness would be the sensitive duel of mine and countermine which must be taking place between the camp of Pa-Kur and the city of Ar. There would be numerous tunnels being worked even now toward the walls of Ar, and, from Ar, countertunnels to meet them. Some of the most hideous fighting in the siege would undoubtedly take place far under the earth in the cramped, foul, torchlit confines of those serpentine passageways, some of them hardly large enough to permit a man to crawl. Many of the tunnels would be collapsed and others flooded. Given the depth of the foundations of Ar's mighty walls and the mantle of rock on which they were fixed, it would be extremely unlikely that her walls could be successfully undermined to the extent of bringing down a significant section, but it was surely possible that if one of the tunnels managed to pass unnoticed beneath the ramparts, it could serve to spill a line of soldiers into the city at night, enough men to overcome a gate crew and expose Ar to the onslaught of Pa-Kur's main forces.

I noted one thing that seemed puzzling for a moment. Pa-Kur had not protected his rear with the customary third ditch and rampart. I could see foragers and merchants moving to and from the camp unimpeded. I reasoned that Pa-Kur had nothing to fear and consequently chose not to employ his siege slaves and prisoners in unnecessary and time-consuming works. Still, it seemed that he had committed an error, if only according to the manuals of siege practice. If I had had a considerable force of men at my disposal, I could have exploited that error.

I brought the tarn down near the far ranges of Pa-Kur's tents, where his camp ended, seven or eight miles from the city. I was not too surprised when I was not challenged; Pa-Kur's arrogance, or simply his rational assurance, was such that no sentries, no signs and countersigns, had been arranged at the rear of the camp. Leading the tarn, I entered the camp as casually as I might have strolled into a carnival or fair. I had no realistic or clearheaded plan, but was determined somehow to find Talena and escape, or die in the attempt.

I stopped a hurrying slave girl and inquired the way to the compound of Mintar, of the Merchant Caste, confident that he would have accompanied the horde back to the heartland of Ar. The girl was not pleased to be delayed on her errand, but a slave on Gor does not wisely ignore the address of a free man. She spit the coins she carried in her mouth into her hand, and told me what I wanted to know. Few Gorean garments are deformed by pockets. An exception is the working aprons of artisans.

Soon, my heart beating quickly, my features concealed by the helmet I had taken from the warrior in the Voltai, I approached the compound of Mintar. At the entrance to the compound was a gigantic, temporary wire cage, a tarn cot. I tossed a silver tarn disk to the tarn keeper and ordered him to care for the bird, to groom and feed it and see that it was ready on an instant's notice. His grumbling was silenced by an additional tarn disk.

I wandered about the outskirts of Mintar's compound, which was separated, like many of the merchant compounds, from the main camp by a tough fence of woven branches. Over the compound, as if it were a small city under siege, was stretched a set of interlaced tarn wires. The compound of Mintar enclosed several acres of ground and was the largest merchant compound in the camp. At last I reached the section of the tharlarion corrals. I waited until one of the caravan guards passed. He didn't recognize me.

Glancing about to see that no one was watching, I lightly climbed the fence of woven branches and dropped down inside among a group of the broad tharlarions. I had carefully determined that the corral into which I dropped did not contain the saddle lizards, the high tharlarions, those ridden by Kazrak and his tharlarion lancers. Such lizards are extremely short-tempered, as well as carnivorous, and I had no intention of attracting attention to myself by beating my way through them with a spear butt.

Their more dormant relatives, the broad tharlarions, barely lifted their snouts from the feed troughs. Shielded by the placid, heavy bodies, some as large as a bus, I worked my way toward the interior side of the corral.

My luck held, and I scaled the interior corral wall and dropped to the trampled path between the corral and the tents of Mintar's men. Normally, the merchant camp, like the better-organized military camps, not the mélange that constituted the camp of Pa-Kur, is laid out geometrically, and, night after night, one puts up one's tent in the same relative position. Whereas the military camp is usually laid out in a set of concentric squares, reflecting the fourfold principle of military organization customary on Gor, the merchant camp is laid out in concentric circles, the guards' tents occupying the outermost ring, the craftsmen's, strap-masters', attendants', and slaves' quarters occupying inner rings, and the center being reserved for the merchant, his goods, and his bodyguard.

It was with this in mind that I had climbed the fence where I had. I was searching for Kazrak's tent, which lay in the outer ring near the tharlarion corrals. My calculations had been correct, and in a moment I had slipped inside the domed framework of his tent. I dropped the ring that I wore, with the crest of Cabot, to his sleeping mat.

For what seemed an interminable hour, I waited in the dark interior of the tent. At last the weary figure of Kazrak, helmet in hand, bent down to enter the tent. I waited, not speaking, in the shadows. He came through the opening, dropped his helmet on the sleeping mat, and began to unsling his sword. Still I would not speak, not while he controlled a weapon; unfortunately, the first thing a Gorean warrior is likely to do to the stranger in his tent is kill him, the second is to find out who he is. I saw the spark of Kazrak's fire-maker, and I felt the flush of friendship as I saw his features briefly outlined in the glow. He lit the small hanging tent lamp, a wick set in a copper bowl of tharlarion oil, and in its flickering light turned to the sleeping mat. No sooner had he done so than he fell to his knees on the mat and grasped the ring.

"By the Priest-Kings!" he cried.

I leaped across the tent and clapped my hands across his mouth. For a moment we struggled fiercely. "Kazrak!" I said. I took my hand from his mouth. He grasped me in his arms and crushed me to his chest, his eyes filled with tears. I shoved him away happily.

"I looked for you," he said. "For two days I rode down the banks of the Vosk. I would have cut you free."

"That's heresy," I laughed.

"Let it be heresy," he said. "I would have cut you free."

"We are together again," I said simply.

"I found the frame," Kazrak said, "half a pasang from the Vosk, broken. I thought you were dead."

The brave man wept, and I felt like weeping, too, for joy, because he was my friend. With affection I took him by the shoulders and shook him. I went to his locker near the mat and got out his Ka-la-na flask, taking a long draught myself and then shoving it into his hands. He drained the flask in one drink and wiped his hand across his beard, stained with the red juice of the fermented drink.

"We are together again," he said. "We are together again, Tarl of Bristol, my sword brother."

Kazrak and I sat in his tent, and I recounted my adventures to him, while he listened, shaking his head. "You are one of destiny and luck," he said, "raised by the Priest-Kings to do great deeds."

"Life is short," I said. "Let us speak of things we know."

"In a hundred generations, among the thousand chains of fate," said Kazrak, "there is but one strand like yours."

There was a sound at the entrance of Kazrak's tent. I darted back into the shadows.

It was one of the trusted strap-masters of Mintar, the man who guided the beasts that carried the merchant's palanquin.

Without looking around the tent, the man addressed himself directly to Kazrak.

"Will Kazrak and his guest, Tarl of Bristol, please accompany me to the tent of Mintar, of the Merchant Caste?" asked the man.

Kazrak and I were stunned, but arose to follow the man. It was now dark, and as I wore my helmet, there was no chance of the casual observer determining my identity. Before I left Kazrak's tent, I placed the ring of red metal, with the crest of Cabot, in my pouch. Hitherto I had worn the ring almost arrogantly, but now it seemed to me that discretion, to alter a saying, was the better part of pride.

Mintar's tent was enormous and domed, similar in shape to others in his camp; however, not only in size, but in splendor of appointment, it was a palace of silk. We passed through the guards at the entrance. In the center of the great tent, seated alone on cushions before a small fire, were two men, a game board between them. One was Mintar, of the Merchant Caste, his great bulk resting like a sack of meal on the cushions. The other man, a gigantic man, wore the robes of one of the Afflicted, but wore them as a king might. He sat cross-legged, his back straight and his head high, in the fashion of a warrior. Without needing to approach more closely, I knew the other man. It was Marlenus.

"Do not interrupt the game," commanded Marlenus.

Kazrak and I stood to one side.

Mintar was lost in thought, his small eyes fastened to the red and yellow squares of the board. Having recognized our presence, Marlenus, too, turned his attention to the game. A brief, crafty light flickered momentarily in Mintar's small eyes, and his pudgy hand hovered, hesitating an instant, over one of the pieces of the hundred-squared board, a centered Tarnsman. He touched it, committing himself to moving it. A brief exchange followed, like a chain reaction, neither man considering his moves for a moment, First Tarnsman took First Tarnsman, Second Spearman responded by neutralizing First Tarnsman, City neutralized Spearman, Assassin took City, Assassin fell to Second Tarnsman, Tarnsman to Spear Slave, Spear Slave to Spear Slave.

Mintar relaxed on the cushions. "You have taken the City," he said, "but not the Home Stone." His eyes gleamed with pleasure. "I permitted that, in order that I might capture the Spear Slave. Let us now adjudicate the game. The Spear Slave gives me the point I need, a small point but decisive."

Marlenus smiled, rather grimly. "But position must figure in any adjudication," he said. Then, with an imperious gesture, Marlenus swept his Ubar into the file opened by the movement of Mintar's capturing Spear Slave. It covered the Home Stone.

Mintar bowed his head in mock ceremony, a wry smile on his fat face, and with one short finger delicately tipped his own Ubar, causing it to fall.

"It is a weakness in my game," lamented Mintar. "I am ever too greedy for a profit, however small."

Marlenus looked at Kazrak and myself. "Mintar," he said, "teaches me patience. He is normally a master of defense."

Mintar smiled. "And Marlenus invariably of the attack."

"An absorbing game," said Marlenus, almost absentmindedly. "To some men this game is music and women. It can give them pleasure. It can help them forget. It is Ka-la-na wine, and the night on which such wine is drunk."

Neither Kazrak nor myself spoke.

"Look here," said Marlenus, reconstructing the board. "I have used the Assassin to take the City. Then, the Assassin is felled by a Tarnsman . . . an unorthodox, but interesting variation . . ."

"And the Tarnsman is felled by a Spear Slave," I observed.

"True," said Marlenus, shaking his head, "but thusly did I win."

"And Pa-Kur," I said, "is the Assassin."

"Yes," agreed Marlenus, "and Ar is the City."

"And I am the Tarnsman?" I asked.

"Yes," said Marlenus.

"And who," I asked, "is the Spear Slave?"

"Does it matter?" asked Marlenus, sifting several of the Spear Slaves through his fingers, letting them drop, one by one, to the board. "Any of them will do."

"If the Assassin should take the City," I said, "the rule of the Initiates will be broken, and eventually the horde with its loot will scatter, leaving a garrison."

Mintar shifted comfortably, settling his great bulk more deeply into the cushions. "The young tarnsman plays the game well," he said.

"And," I went on, "when Pa-Kur falls, the garrison will be divided, and a revolution may take place—"

"Led by a Ubar," said Marlenus, looking fixedly at the game piece in his hand. It was a Ubar. He smashed it down on the board, scattering the other pieces to the silken cushions. "By a Ubar!" he exclaimed.

"You are willing," I asked, "to turn the city over to Pa-Kur—that his horde should swarm into the cylinders, that the city may be looted and burned, the people destroyed or enslaved?" I shuddered involuntarily at the thought of the uncontrolled hordes of Pa-Kur among the spires of Ar, butchering, pillaging, burning, raping—or, as the Goreans will have it, washing the bridges in blood.

The eyes of Marlenus flashed. "No," he said. "But Ar will fall. The Initiates can only mumble prayers to the Priest-Kings, arrange the details of their meaningless, innumerable sacrifices. They crave political power, but can't understand it or manipulate it. They will never withstand a well-mounted siege. They will never keep the city."

"Can't you enter the city and take power?" I asked. "You could return the Home Stone. You could gather a following."

"Yes," said Marlenus. "I could return the Home Stone—and there are those who would follow me—but there are not enough, not enough. How many would rally to the banner of an outlaw? No, the power of the Initiates must first be broken."

"Do you have a way into the city?" I asked.

Marlenus looked at me narrowly. "Perhaps," he said.

"Then I have a counterplan," I said. "Strike for the Home Stones of those cities tributary to Ar—they are kept on the Central Cylinder. If you seize them, you can divide Pa-Kur's horde, give the Home Stones to the contingents of the tributary cities, provided they withdraw their forces. If they do not, destroy the Stones."

"The soldiers of the Twelve Tributary Cities," he said, "want loot, vengeance, the women of Ar, not just their Stones."

"Perhaps some of them fight for their freedom—for the right to keep their own Home Stone," I said. "Surely not all of Pa-Kur's horde are adventurers, mercenaries." Noting the Ubar's interest, I went on. "Besides, few of the soldiers of Gor, barbarians though they might be, would risk the destruction of their city's Home Stone—the luck of their birthplace."

"But," said Marlenus, frowning, "if the siege is lifted, the Initiates will be left in power."

"And Marlenus will not resume the throne of Ar," I said. "But the city will be safe." I looked at Marlenus, testing the man. "What is it, Ubar, that you hold dearest—your city or your title? Do you seek the welfare of Ar or your private glory?"

Marlenus leaped to his feet, hurling the yellow robes of the Afflicted from him, drawing his blade from its sheath with a metallic flash. "A Ubar," he cried, "answers such a question only with his sword!" My weapon, too, had flashed from its sheath almost simultaneously. We faced each other for a long, terrible moment; then Marlenus threw back his head and laughed his great lion laugh, slamming his sword back into its sheath. "Your plan is a good one," he said. "My men and I will enter the city tonight."

"And I shall go with you," I said.

"No," said Marlenus. "The men of Ar need no help from a warrior of Ko-ro-ba."

"Perhaps," suggested Mintar, "the young tarnsman

might attend to the matter of Talena, daughter of Marlenus."

"Where is she?" I demanded.

"We are not certain," said Mintar. "But it is presumed that she is kept in the tents of Pa-Kur."

For the first time Kazrak spoke. "On the day that Ar falls, she will wed Pa-Kur and rule beside him. He hopes this will encourage the survivors of Ar to accept him as their rightful Ubar. He will proclaim himself their liberator, their deliverer from the despotism of the Initiates, the restorer of the old order, the glory of the empire."

Mintar was idly arranging the pieces on the game board, first in one pattern and then in another. "In large matters, as the pieces are now set," he said, "the girl is unimportant, but only the Priest-Kings can foresee all possible variations. It might be well to remove the girl from the board." So saying, he picked a piece, the Ubar's Consort, or Ubara, from the board and dropped it into the game box.

Marlenus stared down at the board, his fists clenched. "Yes," he said, "she must be removed from the board, but not simply for reasons of strategy. She has dishonored me." He scowled at me. "She has been alone with a warrior—she has submitted herself—she has even pledged to sit at the side of an assassin."

"She has not dishonored you," I said.

"She submitted herself," said Marlenus.

"Only to save her life," I said.

"And rumor has it," said Mintar, not looking up from the board, "that she pledged herself to Pa-Kur only that some tarnsman she loved might be given a small chance of life."

"She would have brought a bride price of a thousand tarns," said Marlenus bitterly, "and now she is of less value than a trained slave girl."

"She is your daughter," I said, my temper rising.

"If she were here now," said Marlenus, "I would strangle her."

"And I would kill you," I said.

"Well, then," said Marlenus, smiling, "perhaps I would only beat her and throw her naked to my tarnsmen."

"And I would kill you," I repeated.

"Indeed," said Marlenus, looking at me narrowly, "one of us would slay the other."

"Have you no love for her?" I asked.

Marlenus seemed momentarily puzzled. "I am a Ubar," he said. He drew the robes of the Afflicted once more around his gigantic frame and picked up a gnarled staff he carried. He dropped the hood of the yellow robe about his face, ready to go, then turned to me once more. With the staff he poked me good-naturedly in the chest. "May the Priest-Kings favor you," he said, and, inside the folds of the hood, I knew he was chuckling.

Marlenus left the tent, seemingly one of the Afflicted, a bent wreck of humanity pathetically scratching at the earth in front of him with the staff.

Mintar looked up, and he, too, seemed pleased. "You are the only man who has ever escaped the tarn death," he said, something of wonder in his voice. "Perhaps it is true, as they say, that you are that warrior brought every thousand years to Gor—brought by the Priest-Kings to change a world."

"How did you know I would come to the camp?" I asked.

"Because of the girl," said Mintar. "And it was logical, was it not, to expect you to enlist the aid of your Kazrak, your sword brother?"

"Yes," I said.

Mintar reached into the pouch at his waist and drew forth a golden tarn disk, of double weight. He threw it to Kazrak.

Kazrak caught it.

"I understand you are leaving my service," said Mintar.

"I must," said Kazrak.

"Of course," said Mintar.

"Where are the tents of Pa-Kur?" I asked.

"On the highest ground in camp," said Mintar, "near the second ditch and across from the great gate of Ar. You will see the black banner of the Caste of Assassins."

"Thank you," I said. "Though you are of the Merchant Caste, you are a brave man."

"A merchant may be as brave as a warrior, young Tarnsman," smiled Mintar. Then he seemed somewhat embarrassed. "Let us look at it this way. Suppose Marlenus regains Ar—will Mintar not receive the monopolies he wishes?"

"Yes," I said, "but Pa-Kur will guarantee those monopolies as freely as Marlenus."

"Even more freely," corrected Mintar, turning his attention again to the board, "but, you see, Pa-Kur does not play the game."

16

The Girl in the Cage

KAZRAK AND I RETURNED TO his tent, and until the early morning we discussed the possibilities of rescuing Talena. We turned over a number of plans, none of which seemed likely to succeed. It would presumably be suicidal to make any direct attempt to cut through to her, and yet, if this was the last resort, I knew I would make the attempt. In the meantime, until the city fell or Pa-Kur altered his plans, she would presumably be safe. It seemed unlikely that Pa-Kur would be so politically naïve as to use the girl before she had publicly accepted him as her Free Companion, according to the rites of Ar. Treated as a pleasure slave, she would have negligible political value. On the other hand, the thought of her in the tents of Pa-Kur enraged me, and I knew I would be unable to restrain myself indefinitely. For the time being, however, Kazrak's counsels of patience won me over, convincing me that any precipitious action would be almost surely doomed to failure.

Accordingly, for the next few days, I remained with Kazrak and bided my time. I dyed my hair black and acquired the helmet and gear of an Assassin. Across the left temple of the black helmet I fixed the golden slash of the messenger. In this disguise I freely wandered about the camp, observing the siege operations, the appointment of the compounds, the marshaling of troops. Occasionally I would climb halfway up one of the siege towers under construction and observe the city of Ar and the skirmishes that took place between it and the first ditch.

Periodically the shrill notes of alarm bugles would pierce the air, as forces from Ar emerged to do battle on the plains before the city. When this occurred, inevitably the spearmen and lancers of Pa-Kur, following the lead of siege slaves through the maze of stakes and traps, would engage the men from Ar. Sometimes the forces of Pa-Kur drove the warriors of Ar back to the very walls of the city, forcing them through the gates. Sometimes the forces of Ar would drive the men of Pa-Kur back against the defensive stakes, and once they drove them to take refuge across the now constructed siege bridges spanning the great ditch.

Still, there was little doubt that Pa-Kur's men had the best of things. The human resources on which Pa-Kur could draw seemed inexhaustible, and, as important, he had at his command a considerable force of tharlarion cavalry, an arm almost lacking to the men of Ar.

In these battles the skies would be filled with tarnsmen, from Ar and from the camp, firing into the massed warriors below, engaging one another in savage duels hundreds of feet in the air. But gradually the tarnsmen of Ar were diminished, overwhelmed by the superior forces which Pa-Kur could, with ruthless liberality, throw against them. On the ninth day of the siege the sky belonged to Pa-Kur, and the forces of Ar no longer emerged from the great gate. All hope of lifting the siege by battle was gone. The men of Ar remained within their walls, under their tarn wire, waiting for the attacks to come, while the Initiates of the city sacrificed to the Priest-Kings.

On the tenth day of the siege small engines, such as

covered catapults and ballistae, were flown across the ditches by tarn teams and soon were engaged in artillery duels with the engines mounted on the walls of Ar. Simultaneously, exposed chains of siege slaves began to move the stake lines forward. After some four days of bombardment, which probably had small effect, if any, the first assault was mounted.

It began several hours before dawn, as the giant siege towers, covered now with plates of steel to counter the effect of fire arrows and burning tar, were slowly rolled across the ditch bridges. By noon they were within crossbow range of the walls. After dark, in the light of torches, the first tower reached the walls. Within the hour three others had touched the first wall. Around these towers and on top of them warriors swarmed. Above them, tarnsman met tarnsman in battles to the death. Rope ladders from Ar brought defenders two hundred feet down the wall to the level of the towers. Through small postern gates other defenders rushed against the towers on the ground, only to be met by Pa-Kur's clustered support troops. From the height of the walls, some two hundred feet above the towers, missiles would be fired and stones cast. Within the towers, sweating, naked siege slaves, under the frenzied whips of their overseers, hauled on the great chains that swung the mighty steel rams into the wall and back.

One of Pa-Kur's towers was undermined, and it tilted crazily and they crashed into the dust, amidst the screaming of its doomed occupants. Another was captured and burned. But five more towers rolled slowly toward the walls of Ar. These towers were fortresses in themselves and would be maintained at all costs; hour in and hour out, they would continue their work, gnawing at the walls.

Meanwhile, at several points in the city and at randomly selected times, picked tarnsmen of Pa-Kur, each of whose tarns carried a dangling, knotted rope of nine spearmen, dropped to the wires and the tops of cylinders, landing their small task forces of raiders. These task forces seldom managed to return, but sometimes they were outstandingly successful.

On the twentieth day of the siege there was great rejoicing in the camp of Pa-kur, because in one place the wires had been cut and a squad of spearmen had reached the main siege reservoir, emptying their barrels of toxic kanda, a lethal poison extracted from one of Gor's desert shrubs. The city would now have to depend primarily on its private wells and the hope of rain. It seemed probable that food and water would soon be scarce in the city and that the Initiates, whose resistance had been unimaginative and who were apparently unable to protect the city, would be forced to face a hungry and desperate population.

The fate of Marlenus during these days was in doubt. I was certain that he had entered the city in some manner and was presumably waiting for his chance to strike at the Home Stones of the tributary cities, in order, if possible, to divide the horde of Pa-Kur. Then, in the fourth week of the siege, my heart fell. Marlenus and several men had entered the city, it seemed, but had been discovered—and sealed off in the very cylinder of the Home Stones—indeed, in that cylinder that had been his palace in the days of his glory.

Marlenus and his men apparently had command of the top floor and roof of the cylinder, but there was little hope he could use the Home Stones that now lay within his grasp. He and his men had no tarns, and their retreat was cut off. Moreover, the ubiquitous tarn wire heavily netted in the area of the Central Cylinder would ward off any attempts at rescue, unless perhaps by a large force.

Pa-Kur, of course, was pleased to leave Marlenus precisely where he was, to be destroyed by the men of Ar. Also, Pa-Kur was not so much a fool as to bring the tributary Home Stones to his camp and risk disuniting his horde before the siege was completed. Indeed, it was probable that Pa-Kur had no intention of returning the Home Stones at all but was determined to follow in the imperial footsteps of Marlenus himself. I wondered how long Marlenus could hold out. It would surely depend, in part, on the food and water available and on the persistence of the Initiates' attempts to dislodge him. I was confident that there would be cisterns and canisters of water in the palace, and I supposed that Marlenus, as an enlightened precaution, in view of the unstable politics of Ar, would have outfitted his cylinder as a keep, laying in stores of food and missile weapons. At any rate, my plan for the division of the Home Stones had failed, and Marlenus, on whom I had depended, was, in the language of the game, neutralized if not removed from the board.

In despair, Kazrak and I discussed these matters over and over. The probability of Ar's resisting the siege was minimal. One thing at least remained to be done: there must be an attempt to rescue Talena. Another plan entered my head, but I dismissed it as too far-fetched, as unworthy of consideration. Kazrak noticed my frown and demanded to know what I had thought.

"The siege might be lifted," I said, "if a force could take Pa-Kur by surprise, a force of some thousands of warriors attacking from the unprotected side of the camp."

Kazrak smiled. "That is true. Where will you find the army?"

I hesitated for a moment, and then said, "Ko-ro-ba, perhaps Thentis."

Kazrak looked at me in disbelief. "Are you rid of your senses?" he asked. "The fall of Ar will be Ka-la-na wine to the free cities of Gor. When Ar falls, there will be rejoicing in the streets. When Ar falls, the bridges will be hung with garlands, there will be free Paga, slaves will be freed, enemies will pledge friendship."

"How long will it last," I queried, "with Pa-Kur on the throne of Ar?"

Kazrak seemed suddenly to darken with thought.

"Pa-Kur will not destroy the city," I said, "and he will keep as much of his horde as he can."

"Yes," said Kazrak. "There will be little cause for rejoicing."

"Marlenus had a dream of empire," I said, "but the ambition of Pa-Kur will yield only a nightmare of oppression and tyranny."

"It is unlikely that Marlenus will ever again be a danger," said Kazrak. "Even should he survive, he is outlawed in his own city."

"But Pa-Kur," I said, "as Ubar of Ar, will threaten all Gor."

"True," said Kazrak, looking at me questioningly.

"Why should not the free cities of Gor unite to defeat Pa-Kur?"

"The cities never unite," responded Kazrak.

"They never have," I said. "But surely, if Pa-Kur is to be stopped, this is the time, not after he is master of Ar."

"The cities never unite," repeated Kazrak, shaking his head.

"Take this ring," I said, giving him the ring that bore the crest of Cabot. "Show it to the Administrator of Ko-ro-ba and to the Administrator of Thentis and to the Ubars or Administrators of whatever cities you can. Tell them to raise the siege. Tell them they must strike now, and that you come with this message from Tarl Cabot, Warrior of Ko-ro-ba."

"I will probably be impaled," said Kazrak, rising to his feet, "but I will go."

With a heavy heart I watched Kazrak loop his sword belt over his shoulder and pick up his helmet. "Good-bye, Sword Brother," he said, and turned and left the tent, as if he might have been merely going to the tharlarion corrals or to take his post for guard duty, as in our caravan days. I felt a choking sensation in my throat and asked myself if I had sent my friend to his death.

In a few minutes I gathered together my own gear and put on the heavy black helmet of the Assassin, left the tent, and turned my steps in the direction of the tents of Pa-Kur. I made my way to the interior perimeter of the second ditch, opposite the great gate of Ar in the distance. There, on a hillock overlooking the palisades that rimmed the rampart to the ditch, I saw the wall of black silk that surrounded the compound of Pa-Kur. Inside were the dozens of tents that formed the quarters for his personal retinue and bodyguard. Above them, at several places, flew the black banner of the Caste of Assassins.

I had neared the compound a hundred times before, but this time I was determined to enter. I began to walk with a quickened pace, my heart began to beat powerfully, and I felt the elation of decision. I would act. It would be suicide to attempt to cut my way in, but Pa-Kur was in the environs of Ar, directing the siege operations, and I might, with luck, pass myself off as his messenger; who would be bold enough to deny entrance to one whose helmet bore the golden slash of the courier?

Without hesitation I climbed the hillock and presented myself impatiently to the guards.

"A message from Pa-Kur," I said, "for the ears of Talena, his Ubara-to-be."

"I will carry the message," said one of the guards, a large man, his eyes suspicious. He regarded me closely. Obviously, I was not anyone he knew.

"The message is for the Ubara-to-be, and for her

alone," I said angrily. "Do you deny admittance to the messenger of Pa-Kur?"

"I do not know you," he growled.

"Give me your name," I demanded, "so that I may report to Pa-Kur who it is that denies his message to his future Ubara.

There was an agonized silence, and then the guard stepped aside. I entered the compound, not having a settled plan, but feeling that I must contact Talena. Perhaps together we could arrange an escape at some later time. For the moment I did not even know where in the compound she might be kept.

Within the first wall of black silk, there was a second wall, but this time of iron bars. Pa-Kur was not as careless about his own safety as I had conjectured. Additionally, overhead I could see lines of tarn wire. I walked about the second wall until I came to a gate, where I repeated my story. Here I was admitted without question, as though my helmet were sufficient guarantee in itself of my right to be there. Inside the second wall, I was escorted among the tents by a tower slave, a black girl whose livery was golden and who wore large golden earrings that matched a golden collar. Behind me, two guards fell into line.

We stopped before a resplendent tent of yellow-and-red silk, some forty feet in diameter and twenty feet high at the dome. I turned to my escort and the guards. "Wait here," I said. "My message is for the ears of she who is pledged to Pa-Kur, and for her ears alone." My heart was beating so loudly I wondered that they didn't hear it. I was amazed that my voice sounded so calm.

The guards looked at one another, not having anticipated my request. The tower slave regarded me gravely, as though I had chosen to exercise some long-neglected or obsolescent privilege.

"Wait here," I commanded, and stepped inside the tent.

In the tent was a cage.

It was perhaps a ten-foot cube, entirely enclosed. The heavy metal bars were coated with silver and set with precious stones. I noted with dismay that the cage had no door. It had literally been constructed about its prisoner. A girl sat within the cage, proudly, on a throne. She wore the concealing robes and veils, the full regalia of a Ubara.

Something seemed to tell me to be careful. I don't know what it was. Something seemed to be wrong. I suppressed an impulse to call her name; I restrained an impulse to leap to the bars, to seize her and to crush her to them and to my lips. This must be Talena whom I loved, to whom my life belonged. Yet I approached slowly, almost cautiously. Perhaps it was something in the carriage of the muffled figure, something in the way the head was held. It was much like Talena, but not as she had been. Had she been injured or drugged? Did she not recognize me? I stood before the cage and lifted my helmet from my head. She gave no sign of recognition. I sought for some glimmer of awareness in those green eyes, for the slightest sign of affection or welcome.

My voice sounded faraway. "I am the messenger of Pa-Kur," I said. "He wishes me to say that the city will soon fall and that you shall soon sit beside him on the throne of Ar."

"Pa-Kur is kind," said the girl.

I was stunned, but I revealed not the slightest surprise. Indeed, I was momentarily overwhelmed with the cunning of Pa-Kur and rejoiced that I had followed something of Kazrak's counsels of patience and caution, that I had not disclosed my identity, that I had not attempted to cut my way to her side and bring her out by the blade of the sword. Yes, that would have been a mistake. The voice of the girl in the cage was not the voice of the girl I loved. The girl in the cage was not Talena.

17

Chains of Gold

I HAD BEEN OUTWITTED BY the brilliance of Pa-Kur. It was with a heart filled with bitterness that I left the compound of the Assassin and returned to Kazrak's tent. In the next days, frequenting the Paga tents and markets, I sought, by cornering slaves and challenging swordsmen, to learn the whereabouts of Talena. But the answer, when I received an answer, whether by virtue of a golden tarn disk or mortal fear, was always the same—that she was kept in the tent of red and yellow silk. I had no doubt that these minions of Pa-Kur whom I either cajoled or terrorized surely believed that the girl in the cage was Talena. Of those actually living in the compound of Pa-Kur, it was perhaps only he who knew the true location of the girl.

In despair I realized I had done nothing more than make clear the fact that someone was desperately interested in the whereabouts of the girl, and, if anything, this information would make Pa-Kur redouble his precautions for her security and doubtless attempt to apprehend the individual responsible for the inquiries. In these days I did not wear the garb of the Caste of Assassins, but dressed as a nondescript tarnsman, wearing the insignia of no city. Four times I eluded special patrols of Pa-Kur, led by men I had questioned at sword point.

In the tent of Kazrak, ruefully I understood that my efforts had been futile and that the Tarnsman of Marlenus, so to speak, had at last been neutralized. I considered attempting the destruction of Pa-Kur, but this would not only be unlikely of success but would bring me no nearer my goal of rescuing Talena. Yet nothing but the sight of my beloved would have brought me more satisfaction than driving my sword into the heart of the Assassin.

These were terrible days for me. In addition to my own failures, I received no word from Kazrak, and reports from Ar on the stand of Marlenus in the Central Cylinder became obscure and contradictory. As nearly as I could determine, he and his men had been overcome, and the height of the Central Cylinder was again in the hands of the Initiates. If this had not yet taken place, it was momentarily expected.

The siege was in its fifty-second day, and the forces of Pa-Kur had breached the first wall. It was being methodically razed in seven places, to allow for the passage of the siege towers to the second wall. Moreover, hundreds of light "flying bridges" were being constructed; at the moment of the final assault these would be extended from the first wall to the second, and the men of Pa-Kur would scramble upward toward the looming ramparts of Ar's last defense. Rumor had it that dozens of tunnels, unimpeded, now extended beneath the second wall and could be opened in a matter of hours at various places in the city. The countermining operations of the men of Ar had apparently been desultory or incompetent. It was Ar's misfortune, at this most critical time in its long history, to be in the hands of the bleakest of all castes of men, the Initiates, skilled only in ritual, mythology, and superstition. Worse, from the reports of deserters, it became clear that the city was starving and that water was running short. Some of the defenders were opening the veins of surviving tarns, to drink the blood. The tiny urt, a common rodent of Gorean cities, was bringing a silver tarn disk in the markets. Disease had broken out. Groups of looters from Ar itself prowled the streets. In the camp of Pa-Kur we expected the city to fall any day, any hour. Yet, indomitably, Ar refused to surrender.

I truly believe that the brave men of Ar, in their valorous if blind love for their city, would have maintained the walls until the last slain warrior had been thrown from them to the streets below, but the Initiates would not have it so. In a surprise move, which perhaps should have been anticipated, the High Initiate of the city of Ar appeared on the walls. This man claimed to be the Supreme Initiate of all Initiates on Gor and to take his appointment from the Priest-Kings themselves. Needless to say, his claim was not acknowledged by the Chief Initiates of Gor's free cities, who regarded themselves as sovereign in their own cities. The Supreme Initiate, as he called himself, raised a shield and then set it at his feet. He then raised a spear and set it, like the shield, at his feet. This gesture is a military convention employed by commanders on Gor when calling for a parley or conference. It signifies a truce, literally the temporary putting aside of weapons. In surrender, on the other hand, the shield straps and the shaft of the spear are broken, indicating that the vanquished has disarmed himself and places himself at the mercy of the conqueror.

In a short time Pa-Kur appeared on the first wall, opposite the Supreme Initiate, and performed the same gestures. That evening emissaries were exchanged, and, by means of notes and conferences, conditions of surrender were arranged. By morning most of the important arrangements were known in the camp, and for all practical purposes Ar had fallen.

The bargaining of the Initiates was largely to secure their own safety and, as much as possible, to prevent the utter ravaging of the city. The first condition for their surrender was that Pa-Kur grant a general amnesty for themselves and their temples. This was typical of Initiates. Although they alone, of all the men on Gor, claim to be immortal, in virtue of the mysteries, forbidden to the profane, which they practice, they are perhaps the most timid of Goreans.

Pa-Kur willingly granted this condition. Any indiscriminate slaughter of Initiates would be regarded by his troops as an ill omen, and, besides, they would be useful in controlling the population. Ubars have always employed the Initiates as tools, some of the boldest even contending that the social function of the Initiates is to keep the lower castes contented with their servile lot. The second major condition requested by the Initiates was that the city be garrisoned by only ten thousand chosen troops, and that the balance of the horde be allowed to enter the gates only unarmed. There were a variety of smaller, more intricate concessions desired by the Initiates and granted by Pa-Kur, mostly having to do with the provisioning of the city and the protection of its tradesmen and peasants.

Pa-Kur, for his part, demanded and was granted the usual savage fees imposed by the Gorean conqueror. The population would be completely disarmed. Possession of a weapon would be regarded as a capital offense. Officers in the Warrior Caste and their families were to be impaled, and in the population at large every tenth man would be executed. The thousand most beautiful women of Ar would be given as pleasure slaves to Pa-Kur, for distribution among his highest officers. Of the other free women, the healthiest and most attractive thirty percent would be auctioned to his troops in the Street of Brands, the proceeds going to the coffers of Pa-Kur. A levy of seven thousand young men would be taken to fill the depleted ranks of his siege slaves. Children under twelve would be distributed at random among the free cities of Gor. As for the slaves of Ar, they would belong to the first man who changed their collar.

Near dawn, to the brave sound of tarn drums, a mighty procession left the camp of Pa-Kur, and as it crossed the main bridge over the first ditch, I saw in the distance the great gate of Ar slowly opening. Perhaps I alone of that vast horde, with the possible exception of Mintar, of the Merchant Caste, felt like weeping. Pa-Kur rode at the head of the garrison troops, ten thousand strong. They chanted a marching rhythm as they followed him, the sunlight on their spears. Pa-Kur himself rode a black tharlarion, one of the few I had seen. The beast was bejeweled and moved with a grave, regal stride. I was puzzled as the great procession halted and a palanquin was borne forward by eight members of the Caste of Assassins.

Suddenly I became alert. The palanquin was set down beside the tharlarion of Pa-Kur. The figure of a girl was lifted from it. She was unveiled. My heart leaped. It was Talena. But she did not wear the regalia of a Ubara, as had the girl in the cage. She was barefoot and clad in a single garment, a long white robe. To my amazement, I saw that her wrists were fastened together by golden shackles. A chain of gold was slung to Pa-Kur, who fastened it to the saddle of his tharlarion. The free end of Pa-Kur's saddle chain was then secured to Talena's shackles. The procession resumed to the beat of the tarn drums and Talena, bound in chains of gold, walked, slowly, with dignity, beside the tharlarion of her captor, Pa-Kur, the Assassin.

My wonder and horror must have been written large on my face, because a tharlarion lancer standing beside me regarded me with amusement. "One of the conditions of the surrender," he said. "The impalement of Talena, daughter of Marlenus, false Ubar of Ar."

"But why?" I demanded. "She was to be the bride of Pa-Kur, to be Ubara of Ar."

"When Marlenus fell," said the man, "the Initiates decreed the impalement of all members of his family." He smiled grimly. "To save face before the citizens of Ar, they have demanded that Pa-Kur respect their decree and impale her."

"And Pa-Kur agreed?"

"Of course," said the man. "One key to open the gate of Ar is as good as another."

My head swirled, and I stumbled backward through the ranks of soldiers watching the procession. I ran blindly through the now deserted streets of Pa-Kur's camp and found myself at last in the compound of Mintar. I lurched into the tent of Kazrak and fell on the sleeping mat, shaking with emotion. I sobbed.

Then my hands clutched the mat, and I shook my head savagely to clear it of the uncontrolled tumult of emotion that rocked it. Suddenly I was again my own master, again rational. The shock of seeing her, of knowing the fate that awaited her had been too much. I must try not to be weak in the way of the things I love. It is unbefitting a warrior of Gor.

It was as a warrior of Gor that I arose and donned the black helmet and the garments of the Caste of Assassins. I loosened my sword in its sheath, set my shield on my arm, and grasped my spear. My steps were determined when I left the tent. I strode meaningfully to the great tarn cot at the entrance to Mintar's compound and demanded my tarn.

The tarn was brought into the open. He gleamed with health and energy. Still, the days in the tarn cot, gigantic though it was, must have been confining for that Ubar of the Skies, my tarn, and I knew he would relish flight, the chance to pit his wings once again against the fierce winds of Gor. I stroked him with affection, surprised at the fondness I felt for the sable monster.

I tossed the tarn keeper a golden tarn disk. He had done his job well. He stammered, holding it out to me, for me to take it back. A golden tarn disk was a small fortune. It would buy one of the great birds themselves, or as many as five slave girls. I climbed the mounting ladder and fastened myself in the saddle, telling the keeper that the coin was his. I suppose it was a gesture, nothing but a gesture, but, pitiful though it might be, it pleased me, and, to be honest, I did not expect to live to spend the coin. "For luck," I said. Then, with the first flush of joy I had felt in weeks, I brought the great bird soaring into the sky.

18

In the Central Cylinder

AS THE TARN CLIMBED, I saw the camp of Pa-Kur, the ditches, the double walls of Ar with siege engines like leeches fastened to the inner wall, and, approaching the city, Pa-Kur's long lines of chanting garrison troops, the morning sun flashing on their metal, their march measured by the beat of tarn drums. I thought of Marlenus who, if he survived, might be able to see much of the same sight from the arrow ports of the Central Cylinder. I felt sorry for him, knowing that that sight, if any, would crush the heart of the fierce Ubar. His feelings toward Talena I could not conjecture. Perhaps, mercifully, he did not know what was to be her fate. I knew that I must try to rescue her. How much I would have given to have had Marlenus and his men at my side, few though they might be!

Then, as if the pieces of a puzzle had suddenly, unexpectedly, snapped into shape, a plan sprang into my head. Marlenus had entered the city. Somehow. I had puzzled on this for days, yet now it seemed obvious. The robes of the Afflicted. The Dar-Kosis Pits beyond the city. One of them, one of those pits, must be a blind; one of them must allow an underground access to the city. Surely one of those pits had been prepared years ago by the wily Ubar as an escape route or emergency exit. I must find that pit and tunnel, somehow fight my way to his side, enlist his support.

But first, as part of my plan, I raced my tarn directly for the walls of Ar, swiftly passing the slow procession on the plains below. In a matter of perhaps less than a minute I hovered over the summit of the interior wall near the great gate. As soldiers scattered madly beneath me, I brought the tarn down. No one ventured to repel me. All were silent. I wore the garb of the Caste of Assassins, and on the left temple of the black helmet was the golden slash of the messenger.

Without leaving the back of the tarn, I demanded the officer in charge. He was a dour, hard-bitten man with white hair cropped short. He had gray eyes that looked as though they had seen action and hadn't flinched. He approached sullenly. He did not enjoy being summoned by an enemy of Ar, and in particular by one who wore the habiliments of the hated Caste of Assassins.

"Pa-Kur approaches the city," I cried. "Ar is his."

The guards were silent. At a word from the officer a hundred spears would have sought my heart.

"You welcome him," I said scornfully, "by opening the great gate, but you have not retracted the tarn wire. Why is this? Take it down in order that his tarnsmen may enter the city unimpeded."

"That was not in the conditions of surrender," said the officer.

"Ar has fallen," I said. "Obey the word of Pa-Kur."

"Very well," said the officer, gesturing to a subordinate. "Lower the wire."

The cry, rather forlorn, to lower the wire was echoed along the length of the walls and from tower to tower. Soon the great winches were in motion and, foot by foot, the frightful netting of tarn wire began to sag. When it reached the ground, it would be sectioned and rolled. I was not, of course, concerned with facilitating the entry of Pa-Kur's tarnsmen who, as far as I knew, did not even constitute a portion of the garrison force, but I was concerned with opening the sky over the city in case I, and others, might be able to utilize it as a road to freedom.

I spoke once more, in haughty tones. "Pa-Kur wishes to know if the false Ubar, Marlenus, still lives."

"Yes," said the officer.

"Where is he?" I demanded.

"In the Central Cylinder," growled the man.

"A prisoner?"

"As good as a prisoner."

"See that he does not escape," I said.

"He will not escape," said the man. "Fifty guardsmen will see to that."

"What of the roof of the cylinder," I asked, "when the tarn wire is down?"

"Marlenus will not escape," repeated the officer, adding in a surly tone, "unless he can fly."

"Perhaps you will retain your humor when you writhe on an impaling spear," I said. The eyes of the man narrowed, and he regarded me with hatred, for he well knew what was to be the fate of the officers of Ar.

"Where," I asked, "shall Pa-Kur take the daughter of the false Ubar to be executed?"

The officer pointed to a distant cylinder. "The Cylinder

of Justice," he said. "The execution will take place as soon as the girl can be presented." The cylinder was white, a color Goreans often associate with impartiality. More significantly, it indicated that the justice dispensed therein was the justice of Initiates.

There are two systems of courts on Gor—those of the City, under the jurisdiction of an Administrator or Ubar, and those of the Initiates, under the jurisdiction of the High Initiate of the given city; the division corresponds roughly to that between civil and what, for lack of a better word, might be called ecclesiastical courts. The areas of jurisdiction of these two types of courts are not well defined; the Initiates claim ultimate jurisdiction in all matters, in virtue of their supposed relation to the Priest-Kings, but this claim is challenged by civil jurists. There would, of course, in these days be no challenging the justice of the Initiates. I noted with repulsion that on the roof of the Cylinder of Justice there shimmered a public impaling spear of polished silver, some fifty feet high, gleaming, looking like a needle in the distance.

I took the tarn into the air again. I had managed to bring down the tarn wire of Ar; I had learned that Marlenus still lived and held a portion of the Central Cylinder, and I had found out when and where the execution of Talena was supposed to take place.

I streaked from the walls of Ar, noting with dismay that the procession of Pa-Kur was only a short distance from the great gate. I could see the tharlarion on which he rode, the figure of the Assassin, and the slip of a girl, in her white robe, who, beside the animal, walked like a Ubara, though barefoot and chained to its saddle. I wondered if Pa-Kur might be curious to know who was the rider of that solitary sable tarn which flashed above his head.

In what seemed like an hour, but must have been no more than three or four minutes, I was behind the camp of Pa-Kur and searching for the dreaded Dar-Kosis Pits, those prisons in which the Afflicted may freely incarcerate themselves and be fed, but from which they are not allowed to depart. There were several, easily visible from above because of their broad, circular form, much like a great well sunk in the earth. When I came to one, I would bring the tarn lower. When I had completed my search, I had found only one pit deserted. The others were dotted with what appeared, from the height, to be yellow lice—the figures of the Afflicted. Boldly, giving no thought to the possible danger of lingering infection, I dropped the tarn into the deserted pit.

The giant landed on the rock floor of the circular pit, and I looked upward, my glance climbing the sheer, artificially smoothed sides of the pit, which stretched perhaps a thousand feet above me on all sides. In spite of the breadth of the pit, perhaps two hundred feet, it was cold at the bottom, and as I looked up, I was startled to note that, in the blue sky, I could see the dim pinpricks of light which, after dark, would become the blazing stars above Gor. In the center of the pit a crude cistern had been carved from the living rock and was half filled with cold but foul water. As nearly as I could determine, there was no way in and out of the pit except on tarnback. I did know that sometimes the pathetic inmates of Dar-Kosis Pits, repenting their decision to be incarcerated, had managed to cut footholds in the walls and escape, but the labor involved—a matter of years—the death penalty for being discovered, and the very risk of the climb made such attempts rare. If there was some secret way in and out of this particular pit, assuming it was the one prepared by Marlenus, I did not see what it was and had no time to conduct a thorough investigation.

Looking about, I saw several of the caves dug into the walls of the pit, which, at least in most pits, house the inmates. In desperate, frustrated haste, I examined several of them; some were shallow, little more than scooped-out depressions in the wall, but others were more extensive, containing two or three chambers connected by passageways. Some contained worn sleeping mats of cold, moldy straw, some contained a few rusted metal utensils, such as kettles and pails, but most were completely empty, revealing no signs of life or use at all.

After I emerged from one of these caves, I was surprised to see my tarn across the pit, his head tilted to one side, as if puzzled. He then reached his beak out to an apparently blank wall and withdrew it, repeating this three or four times, and then began to walk back and forth, snapping his wings impatiently.

I raced across the pit. I began to examine the wall with fierce closeness. I scrutinized every inch and ran my hands carefully over every portion of its smooth surface. Nothing was revealed to my eyes or to my touch, but there was the almost imperceptible odor of tarn spoor.

For several minutes I examined the blank wall, sure that it held the secret of Marlenus's entrance into the city. Then, in frustration, I backed slowly away, hoping to see some lever or perhaps some suspicious crevice higher in the escarpment, something that might play its role in opening the passage I was sure lay hidden somewhere behind that seemingly solid mass of stone. Yet no lever, handle, or device of any kind revealed itself.

I widened my search, wandering about the walls, but they seemed sheer, impenetrable. There seemed to be no place in which a lever or handle might be concealed. Then, with a shout of anger at my stupidity, I ran to the shallow cistern in the center of the pit and fell on my stomach before the chill, foul water. I thrust my hand into the slimy water, desperately examining the bottom.

My hand clutched a valve, and I turned it fiercely as far as it would go. At the same time from the escarpment came a smooth, rolling sound as a great weight was effortlessly balanced and lifted by hydraulic means. To my amazement, I saw that an immense opening had appeared in the wall. An enormous slab, perhaps fifty feet square, had slid upward and backward, revealing a great, dim, squarish tunnel beyond, a tunnel large enough for a flying tarn. I seized the tarn reins and drew the beast into the opening. Inside the door I saw another valve, corresponding to the one hidden under the water of the cistern. Turning it, I closed the great gate behind me, thinking it wise to protect the secret of the tunnel as long as possible.

Inside, the tunnel, though dim, was not altogether dark, being lit by domelike, wire-protected energy bulbs, spaced in pairs every hundred yards or so. These bulbs, invented more than a century ago by the Caste of Builders, produce a clear, soft light for years without replacement. I mounted the tarn, who was visibly uneasy in this strange environment. Without much success, by hand and voice, I tried to soothe the beast's apprehensions. Perhaps I spoke as much for my own benefit as his. The first time I hauled on the one-strap, the bird would not move; the second time he lifted into flight, almost immediately scraping the ceiling of the tunnel with his wings, protesting shrilly. My helmet protected me as my head was roughly dragged against the granite of the ceiling. Then, to my pleasure, instead of alighting, the tarn dropped a few feet down from the ceiling and began to streak through the tunnel, the energy bulbs flashing past me to form in my wake a gleaming chain of light.

The end of the tunnel widened into a vast chamber, lit by hundreds of energy bulbs. In this chamber, though empty of human beings, was a monstrous tarn cot, in which some twenty gigantic, half-starved tarns huddled separately on the tarn perches. As soon as they saw us, they lifted their heads, as if out of their shoulders, and regarded us with fierce attention. The floor of the tarn cot was littered with the bones of perhaps two dozen tarns. I reasoned that the tarns must be those of the men of Marlenus, left in the tarn cot when he entered the city. He had been cut off. Left without care for weeks, the tarns had had nothing to feed upon but one another. They were wild now, crazed by hunger into uncontrollable predators.

Perhaps I could use them.

Somehow I must liberate Marlenus. I knew that when I entered the palace my presence would be inexplicable to the guardsmen and that I would not long be able to pass myself off as a herald of Pa-Kur, certainly not when it became clear that it was my intention to depart with Marlenus. Therefore, impossible though it might seem, I must devise some plan to scatter or overcome his besiegers. As I pondered, the fragments of a plan took form in my mind. Surely I was now beneath the Central Cylinder, and the embattled Marlenus and his men were somewhere above me, sealed off by the guardsmen of Ar. At the top of a broad series of stairs I saw the door that must lead to the Central Cylinder and noted with satisfaction that its dimensions were large enough to permit the passage of a tarn. Fortunately, almost at the foot of the stairs lay one of the gates of the tarn cot.

I took my tarn-goad and dismounted. I climbed the stairs that led to the portal into the cylinder, turned the valve, and as soon as the portal began to move, raced down to the tarn cot and swung open that barred gate which lay nearest the foot of the stairs. I stood back, partly shielding myself with the gate. In less than a few seconds the first of the scraggy tarns had lit on the floor of the cot and poked his ugly head through the door. His eyes blazed as he saw me. To him, I was food, something to be killed and eaten. He stalked toward me, around the gate. I struck at him with the tarn-goad, but the instrument seemed to have no effect. The darting beak lunged at me again and again; the great claws grasped. The tarn-goad was torn from my hand.

In that instant a great black shape hurtled into the fray, and the tarn had met his match. Ripping savagely with his steel-shod talons, slashing with his scimitarlike beak, my sable war tarn in a matter of seconds left the attacking tarn a shuddering heap of feathers. With one of the great steel-shod talons on the body of his fallen foe, my tarn emitted the challenge scream of his kind. The other tarns, poking out of the tarn cot, seemed to hesitate and then to notice the open door into the cylinder.

At that moment, to his own misfortune, a passing guardsman of Ar discovered the opened door that had mysteriously appeared in the wall of the first floor of the Central Cylinder. He stood framed for a moment in the doorway and shouted, a shout half of discovery, half of mortal fear. One of the starved tarns, with a leap and stroke of his wings, lunged upward, catching the man in his beak. The man screamed horribly. Another tarn reached the portal and tried to pull the body from the beak of its possessor.

There was another shout from within, and several more guardsmen rushed to the opening. Immediately the hunger-wild tarns surged upward, eager for flesh. The tarns, all of them, entered the cylinder, the palace of Marlenus. In the great hall I could hear the fearful noise of unnatural carnage, the screams of the men, the screams of the tarns, the hiss of arrows. the wild blows of wings and talons. I heard someone shout, a weird, terrified cry, "Tarns!" An alarm bar, a hollow metal tube struck by hammers, began to ring in frenzy.

In two or three minutes I led my own tarn up the stairs and through the opening. I was sick at the sight that confronted me. Some fifteen tarns were feeding on the remains of a dozen or so guardsmen, detaching and devouring limbs. Several tarns were dead; some were flopping about awkwardly on the marble floor, pierced by arrows. There were no living guardsmen in sight. Those who had survived had fled from the room, perhaps up the long, wide, circling stairwell that climbed the inside of the cylinder.

Leaving my tarn below, I climbed the stairs, my sword drawn. When I reached that portion of the stairwell adjoining the upper floors, devoted to the private use of the Ubar, I saw some twenty or thirty guardsmen, behind them a barricade of tile and tarn wire which they had erected. It was not simply that my sword was drawn. To them, my presence was unauthorized, and my Assassin's garb, far from being a safe-conduct, was an incitement to attack. Some of the guardsmen had undoubtedly fought below with the tarns. They were drenched with sweat; their clothing was torn; their weapons, drawn, were red with blood. They would associate me with the tarn attack. Without waiting to call for my identity or engage in any protocol whatever, they raced toward me.

"Die, Assassin!" one of them screamed, and struck downward with his blade.

I slipped under the blade and ran him through. The others were upon me. Much of what took place then is jumbled in my memory, like the fragments of some bizarre, incomprehensible dream. I remember them pressing downward, so many, and my blade, terrible, moving as if wielded by a god, meeting their steel, cutting its path upward. One man, two, three sprawled down the stairs, and then another and another. I struck and parried and struck again, my sword flashing forth and drinking blood again and again. I seemed to be beside myself and fought as if I might not be what I knew I was, what I thought myself to be—Tarl Cabot, a simple warrior, one man. The thought flamed through me in the violent delirium of battle that in those moments I was many men, an army, that no man could stand against me, that it was not my blade or my heart they faced but something I myself only dimly sensed, something intangible but irresistible, an avalanche, a storm, a force of nature, the destiny of their world, something I could not name but knew in those moments could not be denied or conquered.

Suddenly I stood alone on the stairs, except for the dead. I became dimly aware that I was bleeding from minor cuts in a dozen places.

Slowly I climbed the remainder of the stairs until I came to the barricade which had been erected by the guardsmen. I called out, as loudly as I could, "Marlenus, Ubar of Ar!"

To my joy, from somewhere above, around the curve of the stairs, I heard the voice of the Ubar. "Who would speak with me?"

"Tarl of Bristol," I cried.

There was a silence.

I wiped my sword, sheathed it, and climbed to the top of the barricade. I stood for a moment on the crest of the barricade and then lowered myself down the other side. I slowly walked up the stairs, my hands open, free of weapons. I turned the bend in the stairs and, several yards above me, observed a wide doorway, jammed with chests and furniture. It was behind this makeshift rampart, which could be defended against a hundred men, that I saw the haggard but still blazing eyes of Marlenus. I removed my helmet and set it on the steps. In a moment he had burst through the obstruction as if it had been made of kindling wood.

Wordlessly we embraced.

19

The Duel

MARLENUS AND HIS MEN AND I raced down the long stairs to the main hall of the Central Cylinder, where we came on the remains of the grisly feast of the tarns. The great birds, fed, were once again as tractable as such monsters ever are, and with the tarn-goads Marlenus and his men were again in command. In spite of the urgency of our mission, there was a detail that Marlenus did not neglect. He lifted a tile in the floor of the great hall and revealed a valve; with it, he closed the secret door through which the tarns had come. The secret of the tunnel would be kept.

We led our tarns to one of the large circular ports of the cylinder. I climbed to the saddle of my own sable beast and brought it soaring into the air beyond the cylinder. Marlenus followed, and his men. In a minute we had attained the roof of the Central Cylinder and had all Ar and the surrounding countryside spread beneath us.

Marlenus was, in general, well informed of the political situation; indeed, to be so informed required only the vantage point he had so stoutly defended for several days and a particle of awareness. He swore violently when I told him of the proposed fate of Talena, yet refused to accompany me when I announced that I would attack the Cylinder of Justice.

"Look!" cried Marlenus, pointing below. "The garrison of Pa-Kur is well within the city. The men of Ar discard their weapons!"

"Will you not try to save your daughter?" I asked.

"Take what men of mine you will," he said. "But I must fight for my city. I am Ubar of Ar, and while I live, my city will not perish." He lowered his helmet onto his head and loosened his shield and spear. "Look for me hereafter in the streets and on the bridges," he said, "on the walls and in the hidden rooms of the highest cylinders. Wherever the free men of Ar retain their weapons, there you will find Marlenus."

I called after him, but his choice, painful though it must have been, had been made. He had brought his tarn to flight and was descending to the streets below to rally the dispirited citizens of Ar, to call them again to arms, to challenge them to renounce the treacherous authority of the self-seeking Initiates, to strike again their blow for freedom, to die rather than yield their city to the foe. One by one, his men followed him, tarnsman by tarnsman. None left the roof of the cylinder to seek his safety beyond the city. Each was determined to die with his Ubar. And I, too, if a higher duty had not called me, might have chosen to follow Marlenus, ruthless Ubar of that vast and violated city.

Once again alone, sick at heart, I loosened my spear and shield in their saddle straps. I entertained no hope now but to die with the girl unjustly condemned on the distant, gleaming tower. I brought the tarn to flight and set its course for the Cylinder of Justice. I noted grimly, as I flew, that large portions of the horde of Pa-Kur were crossing the great bridges over the first ditch and moving toward the city, the sunlight flashing on their weaponry. It seemed that the conditions of surrender meant little to the horde and that it was determined to enter the city, now and in the full panoply of war. By night Ar would be in flames, its coffers broken open, its gold and silver in the bedrolls of the looters, its men slaughtered, its women, stripped, lashed to the pleasure-racks of the victors.

The Cylinder of Justice was a lofty cylinder of pure white marble, the flat roof of which was some hundred yards in diameter. There were about two hundred people on the cylinder roof. I could see the white robes of Initiates and the variegated colors of soldiers, both of Ar and of Pa-Kur's horde. And, dark among these shapes, like shadows, I could see the somber black of members of the Caste of Assassins. The high impaling post, normally visible on the top of the cylinder, had been lowered. When it was raised again, it would bear the body of Talena.

I was over the cylinder and dropping the tarn to its center. With cries of surprise and rage, men scattered from beneath the suddenly descending gigantic shape. I had expected to be fired on immediately but suddenly remembered that I still wore the garb of the messenger. No Assassin would fire on me, and no one else would dare.

The tarn's steel-shod talons struck the marble roof of the cylinder with a flash of sparks. The great wings smote the air twice, raising a small hurricane that caused the startled onlookers to stagger backward. Lying on the ground, bound hand and foot, still clad in the white robe, was Talena. The point of the sharpened impaling post lay near her. As the tarn had landed, her executioners, two burly, hooded magistrates, had scrambled to their feet and fled to safety. The Initiates themselves do not execute their victims, as the shedding of blood is forbidden by those beliefs they regard as sacred. Now, helpless, Talena lay almost within the wing span of my tarn, so near to me and yet a world away.

"What is the meaning of this!" cried a strident voice, that of Pa-Kur.

I turned to face him, and the fury of what he meant to me ripped through my body, surging like a volcano, almost dominating me. Yet I did not answer him. Instead I called out to the men of Ar on the cylinder. "Men of Ar," I cried, "behold!" I gestured widely to the fields beyond the great gate. The approaching swarm of Pa-Kur's horde was visible, and the dust rose a thousand feet into the air. There were cries of rage.

"Who are you?" cried Pa-Kur, drawing his sword.

I threw off my helmet, flinging it down. "I am Tarl of Bristol," I said.

The cry of amazement and joy that broke from Talena's lips told me all I wanted to know.

"Impale her," shouted Pa-Kur.

As the burly magistrates hastened forward, I seized my spear and hurled it with such force as I would not have believed possible. The spear flashed through the air like a bolt of lightning and struck the oncoming magistrate in the chest, passing through his body and burying itself in the heart of his companion.

There was an awe-stricken silence as the immensity of what had occurred impressed itself on the onlookers.

I was conscious of distant shouting in the streets far below. There was a smell of smoke. There was the faint clash of arms. "Men of Ar," I cried, "listen! Even now, in the streets below, Marlenus, your Ubar, fights for the freedom of Ar!"

The men of Ar looked at one another.

"Will you surrender your city? Yield your lives and women to Assassins?" I challenged. "Are you truly the men of never-conquered, imperishable Ar? Or are you but slaves who will exchange your freedom for the collar of Pa-Kur?"

"Down with the Initiates!" cried one man, drawing his sword. "Down with the Assassin!" cried another. There were shouts from the men of Ar and cries of terror from the Initiates as they cringed or fled. Almost as if by magic, the men of Ar had separated themselves from the others on the cylinder. Swords were drawn. In an instant they would join the battle raging in the streets.

"Stop!"

A great, solemn, hollow voice boomed. All eyes on the roof turned to the sound of that voice. The Supreme Initiate of Ar himself stood forth, separating himself disdainfully from the cowering knot of white-robed figures that cringed behind him. He strode majestically across the roof. Both the men of Ar and those of Pa-Kur fell back. The Supreme Initiate was an emaciated, incredibly tall man, with smooth-shaven, bluish, sunken cheeks and wild, prophetic eyes. He was ascetic, fervent, sinister, fanatic. One long, clawlike hand was raised grandly to the heavens. "Who will challenge the will of the Priest-Kings?" he demanded.

No one spoke. The men, of both sides, fell back even farther. Pa-Kur himself seemed awed. The spiritual power of the Supreme Initiate was almost sensible in the air. The religious conditioning of the men of Gor, based on superstition though it might be, was as powerful as a set of chains—more powerful than chains because they did not realize it existed. They feared the word, the curse, of this old man without weapons more than they would have feared the massed swords of a thousand foemen.

"If it is the will of the Priest-Kings," I said, "to bring about the death of an innocent girl, then I challenge their will."

Such words had never before been spoken on Gor.

Except for the wind, there was no sound on the great cylinder.

The Supreme Initiate turned and faced me, pointing that long skeletal finger.

"Die the Flame Death," he said.

I had heard of the Flame Death from my father and

from the Older Tarl—that legendary fate which overtook those who had transgressed the will of the Priest-Kings. I knew almost nothing of the fabled Priest-Kings, but I did know that something of the sort must exist, for I had been brought to Gor by an advanced technology, and I knew that some force or power lay in the mysterious Sardar Mountains. I did not believe that the Priest-Kings were divine, but I did believe that they lived and that they were aware of what occurred on Gor and that from time to time they made known their will. I did not even know if they were human or nonhuman, but, whatever they might be, they were, with their advanced science and technology, for all practical purposes, the gods of this world.

On the back of my tarn, I waited, not knowing if I was to be singled out for the Flame Death, not knowing if I, like the mysterious blue envelope in the mountains of New Hampshire, so long ago, was doomed to explode in a devouring blue flame.

"Die the Flame Death," repeated the old man, once again jabbing that long finger in my direction. But this time the gesture was less grand; it seemed a bit hysterical; it seemed pathetic.

"Perhaps no man knows the will of the Priest-Kings," I said.

"I have decreed the death of the girl," cried the old man wildly, his robes flutterring around his bony knees. "Kill her!" he shouted to the men of Ar.

No one moved. Then, before anyone could stop him, he seized a sword from the scabbard of an Assassin and rushed to Talena, holding it over his head with both hands. He wobbled hysterically, his eyes mad, his mouth slobbering, his faith in the Priest-Kings shattered, and with it his mind. He wavered over the girl, ready to kill.

"No!" cried one of the Initiates. "It is forbidden!"

Heedlessly, the insane old man tensed for the blow that would end the life of the girl. But in that instant he seemed to be concealed in a bluish haze, and then, sudddenly, to the horror of all, he seemed, like a living bomb, to explode with fire. Not even a scream came from that fierce blue combustive mass that had been a human being, and in a minute the flame had departed, almost as quickly as it had come, and a dust of ashes scattered from the top of the cylinder in the wind.

The voice of Pa-Kur was heard, level and unnaturally calm. "The sword shall decide these matters," he said.

Accordingly, I slid from the saddle of the tarn, unsheathing my weapon.

Pa-Kur was said to be the finest swordsman on Gor.

From far below, the distant shouts of fighting in the streets drifted upward. The Initiates had vanished from the roof of the cylinder.

One of the men of Ar said, "I choose for Marlenus."

"And I," said another.

Pa-Kur, without taking his eyes off me, gestured with his sword toward the men of Ar. "Destroy this rabble."

Instantly the Assassins and the men from Pa-Kur's horde fell upon the men of Ar, who stood firm under the sudden onslaught, meeting them blade for blade. The men of Ar were outnumbered perhaps three to one, but I knew they would give a good account of themselves.

Pa-Kur approached warily, confident in his superior swordsmanship, but, as I expected, determined to take no chances.

We met almost over the body of Talena, the tips of our blades touching alertly, once, twice, each sounding the other out. Pa-Kur feinted, not exposing himself, his eyes seeming to watch my shoulder, noting how I parried the blow. He tested me again and seemed satisfied. He then began testing elsewhere, methodically, using his sword almost as a physician might use a stethoscope, applying it first to one area and then to another. I drove in once directly. Pa-Kur slid the blow lightly to one side, almost casually. While we touched blades almost as if involved in some bizarre ritualistic dance, there was the ringing, the clanging of fiercer swordplay around us, as the men of Pa-Kur engaged the men of Ar.

At last Pa-Kur stepped back, out of the range of my blade. He seemed complacent. "I can kill you," he said. I supposed what he said was true, but it may have been a calculated remark, something to put the enemy off balance, like announcing an unseen mate in chess to provoke an opponent into making an unnecessary defensive move, causing him to lose the initiative. That sort of thing would be effective only once with a given player, but in swordplay once would be sufficient.

I responded in kind, to taunt him. "How is it that you can kill me if I do not turn my back?" I asked. Somewhere within that inhumanly calm exterior there lay a vanity that must be vulnerable. I remembered the incident of the crossbow and the tarn disk over the Vosk. That, in its way, had been a rhetorical gesture on the part of Pa-Kur.

A momentary annoyance flickered through the stony eyes of Pa-Kur, and then a small, sour smile appeared on his lips. He again approached, but cautiously as before, still taking no chances. My ruse had failed. His, if ruse it was, had also. If it had not been a ruse, I would soon know, if only briefly.

Our blades met again, this time in a flash of bright, clean sound. He had begun much as at first, moving toward the same area, only with more familiarity, more rapidity. This led me to puzzle as to whether this was the weaker part of my defense and where his attack would come, or if it was a blind to keep my mind from another area until suddenly he drove through for the kill.

Such questions I forced from my mind, keeping my eyes on his blade. In affairs of the sword, there is a place for outguessing the opponent, but there is no place for anxious speculation; it paralyzes, puts you on the defensive. He had toyed with me. Now I determined not to allow him to control the exchanges. If I was defeated, I determined that it would be a man that would defeat me, not a reputation.

I began to press forward in attack, exposing myself more, but beating back his defense by the sheer weight and number of my blows. Pa-Kur withdrew coolly, meeting my attack effortlessly, letting me weary my sword arm; hating him, I admired him; wanting to destroy him, I acclaimed his skill.

When my attack lapsed, Pa-Kur did not press his own. He clearly wanted me to attack again. After several such onslaughts, my arm would be weakened to the point where it could not withstand the fury of his own offense, which was legendary on Gor.

As we fought, the men of Ar, fighting brilliantly for their city, their honor and loved ones, pushed back the men of Pa-Kur again and again, but from the interior of the cylinder swarmed more men of the Assassin. For each enemy who fell, it seemed three sprang up to take his place. It was only a matter of time before the last of the men of Ar would be forced over the edge of the cylinder.

Pa-Kur and I engaged again and again, I pressing the attack, he withstanding it and waiting. During this time Talena, though bound hand and foot, had struggled to her knees, and she watched us fight, her hair and the folds of her robe blown by the wind that whipped across the roof of the cylinder. Seeing her and the fear for me in her eyes, I seemed to gain redoubled strength, and for the first time it seemed to me that Pa-Kur was not meeting my attack as surely as he had previously.

Suddenly there was a sound like thunder and a great shadow was cast across the roof of the cylinder, as if the sun had been obscured by clouds. Pa-Kur and I backed away from one another, each quickly trying to see what was happening. In our fighting we had been all but oblivious of the world around us. I heard the joyous cry, "Sword Brother!" It was Kazrak's voice! "Tarl of Ko-roba!" cried another familiar voice—that of my father.

I looked up. The sky was filled with tarns. Thousands of the great birds, their wings clapping like thunder, were descending on the city, flying onto the bridges and down to the streets, darting among those spires no longer protected with the terrible defense of the tarn wire. In the distance the camp of Pa-Kur was in flames.

Across the bridges of the great ditch, rivers of warriors were flowing. In Ar the men of Marlenus had apparently reached the great gate, for it was slowly closing, locking the garrison inside, separating them from the horde without. The horde, taken by surprise, was disorganized, unformed for battle. It was milling about in confusion, panic-stricken. Many of Pa-Kur's tarnsmen were already streaking from the city, seeking their own safety. Undoubtedly, the horde of Pa-Kur greatly outnumbered the attackers, but it did not understand this. It knew only that it had been taken by surprise, at a disadvantage by undetermined numbers of disciplined troops that were pouring down on them, while from above, enemy tarnsmen, unchallenged, emptied their quivers into their ranks. Moreover, with the closing of the great gate, there was no refuge in the city; they were trapped against the walls, packed like cattle for the slaughter, trampling one another, unable to use their weapons.

Kazrak's tarn had alighted on the roof of the cylinder, and a moment afterward my father's and perhaps fifty others. Behind Kazrak, sharing his saddle, in the leather of a tarnsman, rode the beautiful Sana of Thentis. The Assassins of Pa-Kur were throwing down their swords and removing their helmets. Even as I watched, my father's tarnsmen were roping them together.

Pa-Kur had seen what I had seen, and now once again we faced one another. I gestured to the ground with my sword, offering quarter. Pa-Kur snarled and rushed forward. I met the attack cleanly, and after a minute of fierce interplay both Pa-Kur and I realized I could withstand the best he had to give.

Then I seized the initiative and began to force him back. As we fought and I forced him back step by step toward the edge of the lofty marble cylinder, I said calmly, "I can kill you." I knew I spoke the truth.

I struck the blade from his hand. It rang on the marble surface.

"Yield," I said. "Or take your sword again."

Like a striking cobra, Pa-Kur snatched up the sword. We engaged again, and twice my blade cut him; the second time I nearly had the opening I desired. It was now a matter of only a few strokes more and the Assassin would lie at my feet, lifeless.

Suddenly Pa-Kur, who sensed this as well as I, hurled his sword. It slashed through my tunic, creasing the skin. I felt the warm, wet sensation of blood. Pa-Kur and I looked at each other, now without hatred. He stood straight before me, unarmed but with all the nonchalant arrogance of old.

"You will not lead me as a prisoner," he said. Then, without another word, he turned and leaped into space.

I walked slowly to the edge of the cylinder. There was only the sheer wall of the cylinder, broken once by a tarn perch some twenty feet below. There was no sign of the Assassin. His crushed body would be recovered from the streets below and publicly impaled. Pa-Kur was dead.

I sheathed my sword and went to Talena. I unbound her. Trembling, she stood beside me, and we took one another in our arms, the blood from my wound staining her robe.

"I love you," I said.

We held one another, and her eyes, wet with tears, lifted to mine. "I love you," she said.

The lion laugh of Marlenus resounded from behind

us. Talena and I broke apart. My hand was on my sword. The Ubar's hand gently restrained mine. "It has done enough work for one day," he smiled. "Let it rest."

The Ubar went to his daughter and took her fine head in his great hands. He turned her head from side to side and looked into her eyes. "Yes," he said, as if he might have seen his daughter for the first time, "she is fit to be the daughter of a Ubar." Then he clapped his hands on my shoulders. "See that I have grandsons," he said.

I looked about. Sana stood in the arms of Kazrak, and I knew that the former slave girl had found the man to whom she would give herself, not for a hundred tarns but for love.

My father stood watching me, approval in his eyes. In the distance Pa-Kur's camp was only a framework of blackened poles. In the city his garrison had surrendered. Beyond the walls the horde had cast down its weapons. Ar was saved.

Talena looked into my eyes. "What will you do with me?" she asked.

"I will take you to Ko-ro-ba," I said, "to my city."

"As your slave?" she smiled.

"If you will have me," I said, "as my Free Companion."

"I accept you, Tarl of Ko-ro-ba," said Talena with love in her eyes. "I accept you as my Free Companion."

"If you did not," I laughed, "I would throw you across my saddle and carry you to Ko-ro-ba by force."

She laughed as I swept her from her feet and lifted her to the saddle of my giant tarn. In the saddle, her arms were around my neck, her lips on mine. "Are you a true warrior?" she asked, her eyes bright with mischief, testing me, her voice breathless.

"We shall see," I laughed.

Then, in accord with the rude bridal customs of Gor, as she furiously but playfully struggled, as she squirmed and protested and pretended to resist, I bound her bodily across the saddle of the tarn. Her wrists and ankles were secured, and she lay before me, arched over the saddle, helpless, a captive, but of love and her own free will. The warriors laughed, Marlenus the loudest. "It seems I belong to you, bold Tarnsman," she said, "What are you going to do with me?" In answer, I hauled on the one-strap, and the great bird rose into the air, higher and higher, even into the clouds, and she cried to me, "Let it be now, Tarl," and even before we had passed the outermost ramparts of Ar, I had untied her ankles and flung her single garment to the streets below, to show her people what had been the fate of the daughter of their Ubar.

20

Epilogue

IT IS TIME NOW FOR a lonely man to conclude his narrative, without bitterness but without resignation. I have never surrendered the hope that someday, somehow, I might return to Gor, our Counter-Earth. These final sentences are written in a small apartment in Manhattan, some six floors above the street. The sounds of playing children carry through the open window. I have refused to return to England, and I will remain in this country from which I departed, years ago, for that distant world which holds what I most love. I can see the blazing sun this July afternoon, and know that behind it, counterpoised with my native planet, lies another world. And I wonder if on that world a girl, now a woman, thinks of me, and perhaps, too, of the secrets I have told her lie behind her sun, Tor-tu-Gor, Light Upon the Home Stone.

My destiny had been accomplished. I had served the Priest-Kings. The shape of a world had been altered, the rivers of a planet's history turned to new channels. Then, no longer needed, I was discarded. Perhaps the Priest-Kings, whoever or whatever they might be, reasoned that such a man was dangerous, that such a man might in time raise his own banner of dominion; perhaps they realized that I, of all on Gor, did not revere them, would not turn and bow my head in the direction of the Sardar Mountains; perhaps they envied me the flame of my love for Talena; perhaps, in the cold recesses of the Sardar Mountains, their intelligences could not accept that this vulnerable, perishable creature was more blessed than they, in their wisdom and their power.

Due, I believe, partly to my arguments and the prestige of what I had done, unprecedented lenience was shown to the surrendered armies of Pa-Kur. The Home Stones of the Twelve Tributary Cities were returned, and those men who had served Pa-Kur from those cities were allowed to return to their cities rejoicing. The large contingent of mercenaries who had flocked to his banner were kept as work slaves for a period of one year, to fill in the vast ditches and siege tunnels, to repair the extensive damage to the walls of Ar, and to rebuild those of its buildings that had been injured or burned in the fighting. After their year of servitude, they were returned, weaponless, to the cities of their birth. The officers of Pa-Kur, instead of being impaled, were treated in the same manner as common soldiers, to their relief, if scandal. Those members of the Caste of Assassins, the most hated caste on Gor, who had served Pa-Kur, were taken in chains down the Vosk to become galley slaves on the cargo ships that ply Gor's oceans. Oddly enough, the body of

Pa-Kur himself was never recovered from the foot of the Cylinder of Justice. I assume it was destroyed by the angry citizens of Ar.

Marlenus, in spite of his heroic role in the victory, submitted himself to the judgment of Ar's Council of High Castes. The sentence of death passed upon him by the usurping government of the Initiates was rescinded, but because his imperialistic ambition was feared, he was exiled from his beloved city. Such a man as Marlenus can never be second in a city, and the men of Ar were determined that he should never again be first. Accordingly, the Ubar, tears in his eyes, was publicly refused bread and salt, and, under penalty of death, was ordered to leave Ar by sundown, never again to come within ten pasangs of the city.

With some fifty followers, who loved him even more than their native walls, he fled on tarnback to the Voltai Range, from whose peaks he could always look upon the distant towers of Ar. There, I suppose to this day, in that inhospitable vastness, he reigns; in the scarlet mountains of the Voltai, Marlenus still rules, a larl among men, an outlaw king, to his followers always the Ubar of Ubars.

The free cities of Gor appointed Kazrak, my sword brother, to be temporary administrator of Ar, for it was he who, with the help of my father and Sana of Thentis, had rallied the cities to raise the siege. His appointment was confirmed by Ar's Council of High Castes, and his popularity in the city is such that it seems probable that in the future the office will be his by free election. In Ar democracy is a long-forgotten way of life that will require careful remembering.

When I returned to Ko-ro-ba with Talena, a great feast was held and we celebrated our Free Companionship. A holiday was declared, and the city was ablaze with light and song. Shimmering strings of bells pealed in the wind, and festive lanterns of a thousand colors swung from the innumerable flower-strewn bridges. There was shouting and laughter, and the glorious colors of the castes of Gor mingled equally in the cylinders. Gone for the night was even the distinction of master and slave, and many a wretch in bondage would see the dawn as a free man.

To my delight, even Torm, of the Caste of Scribes, appeared at the tables. I was honored that the little scribe had separated himself from his beloved scrolls long enough to share my happiness, only that of a warrior. He was wearing a new robe and sandals, perhaps for the first time in years. He clasped my hands, and, to my wonder, the little scribe was crying. And then, in his joy, he turned to Talena and in gracious salute lifted the symbolic cup of Ka-la-na wine to her beauty.

Talena and I swore to honor that day as long as either of us lived. I have tried to keep that promise, and I know that she has done so as well. That night, that glorious night, was a night of flowers, torches, and Ka-la-na wine, and late, after sweet hours of love, we fell asleep in each other's arms.

I awoke, perhaps weeks later, stiff and chilly in the mountains of New Hampshire, near the flat rock on which the silver spacecraft had landed. I was wearing the now so crude-seeming camp clothes I had originally worn. Men can die, but not of a broken heart, for if that were possible, I would now be dead. I doubted my sanity; I was terrorized that what had occurred had been only a bizarre dream. I sat alone in the mountains, my head in my hands. Slowly, with agony, I began to believe that it had indeed been nothing but the cruelest of dreams and that I was now once again coming to my senses. I could not believe this in my heart of hearts, but my mind, forcefully and coolly, required this conclusion.

I struggled to my feet, my heart torn with grief. But then, on the ground near my boot, I saw it—a small object, a tiny, round object. I fell on my knees and snatched it up, my eyes bursting with tears, my heart knowing the full sweep of the saddest joy that can overwhelm a man. In my hand I held the ring of red metal, the ring that bore the crest of Cabot, the gift of my father. I cut my hand with the ring, to make myself bleed, and I laughed with joy as I felt the pain and saw the blood. The ring was real, and I was awake, and there was a Counter-Earth, and the girl, Talena.

When I emerged from the mountains, I found I had been gone seven months. It was simple enough to feign amnesia, and what other account of those seven months would my world accept? I spent a few days in a public hospital, under observation, and was then allowed to leave. I decided to take up quarters, at least temporarily, in New York. My position at the college had, of course, been filled, and I had no desire to return; there would be too many explanations. I sent my friend at the college a belated check for his camping equipment, which had been destroyed with the blue envelope in the mountains. Very kindly, he arranged for my books and other belongings to be sent to my new address. When I arranged for the transfer of my bank business, I was surprised, but not too surprised, to discover that my savings account, in my absence, had been mysteriously augmented, and quite handsomely. I have not been forced to work since my return from the Counter-Earth. To be sure, I have worked, but only at what I wished and for as long as I wanted. I have given much more time to traveling, to reading, and to keeping myself fit. I have even joined a fencing club, to keep my eye alert and my wrist strong, though the puny foils we use are sorry weapons compared to the swords of Gor. Strangely, though it has now been six years since I left the Counter-Earth, I can discover no signs of aging or physical alteration in my appearance. I have puzzled over this, trying to connect it with the mysterious letter, dated in the seventeenth century, ostensibly by my father, which I received in the blue envelope. Perhaps the serums of the Caste of Physicians, so skilled on Gor, have something to do with this, but I cannot tell.

Two or three times a year I have returned to the mountains of New Hampshire, to look again on that great flat rock, to spend a night there, in case I might see once again that silver disk in the sky, in case once again I might be summoned by the Priest-Kings to that other world. But if I am so summoned, they will do so with the understanding that I am resolved to be no pawn in their vast games. Who or what are the Priest-Kings that they should so determine the lives of others, that they should rule a planet, terrorize the cities of a world, commit men to the Flame Death, tear lovers from each other's arms? No matter how fearful their power, they must be challenged. If I should once again walk the green fields of Gor, I know that I should attempt to solve the riddle of the Priest-Kings, that I should enter the Sardar Mountains and confront them, whoever or whatever they might be.